Doctor Donovan's Bequest

Tales from the Slagthorpe Archive

Michael O'Donnell

Doctor Donovan's Bequest

Tales from the Slagthorpe Archive

Matador
9 De Montfort Mews
Leicester LE1 7FW, UK
Tel: (+44) 116 255 9311 / 9312
Email: books@troubador.co.uk
Web: www.troubador.co.uk/matador

ISBN 10: 1 905886-10-1
ISBN 13: 978-1-905886-10-4

Typeset in 11pt Stempel Garamond by Troubador Publishing Ltd, Leicester, UK
Printed in the UK by The Cromwell Press Ltd, Trowbridge, Wilts, UK

Matador is an imprint of Troubador Publishing Ltd

Dedicated with affection to the memory of World Medicine
and all who sailed in her

Contents

The Slagthorpe Archive
(1957–1967)

At 5 o'clock on the morning of July 5th, 1998, Ernest Twigg, 47, Waiting List Adjustment Manager at the Slagcaster NHS Trust *Committed to commitment*, sliced a hole in the mesh fence surrounding the Slagcaster municipal car park. He had requisitioned wire-cutters from the Trust's Engineering Management Resource Centre, claiming an emergency entitlement under Schedule 43, amendment 94.

Once the deed was done, he climbed through the hole and headed for a line of floats drawn up in processional order for the carnival parade that later that day would celebrate the 50th birthday of the NHS. His target was the procession's centrepiece, a three ton lorry loaded with a 15 foot bronze statue of Aneurin Bevan in oratorical mode. (After the carnival his employers, with the help of a donation from BUPA, intended to install it outside the city's new Executive Health Centre.)

The night before, Twigg, who had suffered a series of stress-related disorders after his transfer to the Waiting List Adjustment Department, had stolen the keys of the three tonner from the desk of the Ancillary Vehicle Transportation Manager. He now climbed into the cab, started the engine, and drove the lorry and its load straight through the perimeter fence. As the wheels flung aside fragments of wire mesh embedded in the tyres, Twigg headed for the centre of the city. At the top of Market Hill, he slowed, aimed the lorry at his objective, and leaped from the cab.

The lorry accelerated down the hill, careered across the mini-roundabout at the bottom and hit the Margaret Thatcher Rest Home for Aging Entrepreneurs smack in the middle of its neo-Georgian facade. The force of the impact detached Aneurin from his base and propelled him though the window of the Denis Thatcher dispense bar, across the floor of the Mark Thatcher library, and into the central hallway where he came to rest amid the ruins of the baronial staircase. The aging entrepreneurs, tucked up in their executive suites on the second floor, remained unaware of the damage wreaked below. The only person who might have been at risk was the night porter but, as Twigg knew, he left the premises at 4.30 every morning to boost the black economy with a cash-in-hand paper round.

When Slagcaster Fire Brigade arrived they found that Aneurin had broken open a cavern beneath the staircase. City officials later discovered that this was the walled-up cellar of an old people's home that had stood on the site for forty years until the Slagcaster NHS Trust *Committed to commitment* rationalised its inhabitants into far-off lodging houses. The Trust demolished the building and sold the land to the Philip Morris tobacco company which was looking for a site on which to memorialise its distinguished patron.

Lying in the cellar beneath Aneurin's right buttock, was a battered leather trunk, shaped much like the "treasure chests" that pirates in schoolboy comics dug from the sand on desert islands. The contents of this trunk are now known officially as the Slagthorpe Archive, though doctors of a certain age more often refer to them as Donovan's Bequest.

The archive consists of a handful of medical artefacts, a few photographs, and some 700 sheets of A4 paper on which Doctor Donal Donovan typed, or scrawled in a near impenetrable hand, during the decade he spent as a general practitioner in the South Slagshire borough of Slagthorpe.

Donovan had worked as a senior medical registrar at Saint

Bartholomew's Hospital in London but, for reasons that he hints at in the first paper in this collection, he returned in 1957 to the practice in which his father had been the senior partner. Soon after his return, many of his patients – most of them mothers of young children or women in their second flush of youth – awarded him the accolade their parents bestowed upon his father: *Dear* Doctor Donovan.

The papers in the Archive are an assortment of observations Donovan recorded in his commonplace book, excerpts from his diaries, autobiographical notes, copies of letters, and transcripts of taped conversations. Some scholars have suggested he was making notes for an autobiography, others that he was planning to act as Boswell to his colleague and mentor, Doctor Finbar Aloysius O'Flaherty, described in many of the papers as *singer, poet, intellectual punch-up artist, and much loved general practitioner*.

Little is known of Donovan apart from what exists in the archive. The 1960 edition of the Medical Directory records that he qualified MB BChir in 1954 after training at Cambridge and Saint Bartholomew's Hospital, London. He disappears from the directory in 1969 and from the Medical Register in 1971.

All that we know about O'Flaherty, save for the contents of the archive, is that in 1938 he qualified MB, BCh, BAO at the National University of Ireland in Dublin and in 1946 passed the postgraduate examination that made him a Member of the Royal College of Physicians in London. He never submitted an entry to the Medical Directory but remained on the Medical Register until 1978. His registered address throughout his career was c/o The National Bank, Main Street, Mallow, County Cork. The baptismal register in Mallow's parish church confirms that he was born there.

* * * * * * * * * *

Readers of the Slagthorpe Papers need to be aware of the cultural changes that have affected medicine over the past half century.

In 1998, the year when the Archive was discovered, the public face of medicine wore an earnest expression. The latest management fad was governance by platitude. Every NHS hospital had a Mission Statement incorporated in its title, every ward a platitudinous declaration posted at its entrance. A Sheffield paediatric ward boasted: *The philosophy of care in this ward aims to deliver holistic individualised family centred care meeting the needs of both the hospitalised child and their (sic) families.*

Harold Shipman muttered similar platitudes to his patients before he killed them and Prime Ministers and Health Ministers used them to persuade the populace that the NHS was in vigorous health. Unassuaged by platitude, patients grew increasingly litigious. The most valued doctors in a 1998 hospital were its spin doctors.

In the 1950s and 60s, when Donovan was compiling the Archive, medicine was still a sporting activity. Patients and their doctors took risks, and knew they took risks. People who had lived through a war had learned that survival is a matter of luck and that life is never perfect. When things went wrong they didn't see themselves as victims: they'd had bad luck, drawn the wrong card, fallen foul of what insurance policies called an Act of God. Other wartime traditions lingered. Grown-ups didn't whinge, they shrugged their shoulders and did the best they could. Soldiering on, they called it.

The patients of the 1960s needed that resilience. The NHS, as at every moment in its history, muddled along from crisis to crisis. Junior hospital doctors – and they were labelled juniors well into their 40s – were so dispirited by low pay, poor prospects of promotion, and the reactionary antics of medicine's ruling elders, that they emigrated in large numbers to North America or Australasia.

The hospital service countered the loss of its juniors by importing doctors from the Asian and African Commonwealth. Lured to Britain by the promise of specialist training, these overseas graduates were exploited as cheap pairs of hands. Many received no training. For those who did, the teaching was often perfunctory. Casual unthinking racism was a common ingredient of medical conversation.

1960s medicine was also blighted by professional class distinction. Consultants regarded GPs as their intellectual and technical inferiors ... doctors who had failed to cut the mustard in *real* – by which they meant hospital – medicine. (One of the Slagthorpe papers records an outraged complaint from a consultant who'd seen a GP using a consultants' lavatory.)

True, consultants speaking to GPs on the telephone or happening upon them in a hospital corridor would butter them up because each was a potential referrer of profitable private patients yet medical students rarely heard a teacher commend an action taken by a patient's GP. Even when a GP's letter revealed an astute judgement or diagnosis this would be read out as an entertaining oddity as if a dog trained to bring slippers had, just for once, brought the right pair. A handful of enthusiasts were trying to establish general practice as a specialty of its own but won little more than patronising smiles from the medical establishment

One feature of Donovan's time remains unchanged – the regular prediction of the imminent demise of the NHS. Yet the NHS, though blighted by perpetual reorganisation, still manages – just – to keep going. It's survival owes little to words spun by politicians, health economists, and folk of that ilk but a lot to the human instinct that drives those who actually care for the sick to cope as best they can, however dire the circumstance.

Michael O'Donnell
Loxhill, May 2006

EDITOR'S NOTE
None of the entries in Donovan's commonplace books are dated though it's possible to put an approximate date on some because of the incidents they

describe. The archive contains no diaries, only pages ripped from diaries, and many of these pages are undated. I had intended to present this selection in chronological order but this involved so much guesswork that I gave up the struggle. The order in which most of the papers appear was determined by chance.

A few entries in the commonplace book are written in the first person; most in the third. A few are in the present tense; most in the past. I can define no rule that determines Donovan's choice of person or tense. In editing the papers I have stuck with the original.

Donovan shared James Joyce's dislike of "perverted commas". I have retained his Joycean use of a dash to indicate direct speech and italics to denote other quotations.

M O'D.

EDITOR'S NOTE
The longest of the Slagthorpe papers appears to be the draft for the opening chapter of an autobiography, though narrated in the third person. No other chapters have been found.

Overture and Beginners

In which Donal Donovan re-enters the Kingdom of Childhood and seeks to establish himself as a grown-up.

The Second Sunday after Lupercal. Feast of the Evisceration of the Blessed Stanley of Accrington, Virgin and Martyr. Saturn in conjunction with Mercury. High tide London Bridge 15.37. Moon in its third quarter. Herb of the month: Mrs Stowe's Pussy-willow. At seven in the morning, the man on the Air Ministry roof forecast that rain would become general over England; by seven in the evening, it was unpleasantly particular over the railway embankment at Slagcliffe-le-Willows.

The train had stood motionless for an age and, beyond the rivulets of water that ran down the window, the world was a smear of shadows and reflected gaslight. The young man who had a compartment to himself got to his feet and jerked the leather strap at the base of the window. The window slid down with a thump and Donal Donovan stuck his head out into the rain.

Steam swirled from around the carriage wheels just as it had swirled behind Celia Johnson and Trevor Howard in *Brief Encounter* and as it had always swirled around the wheels that carried him home from boarding school.

At the far end of the platform, a scrawny old man in railway cap, battledress blouse, GPO trousers, bicycle clips, and plimsolls was loading the luggage van with basket after basket of racing pigeons. To Donal he was as familiar as the steam around the wheels: Albert Bicknell, guard, ticket collector, and authorised whistle blower.

The engine driver, equally familiar, had climbed from his cab to watch: Cornelius Molecatcher, a tall gangling man in shiny black cap and greasy dungarees who, for 40 years, had travelled back and forth along the Slag Valley line like an Arkwright shuttle.

Donal withdrew his head from the rain but left the window open. The gap offered a less claustrophobic view of the world than rain-smudged glass.

Slagcliffe Halt is perched on an embankment above the main road into the village and, that night, the municipal gas lamps cast patches of light on tar macadam that glistened like the surface of a river. On the far pavement, two women, their hair coiffured into beehives protected by transparent pixie hoods, tottered past on high heels that made their toes turn in. Once they'd rounded the corner, the only movements on the pavement were the flickering reflections of the pink and violet neon strips on the front of the Regal Kinema. Beyond the Regal was a dark void in which fluorescent screens flickered like fireflies – screens on which, at that moment, two Outspan oranges conversed in cultured accents.

And beyond the flicker of 20th century fireflies, beyond the rain, beyond the clouds, beyond hills and mountains and man-made borders, up there in the furthest corner of the North, Doctor Barbara Moore was on her way from John O'Groats.*

---

*An error that reveals that Donovan wrote this paper some time after the event. Local records suggest he arrived in Slagthorpe in 1957. Doctor Barbara Moore, a Russian dietician did not capture headlines until 1960 when she spent 23-days walking from John O'Groats to Land's End to draw attention to the nuclear threat.

Dr Moore claimed she was fuelled only by fruit juice, honey and cabbage and could exist for months on nourishment absorbed from sunlight and fresh air. After several well publicised walks in Britain she went to the US and

Tramp, tramp, tramp, along a narrow Highland road.

Tramp, tramp, tramp, thoughts of salvation composed in Russian and fragmented English phrases, racing through her brain.

Tramp, tramp, tramp, gastric juices eagerly digesting the last collation of dandelion leaves.

Tramp, tramp, tramp, each footstep earning redemption for mankind's radioactive sins.

Albert Bicknell blew his whistle and Cornelius gave an answering toot from his cab. Then, with much chuffing and clanking, the tank engine and its pair of carriages moved jerkily away from the platform.

Donal was on his way home. The familiar last lap along the Slag Valley line. Home from school, home from university, home from medical school ... but this time just home.

His dad had been a GP at the next stop down the line and had sent Donal away first to school and then to university with instructions to become a respectable citizen. One evening, just a year after Donal had qualified as a doctor, his dad took him aside and spoke emphatically.

—Whatever you do with your life, don't come here. It's all right for the likes of me but I'd prefer you to practice a more fastidious class of medicine. It's what your mother would have wanted.

That mention of the mother her son had never known and whose name was rarely spoken was a signal that, just for once, his dad wasn't teasing his only son.

Two weeks later his dad was dead. So Donal stuck to the course prescribed for him. Until now. Today, twelve years later, he was on his way back. He'd convinced his friends, and almost convinced himself, that he'd grown disenchanted with the style of medicine practised in London hospitals. Only one other person knew he had reached a point where he had to break a routine of which they both

---

walked 3207 miles from Los Angeles to New York. On her return walk to Los Angeles she was hit by a car and died of her injuries.

were part. Without her, his adventure would never have started, but she played her part before it began and had already made her exit.

Just two weeks before, Donal had read an advertisement in the British Medical Journal:

OPPORTUNITY TO PRACTICE REALISTIC MEDICINE.
ASSISTANT WANTED IN FRONT LINE TRENCHES. NO
PROSPECT OF HONOURS, GOLD CHAINS, OR ERMINE. WOULD
SUIT DEDICATED UNWEAVER OF RICH TANGLED PATTERNS.
APPLY IN *SHORT* LETTER TO DOCTOR FINBAR ALOYSIUS
O'FLAHERTY, SLAGFIELD HOUSE, SLAGTHORPE.

Finbar O'Flaherty had joined Donal's dad as an assistant soon after the war and, though Donal had met him only a couple of times, he'd liked him because his dad liked him. When Doctor Donovan senior died, Finbar sent an obituary to the British Medical Journal. The editor of that journal, in which the lives of notorious rogues are commemorated in prose that would seem overblown in *Fox's Book of Martyrs*, refused to publish it, claiming it was *in bad taste*.

Finbar had sent Donal a copy and he still remembered its closing sentences.

Jim Donovan was at ease with general practice. He regarded hospitals as dangerous places that exposed patients with challenged immune systems to opportunist infection and doctors with a challenged sense of security to opportunist temptation to pontificate. He was fond of his patients, even the difficult ones, and he killed very few of them.

That was the last Donal heard of Finbar until he saw the advertisement. He wrote a stumbling letter trying to explain his real reason for wanting to escape from London and its hospitals. Next morning he got a telegram:

Delighted. Come as soon as you can. If you're half the man your father was, you'll be more than I deserve. Bring only stethoscope and full fountain pen. Yours in peace, Finbar.

The next time the train stopped he would be there. Already he had the symptoms that came on every journey home from school: the mounting excitement, the warm glow in the epigastrium, the slight queasiness. And with the symptoms came the expectations: his father waiting at the station, the blazing pyramids of coal in the fireplaces of Slagfield House, the Hornby train hibernating in its box on the top of the wardrobe.

Donal hauled his leather suitcase down from the rack, put on his belted gabardine raincoat, and, as the train jerked into Slagthorpe, stuck his head out the window and looked eagerly along the platform.

His father wasn't there.

Nor was anybody Donal knew or recognised.

He opened the door and exited backwards, leaning in to retrieve his case before slamming the door.

A tall man in long raincoat and brown trilby helped a dumpy woman down from the next carriage and they walked arm in arm through the steam and smoke towards the exit gate. Cornelius Molecatcher gave a toot on the whistle and the train clanked out of the station.

Donal was on his own. The only sound now came from the rain cascading onto the track from the overflowing gutters and he wandered along the platform, lugging his case. There was no one at the gate to collect his ticket, no one waiting for him in the vaulted booking hall.

The booking hall hadn't changed. Its walls were still wartime blanco green and the glass in the doors that led to the station yard was still opaque, coated with crusted dust.

The hole in the wall labelled Ticket Office had its shutter down but a wavering hand had chalked a message on a large blackboard headed **Railway Company Notices**:

Be it known to all who have been granted a safe arrival on the
1931 from Slag Junction that, if Doctor Donal Donovan be among

ye, he should call immediately at my office where he may learn
something to his advantage.
> *Issued by the power invested in me,*
> *Erasmus Dewdrop*
> *By Grace of God, Stationmaster*

Donal lugged his case across the hall to a dark green door on which the brass *Push* plate was polished to the thinness of foil. The bottom of the door had been battered by decades of kicking and he planted his foot where so many had been planted before.

As the door swung open, his eyes started to water. Smoke drifted from a crack in the black-leaded stove at the centre of the room. Beside the stove stood a grey haired man with a head four sizes too large for his body. The unmistakeable Erasmus Dewdrop. Erasmus stared at Donal through wire-rimmed glasses and, while he stared, poured mahogany tea from a blue metal teapot into a George V Coronation mug.

The mug stood in a ring-stained oasis on a table amid piles of papers recording the transactions of the old Slag Valley Railway Company.

Beneath the table a large tweed-covered bottom wiggled from side to side.

—For Christ's sake, shut that door.

Erasmus, whose lips hadn't moved, paused in mid-pour and nodded at Donal who pulled the door to behind him.

The tweeded bottom twitched more vigorously and Donal saw that its owner was jabbing vigorously at the floorboards with a penknife.

The bottom owner cried *Got you* and Erasmus resumed his pour. The tweeds backed out from under the table and their wearer rose creakily from his knees, turned to face Donal and swamped him with images: tufts of fading ginger hair sprouting in every direction, waistcoat impregnated with cigarette ash, horn-rimmed spectacles reinforced in one corner with sticking plaster, red silk handkerchief dotted with horses' heads drooping from top pocket. Doctor Finbar Aloysius O'Flaherty, singer, poet, intellectual punch-up artist and much loved general practitioner.

Finbar thrust a fist under Donal's nose, turned it palm upwards, and opened it.

—What do you think of that, doctor?

—It looks like a bug.

—Bug, how are you? That, my ingenuous lad, is *Coleoptera Aloysia*, the dreaded Slagshire long-horned beetle, first described by the perspicacious Doctor O'Flaherty when he diagnosed a fulminating infection in Stanley Etheringshaw's wooden leg. Get a hungry handful of these lads in your rafters and before you can say *Slagshire Mutual Improvident Building Society*, your mortgaged homestead will come crashing around your ears. It's time Erasmus to call in the insecticide squirters.

—We will fight the good fight, said Erasmus.

As he intoned his response, a lump of wood fell from the ceiling and smashed the coronation mug. Then a rack of wooden shelves collapsed in a flurry of dust, box files, and pots of glue.

Finbar grabbed Donal's elbow.

—Let's get out of here, young Donovan, before these jokers move on to their main course.

The doctors juddered down Slagthorpe High Street in Finbar's pre-war Morris Cowley. Donal sat alongside the driver and his suitcase shared the back seat with a large black Gladstone bag, a scattering of certificates and prescription pads, a pair of Wrigley's obstetric forceps, a sphygmomanometer, and a dog-eared paperback of James Joyce's Dubliners.

They stopped at the traffic lights outside the Picture Palace.

—On your father's last day, said Finbar, he insisted on taking the evening surgery at Slagheaton. He had the pain in his chest before he started but he finished the surgery and drove home.

He nodded towards the cinema.

—That week they were offering an anatomical extravaganza. A painted banner stretched across the façade. Jane Russell's superstructure. One of your poor dad's last sights on this earth.

The traffic lights changed to green and Finbar, who seemed ignorant of the purpose of the clutch pedal, ground the car into a low gear. They jerked forward for some twenty yards until they achieved enough momentum for him to move the gear lever dramatically from bottom to top. The car responded heroically and they were soon back at their cruising speed of 25 mph.

Finbar turned his head towards Donal, winked, and dug him in the ribs.

—It's great to have you here.

Donal longed for him to return his gaze to the road.

—You'll find medicine here is great sport. But we'll leave that till tomorrow. This evening Martha's cooking us up something special and I've blown the dust from a bottle or two of Haut Brion I've been saving for an occasion like this.

A cyclist on the road ahead looked over his shoulder and recognised the car. He rapidly dismounted and carried his bicycle onto the pavement until they passed.

Four hours later Donal sank into anaesthetised sleep and dreamed of Hornby trains and right-handed points and double crossovers. He woke once in the early hours with a dry mouth and a headache but when his alarm re-awakened him at 7.30 the headache was gone and he felt refreshed. No hangover, just a comforting sense of euphoria. Finbar had predicted the condition. The priceless gift of the O'Briens of Haut Brion, he'd said, as they'd sat in high-winged chairs before a blazing fire and polished off the second bottle.

When Donal went downstairs he found kippers, eggs, bacon, sausages, black pudding, mushrooms, and tomatoes sizzling in entree dishes lined up on a hot plate on the sideboard.

Finbar was already at the table, an empty plate in front of him and a cup of tea in his hand as he read the letters page of *The Manchester Guardian.*

—Am I expected to eat all this? asked Donal.

—Only if you want to. We have a few old souls who come in during the morning surgery to finish it off. Does 'em more good than any medicine you or I could prescribe.

Finbar put down the paper.

—You have a satisfied Haut Brion look about you so we'll chuck you in at the deep end. You can take the morning surgery.

As Donal finished his breakfast and dabbed his lips with his napkin, Finbar's housekeeper Martha appeared silently at the door, as if she'd been waiting in the wings. Her demeanour was no less mournful than it had been last night when Finbar claimed *she raises melancholia to an ecstatic plane that drives hedonists frantic with envy.*

—They're ready for you, doctor, she said.

She turned on her heel and Donal followed her down the rambling corridor beneath the stairs towards his father's old consulting room.

The room looked much as he remembered it: the high ceiling fretted with Victorian plasterwork, the net curtained French windows that opened onto the grimy garden, a coal fire flickering in a grate beneath the marble mantelpiece.

—They're in there, said Martha, pointing to the green baize of the waiting room door. The doctor says he'll hang around in case you need him.

Then she left.

A mahogany desk stood in the middle of the room alongside two low filing cabinets. Scattered across the green leather panel in the desk top were a sphygmomanometer, a three years out-of-date drug company calendar, a pile of certificate and prescription pads, a silver inkwell (empty), two thermometers, and a pair of garden secateurs.

In the corner behind him, a chromium plated steriliser steamed and bubbled, gently agitating instruments that lay alongside it on the glass-topped trolley. And along one wall stood a blue leather examination couch with a pink blanket folded across a corner.

Donal crossed to the green baize door and, suppressing a surge of anxiety, flung it open. A noisy babble of conversation stopped instantly and he gazed upon a silent room that seemed filled with rough-looking men, pregnant women, and children with runny noses.

Every head turned and every pair of eyes focussed on him.

—First, please.

The words emerged as a defensive bark.

A large man in a shiny blue suit, and with a white silk scarf wrapped around his neck, rose slowly from his seat and followed Donal into the consulting room. Donal nipped smartly behind the desk, sat down, and tried hard to muster a reassuring smile.

The large man stood at the other side of he desk glowering at him.

—Is Finbar not here?

—Doctor O'Flaherty is not taking this morning's surgery. I'm his assistant. What can I do for you?

—I want to knock on.

—I beg your pardon?

—A knocking on note.

Donal stared at him blankly.

—Best ask Finbar, said the man. He knows. I want a week on't club.

—On't what?

He hadn't meant to mimic the phrase but it was too late now.

—I want a week off.

—So what's the matter?

—Debility. Send for Finbar. He'll tell you. Harry Molesworth. He'll tell you.

—Hang on a minute.

Donal searched for Harry Molesworth's notes in the filing cabinet and removed the card.

—Look up July, said Harry. I knocked on then for a week. Debility. You'll find it there.

Donal looked at the notes.

—All Doctor O'Flaherty did in July was to write the date and make a stroke with his pen.

—That's what I had, said Harry. A stroke. But Finbar always calls it Debility.

—Perhaps we'd better take a look at you. Just take off your clothes and lie up on the couch.

—See here, smart Alec, said Harry aggressively. I've been knocking on with Debility for more years than you've had ham sandwiches. If you think I'm taking my clothes off now you've got another bloody think coming. You run long and have a word with Finbar.

He sat down defiantly. He looked even broader sitting than he did standing so Donal followed his advice.

Finbar was still at the breakfast table, going through his mail. At the other side of the table two elderly men and one woman, who looked as though they'd slept rough overnight, were polishing off what remained of the breakfast.

—This is Sara and Arthur and Stanley, said Finbar. And this is the clever young doctor who's come to join me. Jim Donovan's lad.

The three gave Donal a quick smile before returning to wiping their plates – and the entree dishes – with thick chunks of bread.

Finbar slit open another letter.

—What brings you back so soon?

—Harry Molesworth. His debility.

—The noble Harry, said Finbar without looking up from the letter. Worked for 14 years on the coal face at Slagheaton Colliery and sired six children before his wife upped and offed. Left him with the kids so he went to night school, got a certificate, and became a junior clerk in the Coal Board offices.

—He's a hard worker and they can't get clerks to live up here so the Coal Board kept promoting him till he was just six inches out of his depth. He chews like a beaver at his job but doesn't understand some of it. The only way he can hold it down is to have week off three or four times a year when the tension gets too much. I think it's good medicine to give it him. That way Harry feeds and clothes his children and the Coal Board gets its job done reasonably well.

—So what do I write on the certificate?

—Ergophrenia, said Finbar.

—Of course. Work on the mind. What else?

Sara looked up from her plate and gave Donal a smile of approval.

He responded with a nod then scurried back to the consulting room.

It was empty. Harry had left.

He opened the green baize door.

—Next.

But the waiting room too was empty. They'd all left.

He was a failure. The supreme patient deterrent. He turned back gloomily to the consulting room and, as he did, a patient he'd missed stepped out from behind the door.

And what a patient.

Long blonde hair. Unbelievably long legs that disappeared into a froth of petticoat that caused her skirt to flare mischievously above her knees. A red leather waistcoat over a man's white ballet shirt whose opening at the throat plunged alarmingly towards her umbilicus.

As Donal's jaw dropped, this unbelievable creature fluttered false eyelashes.

—You may remember my mother, she said.

Like a smack in the face with a wet flannel.

—Come in and sit down, said Donal.

Dammit, he did remember her mother. The only possible genetic source of those accoutrements. Blonde and brittle Maye Smerthwaite, Slagthorpe's scarlet woman who, in his father's day, had been the toast of the Slag Common golf club and known to the members as The Hole In One.

This must be Felicia, her only daughter, rumoured to be the product of a careless evening Maye spent behind the tricky bunker near the twelfth green with our local MP, Brigadier Digby Knutsford, RAMC.

—Don't worry about them leaving, said Felicia, for indeed 'twas she. They're all very fond of Finbar. And they didn't realise who you were. I remember you because I used to see you when you came home from Cambridge in your striped blazer. I was only eight but my mother always pointed you out.

—That's Dear Doctor Donovan's boy home from Cambridge, she'd say. That's where you'll go if you're a good girl.

—But I wasn't a good girl. They drummed me out of the convent. Mother St Peter went through my satchel looking for purple hearts and found a packet of Durex. I think she'd prefer to have found purple hearts. I tried to explain that if a girl didn't look after herself no one else would. But she wouldn't listen.

She brushed aside a strand of hair that had fallen across her forehead and produced a smile that threatened to melt Donal's contrived equanimity.

All that stuff about doctors being professionally immune to their patients' sex appeal must have been thought up by a committee of dignified eunuchs. If thoughts were admissible evidence, the General Medical Council could have had him off the register right then.

He tried a hesitant cough.

—What can I do for you?

—Do you like being a doctor?

—Most of the time.

—And are you terribly dedicated?

—Occasionally.

—That's nice. I like a doctor who's keen on his job but doesn't bang on about it.

She perched on a corner of the desk and slipped her waistcoat back from her shoulders.

—Would you like to see my chest?

He blushed, dammit. He blushed.

—Hang on a minute, he stuttered. Tell me what's the matter first.

—I've got a nasty cough. Boozy Knutsford says it's because I smoke too much. But I think I caught a chill on location on the Slagshire moors.

—You're an actress then?

—More a sort of model.

—Perhaps we'd better have a listen to your chest. Take your shirt off and lie up on the couch with the blanket over you. I'll pop outside while you undress.

He waited outside the door for a discreet couple of minutes. Then coughed loudly and returned.

Felicia was not on the couch. She'd removed everything except her tights and was posing before the small mirror above the wash basin narcissistically examining her breasts.

—They're not bad, are they? Yet just because everyone's gone overboard on this flat-titted fashion, I don't get as much work as I did.

—Get up on the couch, said Donal, and nearly smothered her with the pink blanket.

—It tickles, she said and flung it away. Then she climbed onto the couch and lay there as if posing for Playboy.

Finbar's patients, Donal decided, fell into two categories: those who would rather die then remove their clothes and those who couldn't get them off quickly enough.

—Come on, she said. Let's see what you're like at the diagnosis.

He laid his hands over her lower ribs.

—Take a deep breath.

She did.

—Say ninety-nine.

She did.

—I can't feel anything, he said.

—That's funny. I can. You have beautiful hands, Donal. May I call you Donal? And I love your bedside manner.

He snatched his stethoscope from his pocket.

—Breathe deeply, he ordered and plonked the stethoscope between her breasts. The breathing would stop her talking while he worked out how to establish some sort of authority.

For a long ten seconds, he held the stethoscope in place and listened learnedly. Then he glanced down at the edge of the couch and made a disturbing discovery. In the rush and excitement of his first morning he'd overlooked one of life's essentials. The zip of his fly was undone.

Using his right hand to keep the stethoscope in place, he let his left drift idly downwards until it located the clasp on the zip.

—Give a little cough, he said to Felicia, hoping the noise of coughing would camouflage the sound of zipping.

Felicia coughed and he zipped in unison.

He looked down.

Disaster.

As she'd coughed she'd moved and now a good four inches of her tights were enmeshed in the middle of his zipped up fly. He tried surreptitiously to free the zip but it was firmly stuck. He tugged again and Felicia looked down.

—That's a new one on me, she said.

—I'm terribly sorry, he stammered. I'll pay for a new pair of tights, of course, but meanwhile we appear to have established an embarrassing attachment.

—Have you a pair of scissors? she asked.

—Not on me. There's one on the instrument trolley if we can get over there.

She swung her legs from the couch and they started to hop across the room like copulating kangaroos. After two hops they started giggling and after four they collapsed to the floor in hysterical laughter.

—For God's sake, let me take them off, she said Then you can get the scissors.

She slipped off her tights and they both got to their feet, she naked and Donal with her tights dangling from his flies.

—Have you got it sorted then? said a gruff voice.

Donal cast a startled glance over his shoulder.

Harry Molesworth stood at the waiting room door.

—Got it sorted? My debility? My certificate?

Harry walked straight past the naked Felicia and sat in the chair in front of the desk.

—I thought you were never coming back so I went out for a fag.

—Hang on a minute, said Donal.

He went to the instrument trolley, picked up a pair of scissors and, with finely calculated nonchalance, snipped away the tights.

Felicia primped to the couch wiggling her bottom in a provocative way and lay down without benefit of blanket.

—Finbar put you right? asked Harry.

—He did.

Donal wrote Ergophrenia on the certificate.

—Knew he would, said Harry. Thanks.

He picked up the certificate and, as he walked to the door, he glanced at the couch and, for the first time, acknowledged Felicia's presence.

—Next time, Felicia Smerthwaite, don't try to jump the queue.

Donal didn't mention his morning adventure to Finbar though he had to spend more than several minutes after the surgery freeing the snarled zip. Finbar gave him a short list of visits and he enjoyed driving round streets through which he'd walked and cycled as a boy.

Finbar was booked to do the evening surgery at Slagheaton so Donal had to do the one at Slagfield House. Once again the waiting room was packed and he recognised many of the faces that had been there that morning.

But this time every patient stayed and accepted his presence almost with enthusiasm.

When he'd finished and went to lock the outer door of the waiting room he found a handwritten notice taped to its outside.

We are all lucky that I now have the help of dear old Jim Donovan's son Donal, a very clever doctor from London. He will help to improve the standard of medicine I offer you. So, for God's sake, be nice to him.

Yours in peace,

   Finbar Aloysius O'Flaherty

The Happy Medium

With the passing of Madame Blanche, fringe medicine in Slagthorpe will never be the same again. In her time Madame B scavenged across most of the territory: mesmeric healing, spirit surgery, electro-magnetism, herbal douching, earth-thought-force transference, high colonic lavage – she turned each to profit at some stage in her career.

When she died, or as the Slagthorpe Echo put it, *was called to a higher terrestrial plane*, her fame was nationwide but her bread and butter income still came from the rich, obese, and impressionable women who dominate the chintzy front parlours of Higher Drive – Slagthorpe's nob hill.

Higher Drive is a serpentine avenue that winds through the soot-coated shrubbery of Slag Hill. The 1920s builder who dotted its course with mini-Tudor manors and mini-Bavarian Schlosses made up for a lack of aesthetic sensitivity with an unerring sense of the value of a name. Search as you may, you will find no Lower, Middle, or even High Drive, and no matter how hard developers strain to produce grandiose titles for the groves of bungalows and Ideal Homes that nibble like mice at the foot of the hill, they can never erode the superiority of the Higher accolade.

Madame B was a local lass who, until the lure of celebrity demanded a change of image, traded under the name bestowed by her parents, Daisy Ostlethwistle. Back in the 1930s, before her star burst through the murky haze that serves for a sky over Slagthorpe,

Daisy's pretensions caused great amusement among the doctors who practised from Slagfield House. They never guessed the part their practice would play in creating her celebrity.

During Daisy's early days, the junior incumbent at Slagfield House was Donal's father, Dear Doctor Donovan the First, who was playing Doctor Finlay to an intemperate old crook called Cameron. Slagthorpe's Angus Cameron had neither the good sense nor geniality of A J Cronin's creation. He was a cantankerous old devil who made no attempt to keep his medical knowledge up to date and underpaid his junior partner to whom he delegated all night and weekend calls. Yet, though he drank a bottle of whisky every evening, he always had a clear eye for an easy shilling.

In those days, Higher Drive society was dominated by the formidable Gertrude Clackington, relict of a former chairman of the Slagthorpe and District Mutual Improvident Society. When her elderly husband died in the early 1920s his tough young widow, in a piece of entrepreneurial wizardry that bedazzled even hardened Slagshire colliery owners, first became principal shareholder then managing director and finally chairman of Slagthorpe Consolidated Glue. When the Depression came, she bought out the remaining shares and turned the glutinous goldmine into her own private company. With her fortune made and her power unquestioned, her ambition slid into a decline and she settled for growing old gracelessly and enjoying ill health ... much to the profit of Angus Cameron.

Donovan's dad was kept well away from Cameron's cash cow but enjoyed watching from the sidelines whenever Mrs Clackington grew bored with her obsequious GP and suffered one of her attacks of Baffling the Doctors. In the course of ten fraught days, a series of medical knights, and perhaps a Lord or two, would debouch at the Junction to be met by the Clackington Rolls and chauffeured to Gertrude's bijou Schloss perched on the very pinnacle of Higher Drive.

Angus Cameron and a deferential footman – and, according to

Doctor Donovan the First, a stranger would have difficulty telling which was which – would greet the distinguished visitor on the stone steps that led to the main door, and after a brief ceremony which involved the great man handing over hat and overcoat and being led to the cloakroom to warm his hands in a basin of hot water, Angus would perform his humble duty: accompanying the visitor to the bedroom, introducing him to the patient, and standing discreetly in the background.

The Great Man (GM) would then sit on a boudoir chair positioned alongside the head of Gertrude's four poster and generate a sonorous murmur of questions to which Gertrude would respond with deep despairing sighs, sometimes accompanied with a shrug of the shoulders, and occasionally punctuated with an angry grunt.

As the questions drew peacefully to their close, the GM would nod at the uniformed nurse who stood at the far side of the bed. She would lean forward and while the GM turned away and took a discreet interest in one of paintings on the wall, would carefully roll bedclothes up and down to reveal an impressive acreage of Gertrude, concealing only the forbidden territory that lay between the navel and the knees.

A gentle clearing of the throat from the nurse would recapture the attention of the GM who would then approach the bed and use his pre-warmed hands to perform a gentle exploration of Gertrude's available areas. Any attempt to trespass on forbidden territory would be halted by an angry hiss from the patient.

There followed the traditional application of the stethoscope. The GM would place the business end on strategic points fore and aft on his patient's chest, listen with a stone-faced puzzlement that suggested he was in the presence of unique sounds, then demand the ritual incantation of Ninety-nine. After laying aside the stethoscope he would prepare himself for flamboyant demonstration of the percussive art. Placing the palm of his left hand against Gertrude's chest he would rap its middle finger with middle finger of his right to produce impressive resonance. As the last echo died away, the GM would nod once more at the nurse who would hand him a towel and start to rearrange the bedclothes while both doctors retired to the bathroom to consult, the GM wiping his hands with the towel in the manner of Pontius Pilate.

Once in the bathroom the GM would put aside the towel and wash his hands in the basin while discussing with Angus what it might be seemly to tell their patient, seeking words that would express the rarity, indeed uniqueness, of her condition without reaching any definite conclusion. The prepared statement would also hint at her good fortune in at last encountering a doctor who really understood the depth of her suffering. Further tests would, of course be needed.

Once they had agreed on their story and the size of fee this patient would tolerate, they would gossip about strange things that were happening within the trade – who had done what to whom at which Royal College. Only when they judged enough time had passed to impress their patient with the extent of their discussion would they emerge. Angus would stand respectfully in the background while the GM seated himself once more beside the four poster where he would mutter wisely but unpersuasively.

The close of this part of the rubric would be signalled by Gertrude. When she followed one of her attenuated sighs with a raising of her eyes towards the lace fringe of her bonnet Angus knew it was his duty to step forward and usher the visitor quickly downstairs and into the Rolls.

Once the GM had been dispatched Angus would re-climb the stairs slowly, weighing his despondency against the evening's profitability, and knowing that when he re-entered the bedroom Gertrude would issue a stinging rebuke followed by a demand that he find some person better suited to diagnose the complex origins of her suffering.

The highly-ritualised event would close with Angus driving recklessly down Higher Drive eager for the taste of whisky and

wondering which of his old medical teachers he could call on next
to visit Gertrude. At the same moment the GM sitting in the
Slagshire Pullman sipping British Rail Burgundy would meditate
upon the enigmatic nature of his trade. Yet, even as increasing
distance separated the doctors, there would come a moment of
harmonious telepathy when each, now re-established in his own
world, would comfort himself by counting his guineas.

It was, of course, clear to anyone unblinded by the lure of gold
that Angus and the procession of GMs could do little to alleviate
Gertrude's suffering. The only person with the power to do that
was Gertrude. She wasn't feigning illness. She felt genuinely
debilitated but because everyone found it more profitable to cosset
her than to cajole her, she suffered from a surfeit of solicitude. And,
being of suspicious mind, the more attention she got, the iller she
thought she was.

As is the way with nature, her illness was self-limiting. The days
she spent in bed allowed her to rekindle the restless energy that had
run low and one morning when the energy was restored and
bursting to be released she would rise from the four poster and
signal her return to normal health by firing a couple of managers
and sacking a few servants. Then, for a month or so, Angus
Cameron's gold mine would lie dormant.

No one knows how Gertrude first heard of Madame Blanche
who had already spent half a lifetime operating as a low-grade
medium in a dingy lair near the cattle market where she earned a
crust from palm reading, crystal gazing, Saturday evening séances,
and occasional assistance to young ladies in trouble. News of her
services was passed by word of mouth and she recruited séance
clients by hanging around the fringes of funerals dressed in antique
gown and coat of black, with the veil on her sombre toque pinned
to one side so she could stare at the bereaved with a discomfiting
fixation.

Maybe Gertrude spotted Blanche at a funeral or a memorial
service or heard her mentioned at a Higher Drive soiree but meet

they certainly did and Doctor Donovan the First would recreate the scene – with assumed voices and elaborate pantomime – of the first historic consultation. (He had not been present but received a colourful account from Gertrude's nurse of the time who was one of his patients.)

Gertrude was suffering another attack of Baffling the Doctors and the procession of GMs had, as usual, failed to alleviate it. This time she decided to cut out the middle man and ordered her nurse to tell Doctor Cameron she needed no further attention from him. She then commanded her butler to summon Madame Blanche.

The scene opened with Gertrude sprawled as usual amid the lavender-scented pillows of the vast four-poster but with sharp eyes fixed on a far corner of the room where Madame Blanche, who had insolently ignored her patient when she entered, sat oscillating gently in a rocking chair. She was, as always, clad entirely in black with the silk toque fixed firmly in place with giant hatpins.

For five long minutes not a word was spoken. Then suddenly the rocking stopped and Madame Blanche's head fell back and her arms flopped against the sides of the chair as she collapsed into a trance. For a few minutes there was silence. Then she started to emit a stream of high-pitched gibberish at first softly but mounting in crescendo till it filled the room.

The gibberish stopped as suddenly as it had begun and Madame B started to froth at the mouth. Then, as her eyes rolled towards heaven, she emitted a piercing shriek:

—It's your duodenum.

Gertrude was clearly impressed, indeed frightened. For a moment she looked as if she were about to duck her head beneath the sheet but before she could move Madame B was at it again.

This time the gibberish was even louder, was indeed painful to Gertrude's ears before it turned to moaning, whistling, and genuinely eerie hooting which ended with a cry this time less terrifying than triumphant:

—High colonic lavage.

That was the moment when Miss Clackington *knew* that extraterrestrial forces had rallied to her aid.

Madame Blanche was revived with generous helpings of Courvoisier and, as soon as she recovered, went into action with the apparatus she just happened to have handy. With that magnificent suspension of reason that is pathognomonic of the fringe enthusiast, Gertrude, who in all else was a shrewd and intelligent woman, showed not one flicker of suspicion when Madame Blanche explained that, when it came to colonic lavage, she was Slagshire's only really high operator in a field where connoisseurs measure efficacy in terms of altitude.

After three brief but expensive treatments, Miss Clackington's attack of Baffling the Doctors switched dramatically into her first Miraculous Cure – the first of many to be attributed to the magical administrations of Madame B.

Blanche next persuaded Gertrude to have a twice-weekly prophylactic lavage to wash away any accumulation of noxious substances. Within a month her lower bowel had grown so dependent on this stimulation that, without it, it could not go about its normal business. If Gertrude missed a treatment she was immediately afflicted by the dreaded constipation and had to have a course of the Extra-High – and naturally extra-expensive – lavage that Madame Blanche was happy to provide.

Thus it was that Daisy stole Angus Cameron's gold mine and once Miss Clackington had trumpeted the glad news across the bridge and coffee tables of Higher Drive, Madame Blanche was appointed official irrigator to every expensively nurtured colon on the hill. Within months she acquired a Black Box, a cosmic ray brine bath, and an infinite array of herbal distillations with which she bewitched insecure Slagshire tycoons and wealthy Slagshire widows who queued at her door for a dip in the stimulating waters of unorthodoxy.

For ten years Madame Blanche reigned as the unchallenged queen of the Slagthorpe fringe. Even the Bishop's wife in far off

Slagcaster, a fiercely intelligent woman whose scepticism had been honed by years of contact with the clergy, used to boast of having *My little woman in Slagthorpe* – much as others would boast of *My little physician in Vienna* – to put things right when orthodox medicine failed in its duty.

Madame Blanche's practice triumphantly survived the war – not surprisingly because her treatments were essentially designed for life's non-combatants – but Doctor Donovan the First reckoned that the coming of the NHS would put an end to it. He reckoned wrong.

Far from driving Daisy out of business, free medicine available to all strengthened the appeal of her unorthodoxy. With specialists and operations available to every Tom, Dick and Harry, citizens of Higher Drive could maintain social superiority only by indulging in treatments that were clearly too expensive for the masses. Mysterious courses of injections, stimulation of the natural vital processes, and other treatments that had the cachet of being unavailable under the National Health, replaced the Black Box and the trusty high lavage.

The NHS opened other opportunities. Before 1948 Daisy's success came from her ability to ape the antics of exploitive doctors. Now she could tackle the profession head on and deride their irresponsible treatments. This new aggressive attitude, and the arrival of nationwide television in the early nineteen fifties, brought Madame Blanche national recognition. Media hungry for anything new or different competed to devour her. Sunday papers, glossy magazines and television chat shows doted on her and it was a thin week if her face or utterances failed to crop up somewhere.

Daisy's next Great Leap Forward came in 1959 when Gertrude Clackington shuffled off her mortal shackles and moved reluctantly to the great four poster in the sky. (Finbar, who by then had become an occasional astringent force in Gertrude's life had to certify her death and attributed it to enema addiction.) Under a trust fund set up through Gertrude's will, Daisy was installed as director of the

Slagthorpe Consolidated Glue True Medicine Clinic dedicated not just to relieve affliction but to campaign against vaccination, fluoridation, and other unnatural processes that doctors conspired to inflict upon the innocent.

Daisy retained her flair for diagnosing a need just before it welled into public consciousness. She was one of the first to spot that Mother Nature was about to be re-enthroned as a benevolent matriarch and no longer reviled as the malevolent force who wreaked natural disasters or caused death from natural causes. The Slagthorpe Consolidated Glue True Medicine Clinic soon became the headquarters of the national chain of Madame Blanche Natural Food Stores and natural became the most powerful adjective in Madame Blanche's business: natural food, natural remedies, natural cosmetics ... she could scarcely invent them rapidly enough to keep pace with the demand. It was a business of which entrepreneurs dream: cheap ingredients bought in bulk and resold in small quantities at extravagant prices. The only expensive ingredient was the nostalgic packaging.

Madame Blanche Natural Products were soon available in every High Street and there was talk in the financial pages that Madame Blanche Enterprises was poised to extend its empire overseas when it suddenly lost its empress, struck down in the prime of her seventy-fourth year by an attack of irony. Daisy succumbed to smallpox contracted from a guru she'd imported to take over her transcendental meditation department.

Finbar gave the news to Donal at lunchtime when he returned from his morning visits.

—Have you read about Daisy? asked Finbar, waving a copy of the Echo. Poetic justice is alive and well and living in Slagthorpe. She got her quietus from her own Slagarishi. Your father should have been with us at this hour.

He put his arm around Donal's shoulder and led him towards the dining room.

—Now let me give you the epilogue. The Echo doesn't include

it because it was delivered only last night. Have you met Mortimer Dreer yet, our medical officer of health? He's a miserable old sod but yesterday evening brought the first smile I've ever seen on his gloomy chops. He had to run a special session at the True Medicine Clinic to vaccinate all those who'd attended last week's anti-vaccination meeting. And Mortimer, I'm reliably informed, got a 100 per cent turnout of eager and co-operative clients.

—Enjoy that thought, my lad, while you set about Martha's tripe and onions ... one hundred per cent natural of course.

Let's Play Doctors and Nurses

From the crest of the low ridge that marks the northern fringe of Slagthorpe a soot-stained gothic building glowers across the town. A self-important grammar school founded by nineteenth century burghers in search of honours? The eyrie of a demented Victorian industrialist? No. This is the Slagthorpe Memorial Hospital, powerhouse of Slagthorpian medicine and known to every local as the Slaughterhouse.

The nickname implies no criticism of Slagthorpian surgery but celebrates the hospital's location. The architect refused to disfigure the façade with anything as vulgar as a gateway so the main entrance is at the back of the building just a stone's throw away from the cattle market. (Not that it is always stones that are thrown from the cattle market, as Doctor Abu Ben Adam, the Memorial's friendly casualty officer, will readily testify.)

The hospital is not, as many think, a memorial to Slagshire heroes who fell in the First World War. It was erected in 1902 by the first Lord Slag ostensibly in memory, but in truth in gratitude, for the death of the first Lady Slag and shortly before he married the second Lady Slag, Marietta Enrevanche, a Gaiety girl who earned her footnote in history by dancing before the future king clad only in the Prince of Wales feathers.

A week ago last Tuesday, the Memorial was the scene of one of those minor eruptions – a small earthquake in Chile on the Emotional Scale – that occur when people who have to keep their emotions on a tight rein are forced to work closely together. In boarding schools these catharses tend to occur around the age of puberty. In the equally neurotic hospital environment they occur when doctors and nurses temporarily regress to a mental age of round about five.

At the Memorial, the person with most experience of these emotional catharses is the Senior Surgeon, Lionel Tetchy. Years before surgeons could pronounce *electrolyte levels*, let alone knew what they were, Lionel decided that practitioners of his craft needed only two attributes: a high level of technical skill and a memorable personality. He achieved the first by devoting his years as a registrar exclusively to operating or – as the more macho surgeons prefer to call it – *cutting*. If other registrars wanted an afternoon, an evening, or a night off Lionel was always happy to stand in and do the emergency surgery.

After a time, his willingness and his efficiency began to impress his seniors and they came to rely on both. If an out-of-hours problem arose they could save themselves a tedious journey to the hospital by suggesting over the telephone that young Tetchy take a look at the patient and, if need be, get on with what was necessary.

So proficient did young Tetchy become that, at a time when surgical preferment was fiendishly difficult to achieve, he was appointed a consultant surgeon after his first interview. Not only that but he won the job at the Slagthorpe Memorial in the face of competition from the nephew of a member of the appointments committee and the son of a close friend of the chairman

Lionel acquired the second essential attribute of a surgeon on his very first morning in a Memorial operating theatre. He made his debut as a Personality by picking up a gall bladder he had just removed and flinging it in the face of a somnolent anaesthetist.

From that humble beginning, he set about enhancing his reputation. He insulted his patients, hurled instruments at the theatre sister and obscenities at his juniors, invited self-important members of the hospital management committee to indulge in impossible anatomical acrobatics, and made it clear he was a chronic sufferer from haemodementia or, as non-doctors call it, bloody mindedness.

As time wore on his fellow consultants' irritation turned to acceptance and eventually he earned the right to be known as a Character, the highest accolade surgeons can bestow on those few colleagues they really respect. And surgeons, as every impecunious pathologist knows, are no fools. The ruder Lionel was to his patients, the larger grew his private practice.

A well upholstered Slagthorpian enjoys nothing better, it seems, than being insulted by an expert. When Lionel told Councillor *Big Maggie* Ramsbotham JP that her haemorrhoids were caused by sitting on too many constipated committees, she responded by giving him a silver cigar box. When he told the Rev Enoch Trismus, perpetual curate of St Mary's and All Slag, that the indication for removing the reverend prostate was the continuing safety of the spinsters of the parish, he received a silver salver inscribed with a brief but illuminating reference from the Book of Job.

Conscious of the power of dogmatic assertion, Lionel, like every other Character, carries a collection of glib aphorisms in his surgical haversack.

—The only value of an anaesthetic is that it prevents the patient from asking tedious questions during an interesting operation.

—Biochemical tests are like short skirts. What they reveal can be interesting but what they conceal is fundamental.

Regular grumpy enunciation of these aphorisms produces that sycophantic chuntering from registrars and housemen that Lionel considers is the mark of A Good Team.

A dominant trait in the Character that Lionel plays is misogyny. The role comes easily. His mother died when he was an adolescent and since her death only two women have earned his affection. The first is his wife, a former theatre sister whom he married only after he'd trained her to serve his needs in the way he likes them served; the second is his current theatre sister, a chirpy tomboy whom he calls A Decent Chap and is the only person licensed to contradict her master.

His relations with other nursing staff have always been strained, possibly because he always refers to nurses as virgins. Out-patients, unused to the traditional licence granted to Characters, are often discomfited by the instruction to leave their particulars with the virgin at the desk. Inpatients are similarly disturbed when Lionel, examining a patient in the ward, thrusts his head through the curtains that surround the bed and bellows:

—Buck your ideas up, sister, and send us another virgin.

Lionel sees enemies everywhere but long ago decided that his arch enemy was the Memorial's Matron, Olivia Binnington, chiefly because, in Olivia's eyes, Lionel is no enemy at all. She admires his skill as a surgeon and finds it sad that an intelligent adult should so often behave like a spoilt child.

Like Lionel, Olivia is not a native Slagthorpian. She grew up in Slagcaster where her father was a clerk in the Finance Department of the Slagshire County Council. (She was christened Olivia because Twelfth Night was a set book when he did his Matric.) She drifted into nursing in the late 1920s, largely to please her parents. It was a respectable job for a respectable girl, not well paid but free from any contamination by Trade.

Her father thought it would give her a leg up the social ladder onto which he had managed to clamber. Her mother's thoughts were more particular. She hoped Olivia would meet a nice young doctor, become his wife, live in a large detached house, have a maid and gardener, maybe even a cook and chauffeur, read *The Lady*, master the Culbertson system, and provide her mother with well-spoken grandchildren who would go to smart schools.

Before she had made any decisions of her own Olivia found herself installed in the Preliminary Training School attached to the SRI, the Slagcaster Royal Infirmary. There she was taught how to wash bedpans by a Sister Tutor who inspected the results with the assiduity of an army sergeant, seeking out specks of dirt by squinting down hollow bedpan handles as if they were rifle barrels.

She was also taught how to perform blanket baths on three life-size dolls. Two were adults, Lady Gertrude and Mrs Snooks; the third was an innominate baby of indeterminate gender. The Lady Superintendent forbade the use of a male doll and instructors had to adopt a euphemistic approach to the washing of a man's dangerous equipment.

—After the second change of water, the Sister Tutor would explain, you will hand the flannel and towel to the patient and say, I'm sure you'd like to finish yourself off Mr Snooks while I go and prepare your mouthwash.

After six months indoctrination in the basic skills, Olivia and her fellow students moved to the Slagcaster Nursing School, dogsbodying as probationers on the SRI wards, bashing the books, and clocking in for lectures. If, after four years, they had proved they had the stamina and could pass the exams they would become qualified nurses.

Training as a nurse in the late nineteen twenties was a bit like entering a religious order: life as a probationer was as harsh as that of a novice in a convent. The hours were long and a trainee nurse had to seek permission, only rarely and grudgingly given, to stray outside the hospital or the gloomy nurses' hostel. The day shift lasted from 9 am to 8pm and the night shift from 9pm to 8am. Probationers on the day shift were allowed a two hour break in which to attend lectures and grab a meal. They were expected to cram study for exams into the space between shifts and had to attend lectures during their one day off a fortnight. Each spell of night duty lasted for three months but, after 30 consecutive nights, nurses were allowed three nights off … just long enough to disrupt the sleep pattern they'd established over the previous month.

When Olivia started at the SRI, the hospital's matron and Lady Superintendent of the Nursing School was the dreaded

Dame Hermione MacPherson, whose wizened face – a feminised version of Lord Beaverbrook's – still scowls at visitors from her portrait in the SRI entrance hall. Dame MacFearsome, as she was known to everybody except herself, believed that the only way to toughen young gels coming into the profession and prepare them for the nasty things they would have to do was to impose stern discipline. Rewards were few – the satisfaction of a job well done was considered its own reward – but punishments were many. Most involved humiliation before an audience of other nurses or even patients.

In the MacFearsome Catalogue of Nursing Depravity, the three deadliest sins were undue display of emotion, fraternising with doctors, and idleness. The greatest of these was idleness: junior nurses who had nothing to do were expected to go to the sluice and wash and re-wash bedpans that were already clean until summoned to another task by the ward sister.

At the Slagcaster Nursing School, as at boys' public schools, privilege came with promotion. Trained nurses suffered fewer restrictions than probationers, staff nurses fewer then trained nurses, and so on. The system, as in public schools, encouraged bullying: seniors were determined that their juniors should suffer just as much as they did when they were lower down the ladder.

Dame MacFearsome was given to making surprise inspections of the wards to ensure that every rule, no matter how petty, was enforced. The coal scuttle by the ward fire had to be to the right of the fireplace, fire tongs, coal shovel and poker had to lie parallel against the fender exactly three inches apart, and all four castors on every bed had to be lined up fore and aft with no deviation to left or right.

One day Olivia was gossiping with another nurse in the ward kitchen when she remembered she'd left a patient perched on a bedpan. She scuttled back to the ward bang into the middle of one of Matron's lightning inspections.

—Nurse, bellowed the MacFearsome basso-profundo.

Olivia just managed to retain her balance as she skidded to a halt on the polished wooden floor.

—Has a patient suffered a serious haemorrhage?

—No, Matron.

—Is the ward kitchen on fire?

—No, Matron.

—Then why have you run from the kitchen to the ward? A nurse may run only for haemorrhage or fire. You know the rule, I presume.

—Yes, Matron.

—Well, walk, nurse, walk. It's not a matter of safety but of dignity. When I enter my office at six o'clock tomorrow morning I will find on my desk a 1000 word essay in which you will have explained why a nurse should walk with dignity.

Despite the night's sleep lost to pen-chewing composition, Olivia didn't grumble. But then she was the only nurse who never complained about the petty rules or the disciplinary humiliations. She didn't complain because she was happy: had never been happier at any time in her life. Despite the long hours, the bullying, the permanent backache and the burning feet, she had fallen in love with nursing. She could think of nothing she would rather do. She wasn't the only person to benefit from her contentment: her good natured approach to the job cheered her patients who often felt better just for seeing her.

During her four years as a probationer Olivia rarely strayed outside the hostel or the hospital. When others in her set learnt how to sneak out to go to the cinema or dances with their boyfriends, she stayed in and got on with her studies, fascinated by everything she read, eager to make herself better at her job. In her final exam her marks set a new high for the SRI. Only after she had telephoned her parents to announce she was a full-blown nurse and started to search around for others with whom to share the joy, did she discover that the only real friends she had made over the past four years had all been patients. True, she had had two chums in her first year set but she'd lost contact with both when they gave up the struggle and sought nine to five jobs: one as a secretary, the other as a sales lady in *Dianna's*, Slagcaster's premier couturier, who specialised in silver fox furs and overpriced county tweeds.

As a star student, Olivia was appointed a staff nurse at the SRI where she continued to make friends with patients while enjoying casual acquaintance with nurses. Staff nurses liked her because she was always happy to cover for them if they wanted to sneak off on emotional errands; her juniors liked her because she never bullied them but tried to get them to share her enthusiasm for her work.

A few of her contemporaries managed to nab themselves a doctor and moved to distant territories. Occasionally they would invite Olivia to visit and, though she was impressed by the luxury of their surroundings and enjoyed the gossip about old times, she didn't feel envious. She never dreamed of swapping her life for theirs. She was too happy where she was.

Not that she fought shy of doctors. She had her share of evenings drinking too much beer in the pub, of rough and tumble on the back seats of cars, and uncomfortable acrobatics on the narrow bed in the On-Call doctor's room. She even spent one week-end at the Grand Esplanade Hotel in Slagton Regis with a handsome young Scot who was training to be a surgeon. He spent most of their time together talking about what he was going to achieve; in return Olivia offered him the loving care she offered to her patients. He still sends her a Christmas card every year, giving the latest details of his ever growing family, which now runs to a couple of grandchildren.

In 1936 one of MacFearsome's last decisions before she walked with dignity into the hereafter was to appoint Olivia as the sister in charge of the SRI's respected orthopaedic ward. Two years later when Olivia's career was riding high she, who had witnessed countless tragedies in the lives of others, suffered the first real tragedy in her own. Both her parents were struck down by lobar pneumonia. The infection proved impervious to the magic of the new M&B 693 and her mother died just 12 hours after her father.

For the first time in her life Olivia knew the meaning of depression. She kept soldiering on at the SRI but, when she went outside the hospital, she found that too many corners of the city stirred memories of the life she had shared with her parents. The outbreak of war gave her a respectable reason for leaving Slagcaster.

The SRI reluctantly accepted her resignation and she got a job as an auxiliary staff nurse at a military hospital that had just opened in a requisitioned country mansion in Derbyshire. When she arrived most of the patients were survivors of Dunkirk. Their wounds, their burns, and their shattered bones had been dealt with elsewhere and they came to Wadsworth Hall to recover their wits and their strength. On summer days the young patients, wearing the white shirts, red ties, and blue pyjama-like uniforms issued to those who'd been damaged by war, lounged beside the swimming pool, ambled around the park, or sprawled indoors in ornate chairs which still bore the imprint of the bottoms of the gentry.

Olivia had been at Wadsworth Hall for six months when, suddenly and unexpectedly, she fell in love. For the first time, her life was invaded by a presence that distracted her attention from her work. She was used to being emotionally involved with her patients but her involvement with one patient now dominated every moment of her day. Eddie was an Army pilot whose legs had been broken and burned when he crash-landed his reconnaissance plane at an aerodrome in Kent.

His broken bones had been set at a hospital near Oxford and the fractures had reunited. He was transferred to Wadsworth Hall for the treatment of his burns, a long and tedious process that involved regular cleansing, dressing and re-dressing of the damaged skin. For weeks Olivia sat on the side of his bed persuading him that he would soon be walking again, flying again. Later, when her first prediction proved true, she took time off – for the first time in her career – and walked with Eddie through the dales. He talked about his childhood, how he had grown up in a Barnado's home and had never known his family. He occasionally held her hand or put his arm around her shoulder if they were walking down a difficult path but not once did he try to kiss her.

Love, Olivia decided, was a disease. The sad thing was that Eddie showed no signs of being infected. Still, her condition wasn't fatal and she decided to enjoy its sweet and sour symptoms until Eddie was discharged from Wadsworth. With luck her symptoms would fade once he walked out of her life. The day he received his discharge date, they took a last walk through Dovedale and that evening in a village pub Eddie, the man who had never kissed her, asked her to marry him.

A week later on a misty autumnal morning the hospital chaplain performed the ceremony in the chapel in the grounds of Wadsworth Hall. There was no time for a honeymoon. Eddie had been posted to a training camp in Lincolnshire. To Olivia's unspoken relief he'd accepted that his flying days were over and the army had decided to retrain him as an air controller. The newly weds rented a cottage in a village near the hospital. Olivia continued to nurse and Eddie sped home on his motorbike at weekends and sometimes for a night during the week. Olivia had never been happier. She felt she was living in one of the films they showed on Sunday evenings in the Wadsworth Ballroom. Their cottage with wisteria above the windows, honeysuckle round the door, was just the sort of place where Wing Commander Michael Redgrave would join Mrs Wing Commander Rosamund John for a weekend.

When Eddie finished his retraining course, the army posted him back to his old unit in Kent. The night before he left he and Olivia had dinner in the village pub. They decided that she would move to a hospital near Edenbridge which was advertising for staff, then they went home and sank a bottle of champagne. At five next morning Olivia stood in the cottage doorway and waved Eddie off on his motorbike. He always left early to get back to his unit before dark: he didn't like driving with a blacked-out light. That night he rang, as he always did, to tell her he'd arrived safely

Three days later, while she was in the ward changing the dressings on a young man's amputation stump, an orderly came in and handed her a telegram. *Deeply regret to inform you … killed on active service.* She kept the news to herself and stayed on the ward for the remaining thirty minutes of her shift. She then spent four hours negotiating with wartime telephone operators before she managed to get through to the adjutant's office in Kent.

The duty officer told her that, the night before, Eddie had been sent to collect a package from the Signals Office at Shorncliffe. There was no company transport so he took his own bike. Division was holding a night exercise and some idiot had left a broken-down truck unguarded on one of the narrow roads near Lydd. Eddie had run smack into it. He hadn't suffered, said the adjutant. Dead on arrival at the military hospital. There'd be an official enquiry, of course.

The next morning Olivia spoke to the Matron who reluctantly accepted her resignation. The following day she spent fourteen hours on two trains, crowded with soldiers and their kit, travelling to Kent for the military funeral. Eddie's unit gave her a room in the mess for the night.

She was the only civilian at the funeral, the only family he had. Afterwards she shook hands and sipped beer with some of Eddie's friends whom she knew by name but had never met. When she returned to the cottage to pack her few worldly goods, she removed her wedding ring and her cheap engagement ring, put them in their boxes and stuffed them with a tiny package of letters into the bottom of her suitcase. She never wore them again.

Once again Olivia turned her back on the past. Reverting to her maiden name, she applied for a job at one of the new EMS (Emergency Medical Services) hospitals set up to treat civilians and members of the Services. Her application was accepted.

The hospital was housed in prefabricated huts erected in the grounds of another country house, this time in Warwickshire. Olivia moved into the nurses' home and stayed there for the rest of the war treating young men who had been wounded in Africa then Italy, then France and Germany. She treated them with skill and compassion but she never mentioned Eddie … to them, or to the people she worked with.

On VE Day she danced in the streets; on VJ Day she went to a Victory Hop at a local dance-hall. The following morning, fighting off a hangover, she flipped through the classified ads in *Nursing Mirror*. A name from the past caught her eye. The Slagthorpe Memorial was advertising for an Assistant Matron. She applied, went for an interview, and got the job. A year after her arrival at the Slaughterhouse, the Matron's liver, eroded by gin, finally surrendered and the Memorial's governors installed Olivia as the new queen bee.

She had been Matron for eighteen months when Lionel Tetchy was appointed a consultant. Five years, later thanks to the exodus of the elderly parties who had kept the Memorial going during the war, he became the senior surgeon. By then, he had fought and subdued every member of the staff − except the Matron. The very sight of her began to irritate him. She was far too comfortable and composed … a cat who walked on her own.

Olivia still had the restrained glamour of a heroine in a post-war British film. She was tall and slim, her dark hair tinged with grey; the smile that had consoled so many patients was still warm and reassuring; the calm self confidence had now matured and gave her an air of detachment. In the eyes of the Senior Surgeon, her crime was that she had never surrendered to Lionel the Character. No matter how vigorous his verbal assaults she always responded with equanimity. Even on the morning when he grabbed the lapels of her cape and gave literal demonstration of his desire to shake sense into her, her only response was a calm and reassuring smile that carried not a hint of mockery.

Lionel grew obsessed with the need to puncture that serenity and last month he grabbed his opportunity when a young sister, who had come to the Memorial after working in a more civilised surgical department, lodged a formal complaint about Lionel's behaviour. Olivia reluctantly accepted the young woman's resignation but the hospital management committee, compelled by regulation to investigate the incident, set up a formal inquiry. Thus it came to pass that a week ago last Tuesday the Memorial suffered its most recent small earthquake in Chile

The committee of inquiry convened in the Governors' Hall. The hospital secretary presented the case for the prosecution, making it clear he did so only because it was part of his job and punctuated a few tentative assertions with wary glances at the accused.

Lionel replied with an irrelevant, obscene, and only slightly amusing story.

The committee next called Olivia who described how the insulted sister had come to her in some distress and had literally wept on her shoulder.

—And what was the nature of the insult? asked the chairman.

Before Olivia could reply, Lionel leaped to his feet.

—There was no insult, he barked.

For a moment he stood silent and cast his eyes around the room till he was sure he had the attention of his audience

—I just told the young woman to go to the devil.

Then, turning towards Olivia,

—But I didn't expect her to take me literally.

The committee members, most of whom feared they might one day be stretched on the table beneath Lionel's knife, offered the traditional responses to a sally from a Character. Three smiled and the other two managed a burst of sycophantic laughter.

Lionel flashed a triumphant glare at his adversary. Olivia shrugged her shoulders.

—You may resume your seat, matron, said the chairman, then droned on for another ten minutes.

—Unfortunate incident … misunderstanding … need for better communication … useful lesson … storm in teacup … time to move on … drone, drone, drone.

Eventually, after extracting nodded acquiescence from his colleagues, he announced the verdict. We all, he was sure, could learn from this unfortunate misunderstanding but the complaint was dismissed and no further action needed to be taken.

Lionel aimed another triumphant glare at his enemy then swept from the room and, gathering a posse of the sort of doctor who likes to be seen hob-nobbing with a Character, headed for the saloon bar at the Slagshire Cheese.

—Landlord, bellowed Lionel as he entered the pub. A magnum of your best champagne and drinks of their choice for your estimable clientele.

Orders were taken, drinks served, and glasses raised in benediction to the provider. Lionel leant his back against the bar and addressed the champagne-sipping acolytes.

—I wish you could have seen the Queen virgin. Smile as sweet as sugar icing. Certain I couldn't lay a finger on her. Well, she's not so certain now.

The sycophants responded with shallow cackling.

—Women like that are a menace in a hospital. Intellectual puddings … lives wasted. I doubt that one exciting moment has intruded on that virgin's life.

He raised his glass.

—Here's to the Queen Virgin and her virginettes. Let them sob on one another's shoulders till the ugly cows come home.

The toast was drunk to noisy acclamation and followed by a chorus of *Why was he born so beautiful?* Another chapter for the folklore. Another triumph for the Character.

When Olivia left the Governors' Hall she popped into Alderman Satterthwaite Ward to make sure the two new nurses from Jamaica weren't being put upon. Then she climbed the spiral staircase in one of Memorial's gothic towers till, at the top, she reached the circular hallway of the Matron's Flat: sitting room, bedroom, tiny bathroom and even tinier kitchen. She opened a cupboard in the sitting room, took out a couple of bottles and a glass, and poured herself a gin and It. With glass in hand, she settled in the large armchair that faced the window overlooking the hospital park.

As she sipped her drink and gazed down on spindly trees and grass speckled with bare patches of hard-packed earth, she conjured up the vision that would sustain her for the fourteen months that remained before she retired: a bungalow high on the cliffs at Slaghaven, wisteria above the windows, honeysuckle round the door, a ghostly resonance of Michael Redgrave and Rosamund John, and a sign on the wicket gate, *Dunursin*.

EDITORS NOTE
Extracts from three papers in the archive which deal with an unusual group
of patients registered with the Slagfield House practice and one patient of
particular significance.

A Lady of some Consequence

At the north-east corner of Slag Common stands a curious
collection of buildings. At the centre is a Palladian villa built in the
early 19th Century. To its right is a quadrangle rendered in the
style of 1930s Tudor stables; to its left a quarter-scale reproduction
of Eton College chapel. This intriguing complex houses not just
the Convent of St Euphemia, home of the Sisters of Divine
Improvidence, but the thriving St Euphemia Collegiate School for
Young Ladies.

The villa was built by a Slagthorpian entrepreneur who made
his fortune in the slave trade and came home to live the rest of his
life in style. Two generations later his descendants acquired the
sense of cultural superiority that comes with unearned income and
moved South in search of minds of similar refinement. Their
lawyers could find no Slagthorpian prepared to buy the villa so it
was left to crumble, at first invaded and finally engulfed by the
scrub that thrives in that corner of the common.

Then, in the mid nineteen twenties, Mother St Peter-Without-
Chains, St Euphemia's spiritual and temporal leader – though not
necessarily in that order – arrived on a scouting mission from
Ireland charged with finding a site for a new convent and school.
She was quick to spot the potential of the ruin on the common and
acquired it at a knock down price. In a barter deal with immigrant
Irish navvies – they offered their labour in exchange for spiritual

consolation, hearty meals of bacon and cabbage, and minimalist wages – she restored the villa, installed the nuns, and cleared the surrounding land. She then added the Tudor blocks, one by one, to house the expanding Collegiate School for Young Ladies.

The notion of Young Ladies, carefully nurtured by Mother St Peter, is the source of the convent's prosperity, appealing as it does to upwardly mobile Slagthorpians who want to give their girls a bit of *tone*. The educational skills of the Sisters of Divine Improvidence are devoted to producing nothing less – and indeed nothing more – than acceptable Young Ladies.

In the Junior School technical skills like reading and writing yield precedence to Elocution, Manners, and Sitting Up Straight at Table; in the Upper School practical subjects like Forms of Address and Occasions When Gloves Should be Worn are deemed more rewarding than vulgar dabbling in the laws of thermodynamics, or tedious exploration of the works of Shakespeare or the dangerous Voltaire.

Mathematics are not wholly spurned. The curriculum devotes much time to the addition, subtraction, multiplication and division of pounds, shillings, and pence, the mental calculation of compound interest, and the analysis of balance sheets. Logarithms, the calculus, and suchlike fooleries earn the same contemptuous rejection as recognised sources of sedition such as Relativity or the dreaded Evolution.

Biology is never taught – indeed it tops Mother St Peter's list of dangerous subversions – but History is quite acceptable as long as it consists of tales of saintly kings and queens who, with the help of wise ecclesiastical counsellors, dispense gracious bounty to an ungrateful peasantry.

The only foreign language taught is French. But then the Sisters of Divine Improvidence are members of a French order. The religious order *Les Dames d'Improvidence* was founded in a remote corner of South-West France a decade or two before the Revolution when a handful of aristocratic ladies decided they preferred their own company to that of aristocratic gentlemen and created a convent to which they could withdraw and justify their lives by ministering to the poor.

Visitors who know this history wonder why they never meet a French nun at St Euphemia's, indeed never meet one who isn't Irish. The reason is that, in the mid nineteenth century, *Les Dames* sent emissaries from France to establish a satellite community in a small town in the West of Ireland driven no doubt by the same enthusiasm to civilise the ignorant that now leads Sister Agnes to encourage girls in the junior school to hand over pennies to save the souls of African pagans.

The later migration from Ireland which established a satellite in Slagthorpe was motivated less by missionary zeal than by the realisation by the Irish Reverend Mother that her only hope of retaining her sanity was to get Mother St Peter out of the Irish convent and into a place of her own.

The decision bore rich fruit and today St Euphemia's is a monument not just to *Les Dames* but to Mother St Peter. When the impecunious clutch of nuns arrived in Slagthorpe, it was she who knocked on the door of every mini-mansion on Slag Hill soliciting alms and superior pupils. She it was who persuaded her fellow *Dames* that the survival of their order in England depended less on ministering to the poor than on ministering to the rich. She it was who recruited the fire-breathing preacher Father Neil Obstat to frighten wealthy Slagshire widows into trying to buy themselves a place in Heaven with a hefty donation to the building fund. She it was who hired and cosseted the labourers with barter deals. And she it was who briefed the architect and, when he retired demented to the Slagshire County Asylum, completed the plans and became Site Manager and Officer of Works.

It was also Mother St Peter who, during the nineteen thirties, organised the jumble sales, garden parties, and County Balls whose proceeds built the playing field pavilion, the tennis courts, the indoor riding school fashioned after the one in Vienna (with details

of interior design copied meticulously from Austrian postcards)
and, last in a shrewd order of priorities, the chapel where any
substantial benefactor had his or her name inscribed on made-to-
measure marble.

Five years ago when the thriving St Euphemia business seemed
to have achieved its full potential, Mother St Peter struck again
when she heard that the chairman of the Slagshire Friendly
Insurance Society had been moved into lodgings provided at His
Majesty's expense. When he was forced to sell the Old Manor on
Slag Hill, she blasted all competition aside and acquired this fine
example of Edwardian Baronial to house the St Euphemia
Finishing School.

Though the new establishment is happy to accommodate
Young Ladies who graduate from the Collegiate School, provided
they have adequate financial upholstery, it is really designed to
serve the needs of South American millionaires whose daughters
have reached a difficult age or are going though a bad patch. The
school offers the girls a high gloss English finish in safe Catholic
surroundings. Their mothers can escape the tedious traumata
associated with their daughters' adolescence, and their fathers can
congratulate themselves on getting the girls away from the
influence of local Lotharios.

That is the theory but, though the pupils do acquire a few
social graces and a useful second language, the most enduring gift
the school bestows is a taste for the forbidden fruits that the parents
feared were too readily available at home. Mother St Peter is not
blind to what goes on. Recently when newspapers ran a spate of
stories about impecunious playboys running off with South
American heiresses, she could scarce conceal her pride that so
many of the new celebrities were Old Euphemians.

Only once has Mother St Peter been near to coming unstuck.
In 1949, having painfully suppressed her entrepreneurial instincts
during the war, she built a new gymnasium. It was beyond her
comprehension that life could be encumbered with such things as

planning permission or building regulations and, only after Father Neil Obstat had performed the Opening Blessing, did she receive a stern letter from the Slagthorpe Corporation threatening her with criminal prosecution for flagrant disregard of planning regulations.

She was so troubled that she spent a night in prayer followed by a more productive day reading the small print of the building regulations. The following morning she announced that her gymnasium was exempt from regulation because it was a war memorial. The planning officers backed off and the school doctor Finbar O'Flaherty suggested she should install a plaque above the door: *Dedicated to the fallen from St Euphemia's.*

* * * * * * * *

EDITOR'S NOTE
In most papers in the archive, Donovan writes about himself in the third person. The following excerpt comes from one of the few he wrote in the first person. It is also written in longhand. The many corrections and spelling mistakes (here corrected) suggest that this was a draft written soon after the event. Donovan may have intended to polish it up later but no other version exists.

Proclaim it triumphantly and with joy. After a week of mounting dread I have survived Trial by Ordeal. At two minutes before eleven of the clock this morning I, Donal Patrick Donovan, explored the body of a nun. Without flicker of eyelid or tremor of lip, I gazed on cropped hair and slender neck unshrouded by a cowl and laid hands upon the naked skin of breast and belly. And I have survived. My hand hath touched forbidden flesh yet hath not withered. I walked from the sickroom with a sense of liberation I've known only once before, when I danced along a corridor after the last of my medical exams.

Some might think that examining a nun is no great achievement for a man who has delivered babies, helped surgeons to grope around in people's innards, and gazed on mangled bodies in wrecked cars. But consider my childhood.

In the selfsame building where I survived my Trial is my first schoolroom where I was parked one morning when I was four, where Sister St Agnes gave me a peardrop for being a good boy, where Sister St William taught me how to tie my shoelaces with a brown lace threaded through eyelets in a piece of cardboard, and where I used my Dad's loose change to save Black Babies.

For just a penny handed to Sister St Philomena I could choose my own Black Baby from the box of cardboard cut-outs she kept on the top of the radiator and pin it to the bottom step on the chart on the wall. For another penny I could move my baby one step up the staircase until, when half a crown had gone to the Foreign Missions, my baby reached the top and was received into the arms of Jesus. In that world, nuns became surrogate mothers, less predictable, less lovable than the real thing, but just as untouchable – untouchable, that is, in the way that doctors touch you.

Today, as we descended the stairs from my triumph in the sickroom, Sister St Matthew, the young Infirmarian who had trained as a nurse before entering the convent, whispered … yes whispered as if we were still sharing forbidden secrets,

—Mother St Peter would like a word with you, doctor, before you leave.

It wasn't a request but a command. She led me to the convent parlour and left me there on my own. This was the room where Dad would sometimes bring me, even before I started school, to show me off. A procession of nuns would come in, each raising her arms in joy at the sight of the doctor's little boy, then bend to kiss me. When I drew back, they teased me for being shy. They didn't know that what really put me off was the bristly hair on their upper lips.

Today I discovered that the parlour is exactly as it was: flocked green wallpaper; an abundance of brocade in gold and sable; a Chinese carpet so thick you feel you are treading on a trampoline; a mahogany table with mirror polished surface, a central bowl of fresh-cut flowers, and a far from artless selection of table-top books: Treasures of the National Gallery, The Noble Horse at Work and Play, A Life of St Aloysius Gonzaga, The English Country House. This is where Mother St Peter receives distinguished visitors: bishops, parish priests, potential benefactors, parents of prospective pupils and, this morning, a doctor who had examined his first nun.

The room even smells the same – mustiness and furniture polish plus a hint of the mildew I still associate with priests and churches and once assumed was the odour of sanctity. The carpet is almost certainly the one on which the small embarrassed boy stood alongside his father. Once the ordeal by kissing was over I was allowed to sit on a straight-backed chair too high for my feet to reach the ground while the nuns retired twittering to a corner and Dad sang to them in his light tenor voice. The twittering would stop and I would hear an occasional sniffle while Dad sang Irish ballads that reminded them of the homes and parents and brothers and sisters they had left behind.

Finbar, I'm told, keeps up the tradition and enhances the memories of times past by addressing the nuns by their real names which he found on their NHS records. Sister St Ethelburgha reverts to Marie O'Rafferty; Sister St Agathonicus to Bridie Madigan. Was he teasing me, I wonder, when he told me that when alone with Mother St Peter he calls her Maggie Reilly?

This morning, while I waited, I went to one of the tall windows and pushed back the lace curtain an inch or two. Outside, four small boys were kicking a leather football across the asphalt of the playground where I regularly grazed my knees and took them tearfully to Sister St William to have them dabbed with her painless *white iodine.**

---

*Hydrogen Peroxide which, unlike brown Tincture of Iodine, did not cause painful stinging. Small boys grazed their knees often because most wore short trousers up to the age of 12 or even 14.

St Euphemia's educates just a handful of boys, acceptable only if they came from the right sort of family: Catholic middle-class, or any-religion rich. They are admitted to the kindergarten and can stay until they approach puberty, an affliction which Mother St Peter believes can strike as early as the age of eight. This means that all boys must leave before their ninth birthday so they are not just outnumbered but out-aged. Like members of any persecuted minority, they quickly learn the ambivalences of humanity. I never knew whether the next big girl who stepped in front of me would want to mother me or thump me.

As I watched from the parlour window, six or seven girls danced onto the playground with an energy that suggested they had just been let out of class. They moved eagerly towards the footballers but the boys, who spotted them coming, had already picked up their ball and were exiting around the corner.

I heard a soft brushing noise behind me. When I turned, I found the parlour door had opened silently and I shared the room with a familiar ageless figure.

For a moment Mother St Peter-Without-Chains stood quite still. Then she lightly clapped her palms together and raised her fingers to her chin.

—Oh, Doctor, she said. You are the image of your father … Dear Doctor Donovan.

She glided across the room, as if on wheels. Dear God, I hoped she wasn't going to kiss me. She stretched out her hand and we made contact in a formal handshake.

—It's very nice to have you back in the town. And very kind of you to offer to look after us.

I didn't explain that it was Finbar who, unasked and in the face of some opposition, made the offer on my behalf.

—I'm sorry if I've delayed you. I just wanted to have a look at you before you dashed away.

She gave me a smile that from anyone else would be blatantly seductive.

—And I thoroughly approve of what I see. Dear Finbar must be proud to have you working with him.

I had a go at the self-deprecating smile that proved useful when I was a schoolboy but Mother St Peter was already leading me from the room.

As we walked along the corridor, she asked,

—And how is our patient?

I offered a few platitudes about the nun I'd seen. Her problem I suspect is a mixture of boredom and sexual frustration but I didn't say so ... though I suspected Mother St Peter had made the same diagnosis. I used the sort of euphemisms I detest: *Overtired, Run down*. My first visit was not the time to start rocking the boat

We reached the front door.

—I think I understand what you're saying doctor. I'm the first to admit that we have some odd creatures here, though it would never do to let that be known outside. Or am I being a bit old fashioned? From what I read in the papers these days, it would seem that anything goes.

She had her hand on the rosary that hung from her belt and she rattled its large wooden beads.

—I came to the conclusion long ago, doctor, that there's only one really convincing argument for the existence of God. For over thirty years we've had twenty-eight women of uncertain age locked up together in this house and we haven't had one murder.

Once again she produced the enigmatic smile, then gave a final, more gentle, rattle to the beads before raising her hand to open the door.

—It was very kind of you to call, doctor. I hope we're not too great a trouble to you.

And even as a polite response rose to my lips, the door closed on Mother St Peter and her smile.

* * * * * * * * * *

EDITOR'S NOTE
This third excerpt comes from typed pages pasted into one of Donovan's
commonplace books.

A dark damp November evening. Half an hour to go to dinner.
Finbar asleep in his favourite chair. Martha tapped gently on the
Manchester Guardian that lay tented over his face. Finbar growled,
shook his head, then slid the newspaper down and peeped over the
top. Martha recited the telephone message she'd received. Moving
with unaccustomed speed Finbar swung his legs sideways and
rolled rather than rose from the sofa. Once upright, he toddled
along to the surgery, pulled out a drawer in one of the filing
cabinets, and searched through the tightly packed NHS records.

When he found the record he was looking for, it was blank. Just
the patient's name and address on the front of the envelope,
written there when the Clerk to the Slagshire Executive Council
issued it in 1948. Finbar, puzzled, stuck a finger into the envelope
to see if it contained a folded letter or note. It was empty. He
stuffed the record into his jacket pocket and toddled out to the car
shielding his head from the drizzling rain with the *Manchester
Guardian*.

As he drove along the High Street, a fork of lightning crackled
across the sky, a clap of thunder exploded in the heavens, and every
light in the town went out. A second lightning fork outlined the
twin cupolas of Satterthwaite's Haberdashery Emporium in
ghostly silhouette. This time the simultaneous explosion seemed to
unleash a barrage of hailstones that drummed on the roof of the
car.

Within seconds the hailstorm stopped as abruptly as it started,
swept away by gusts of wind that drove the rain horizontally at the
windscreen. The wipers expired without a struggle. Finbar wound
down the driver's window and thrust out his head to get a sight of
what lay ahead.

In an instant, his spectacles were as opaque as the windscreen and he flung them onto the seat alongside him. He kept the accelerator pushed flat against the floor and the old Morris Cowley, jerking along in top gear, thrust itself at the wall of water like a North Sea trawler forcing its way back to port. Finbar hoped young Donal was doing his stuff.

Eventually the Morris made it to the convent gates and struggled triumphantly up the drive. One of the lay sisters who worked in the kitchens and did the menial jobs around the convent was waiting in the main porch. The only visible light in the building was the paraffin lantern she held high in front of her. As the car approached, she swung it to and fro as if guiding the good ship Morris into harbour. Finbar gave her a wave and switched off the engine. He retrieved his spectacles and dashed through the rain to the porch.

Once he reached shelter he leaned forward and shook his head like a dog trying to dry itself, ran his fingers through his hair, and wiped his face with the horse-headed handkerchief. The lay sister watched in silence and, when he was done, led him briskly, still without a word, up the curved staircase to the first floor of the old villa.

He wasn't sure where they were going but was surprised that they had to climb a less ostentatious staircase to the second floor. He was even more surprised when he had to follow the swinging lantern up narrow uncarpeted stairs to the garret which, when the villa was built, had housed the beds of the lowliest servants.

At the top of the stairs they edged along a narrow passage to a door so low that, when his guide pushed it open, Finbar had to stoop to get through. When he raised his head, he found he had entered a scene from a Verdi opera.

The long low room was under the eaves of the house. The only light came from candles that threw dancing shadows across the bare beams of the roof and along whitewashed walls free of decoration save for a crucifix and a simple ceramic image of the head of the Blessed Virgin. He didn't know it then but this evening

was the first time that anyone other than herself had entered
Mother St Peter's bedroom.

The candles – tall slim ecclesiastical candles – were held by a
group of nuns who knelt tightly-packed at one end of the room
reciting repetitive decades of the rosary in a low undulant murmur.
At the opposite end was a truckle bed on which, propped up on
pillows, lay an old lady in white nightgown and linen bonnet. At
one side of the bed knelt the young Infirmarian, Sister St Matthew;
at the other stood the young Doctor Donovan radiating insecurity.
Finbar strode across the room and, for a moment, put a hand on
Donovan's shoulder. Then he spoke softly to the old lady .

—What the hell have you been up to, Maggie? Scaring the life
out of Jim Donovan's boy.

Mother St Peter opened her eyes, turned them slowly towards
Finbar, and smiled.

A single voice emerged from the murmur at the other end of
the room.

—The fourth sorrowful mystery. The carrying of the cross.

The murmuring resurged.

—Our father who art in heaven, hallowed be Thy name ...

Mother St Peter closed her eyes again. Her face was pale, and,
in the candlelight, her lips were the colour of blue-black ink. Donal
tugged at the shoulder of Finbar's jacket pulling him closer so he
could whisper into his ear.

—I think she's had a massive coronary. She suddenly collapsed
with pain in her chest. By the time I arrived, she'd insisted they
carry her up here and put her to bed. This has always been her
bedroom, it seems. They've sent for a priest but both priests are
out. I've given her some morphia and the ambulance is on its way
but I'm beginning to wonder whether they'll make it in time. She
has very little pulse and what little she has is irregular. I thought
she'd gone just before you arrived and I gave her some intravenous
coramine.

—There's nothing more you could have done.

Finbar turned back to the bed, picked up one of Mother St Peter's hands, and placed it gently between his palms, as if to warm the waxen fingers.

Then he bent his head close to her ear.

—You're on your way home, Maggie, he whispered.

Her lips started to form a smile but her eyes stayed closed.

Very softly Finbar began to sing the Percy French melody.

—Come home Maggie Reilly to Ballyjamesduff. Come home Maggie Reilly to me ...

Now Mother St Peter did open her eyes and with great effort turned her head towards Finbar. Then, slowly and deliberately, she winked.

At the very moment of winking, her head fell forward and one short breath rattled in her throat. Then nothing. Donal grabbed his stethoscope but Finbar signalled him to put it aside.

Finbar gently eased his patient's head back onto her pillow and, as he did, a sizzling streak of lightning struck a tree in the convent garden. There was a deafening crash of thunder, the top sash of the dormer window slid down, and a gust of wind swept through the room extinguishing all the candles. The confident murmur of prayer from the nuns in the corner turned to a whimper of fear and for a moment even Finbar was shaken.

The only person to retain her composure was the young Infirmarian. She leaned towards Finbar.

—Fear not, doctor, she said softly. 'Tis only Mother St Peter passing through the eye of a needle.

Prime Angus

The chief health hazard in the Slag Valley is not, as you might expect, the black smoke that belches from the chimneys of Slagshire Consolidated Glue. Nor the high-pitched decibels that emanate from the String Vest Manufactory. Local doctors, asked to nominate the greatest threat to the well-being of their patients, would plump unanimously for Slagthorpe's friendly Scots family butcher, Angus MacSteak.

The name Angus MacSteak is inscribed in gold script on a black glass panel above the High Street shop. Yet when Angus's dad ran the business between the wars a less ornate sign proclaimed it as *Atherton's. Your Friendly Family Butcher*. In those days, when Angus was not Angus but Cyril, he used to help his dad in the shop at weekends and during the school holidays. He was an observant lad and grew impressed by the partiality that members of Slagthorpe's suit-wearing class expressed for the flavour of Scottish beef. He was equally impressed by the success of Macfisheries who had a branch just five doors down from Atherton's in the High Street.

So in 1949, when Atherton Senior retired to a seaside bungalow near Slagton Regis and young Cyril inherited the business, he changed not only his name but what he likes to call the *ethos* of the business. He dyed his hair sandy and took to quoting *Rabbie Burns* in a stage Scottish accent and to dropping *wee Scottish phrases* into his conversation.

Angus serves fine meat and his standards of hygiene are beyond reproach. So the vehemence of the medical consensus on his threat to health might puzzle a stranger. Especially one who has caught a glimpse of Angus behind his marble slab dispensing best end of neck with a winning smile or slipping old Miss Haythornthwaite a free package of assorted giblets with a consoling murmur of *O wad some Pow'r the giftie gie us* ... What outlandish power, the stranger might wonder, does this genial man possess that unites the medical profession in antipathy?

The answer is that, in his spare time, Angus is the founding director and sole member of the Slagthorpe First Aid Vigilantes. At the first rumour of a road accident, a collapse in the street or even a sprained ankle, he will halt his cleaver in mid swing, grab the first aider's portmanteau he keeps on a shelf beneath the cash register and dash to the scene.

His arrival brings little comfort to the afflicted. It's not just the blood-stained apron that puts them off but Angus's overwhelming efficiency. By the time the most fleet footed nurse or doctor can get there, the victim will be swathed from head to toe in bandages wound on with the mathematical precision that is the mark of a competition winner and Angus will be engaged in Maintenance of Morale, which figures large in first-aid manuals, by giving spirited excerpts from Tam O'Shanter – with actions.

Angus's problem is that his training has been high on first-aid competitions, where points are won by sticking obsessively to the instructions in the manual, and low on practical experience. Yet he retains the enthusiasm that carried him from the Boy's Brigade to the St John's Ambulance to wartime ambulance driver in Slagton Bay, a conurbation totally ignored by enemy forces. (That is if you discount the Luftwaffe pilot who parachuted into the field alongside Stan Oakroyd's farm and whom Mrs Stan, impressed by his uniform, took in and gave a cup of Bovril thinking he was one of the side-car men from the Royal Automobile Club.)

When VE-day robbed Angus of both uniform and ambulance, he founded the First Aid Vigilantes with an eagerness matched only by his reluctance to recruit other members. The challenge of helping the afflicted so invigorates him that he doesn't like to dilute the effect by sharing it.

When it comes to the practicalities, any insecurity Angus might feel because of his lack of experience is overwhelmed by the confidence engendered by his triumphs in first-aid competitions. By the time a doctor or ambulance arrives at the scene of an incident, no matter how trivial, Angus will have applied not just bandages but complicated splints, poured brandy down a reluctant throat, and labelled the victim with a neat docket recording temperature, pulse, respiration and pattern of bowel movements over the previous week.

Slagthorpians resent this tour de force if they've suffered only a sprain, so Angus's clientele – apart from innocent visitors who admit to an indisposition and are overwhelmed before any local can protect them – are the local meths drinkers who collapse regularly in the purlieus of his shop and accept the bandaging in return for the brandy.

There was a time when Angus's enthusiasm earned him a couple of useful perks: a free place on the touchline at Slagvilla when the Rovers were playing at home and a free seat at the Hippodrome when the Slagthorpe and District Operatic and Thespian Society put on its annual musical extravaganza.

He lost the Slagvilla concession in the middle of the local Derby with Slagheaton Thursday, when the Rovers' wizard of the dribble, Twinkletoes Gilhoury, suffered a nasty sprain of his ankle. As he lay on the ground, his team mates rushed from all parts of the pitch to form a protective screen between him and Angus but they underestimated the determination of a true vigilante and in the resulting fracas the referee – a literal-minded stranger who misinterpreted the compliment intended by *Fair fa' your honest sonsie face* – not only took Angus's name but awarded a penalty against the Rovers. That evening Angus was relieved of his honorary post and denied further admittance to the ground.

The Thespians terminated their arrangement after an equally unfortunate incident on the night that Cynthia Clack, Slagthorpe's first lady of song, pulled a hamstring while straining for a top C in the gypsy czardas she'd inserted in the first act of the Thespians' musical adaptation of *Rebecca of Sunnybrook Farm*. The plaster cast Angus applied during the interval not only restricted her gay abandoned movements in Act Two but, during the romantic pas-de-deux in Act Three, dealt Reg Harbottle, tenor, such a grievous blow that Mrs Harbottle won compensation from the Thespians for the deprivation of her conjugal rights.

These setbacks failed to dampen Angus's enthusiasm. He bided his time, confident that fate would offer him a chance to re-establish himself. A fortnight ago last Thursday it seemed that fate had so provided.

Twice a week Angus takes his van down the Slagheaton Road to deliver two hundred-weight of his patented Cornish Pastyfilla to the works canteens of the factories on the trading estate. His last call on that fateful Tuesday was to the Laughing Ebenezer Joke factory.

He had unloaded two drums of Pastyfilla, slipped the traditional half pound of steak to the canteen manager, and was about to back the van out of the yard, when the sign he had so often prayed for was given unto him. The alarm bells rang on the main factory floor heralding what the Slagthorpe Echo later described as *a cataclysmic moment*. A build up of pressure behind a clogged valve caused a blowback in the Laughing Ebenezer's itching powder blender.

Within minutes a cloud of concentrated itch provoker billowed out of the blender room and swept along the whoopee cushion production line straight into the inspectorate where Mavis Clatterbridge and her team of young ladies test each cushion to ensure it produces an adequately vulgar note. Within seconds the girls were scratching frenetically. Mavis led them into the uncontaminated air in the factory yard where, in a desperate

attempt to conquer the dreaded Ebenezer itch – *One puff and watch
'em squirm!!!* – they first rolled on the cobbles and then frantically
tore off their clothing.

Their antics brought Laughing Ebenezer to a halt as every man
on the premises rushed to a window overlooking the yard. Every
man, that is, except Angus. With a radiant calm and a few barked
orders he organised *a wee human chain* of uncontaminated ladies
from other parts of the factory to link him with Rumbold's chemist
shop on the corner where, quoting an emergency wartime order
that had yet to be revoked, he commandeered Mr Rumbold's
entire stock of oily calamine lotion.

Next he commandeered a spray-gun from the factory paint
shop and, as the human chain passed him the bottles of calamine,
he isolated each writhing figure in the yard and, with ribald
encouragement from the men at the windows, applied two
generous coats of the oily lotion. Thanks to this commendable
initiative, the chaos in the yard slowly subsided as each girl lost her
itch, rediscovered her embarrassment, grabbed her clothes, and
sprinted back into the building.

One of the last in Angus's queue of eager patients was Deirdre
Ratband, this month's regional winner in the Miss Slagshire Co-op
Tiptilted Bra competition and fancied favourite to sweep all the
prizes (probably off the mantelpiece) in the area finals. Angus had
given her a comprehensive undercoat and was readjusting his
nozzle to deliver a delicate fine-gloss finish when who should
rumble into the yard on his brewer's dray but burly Alf Ratband,
boxer, wrestler, bass drum basher in the Slagheaton Colliery Silver
Band and Deirdre's dad.

Alf, though sluggish in the intellectual department, is pretty
nifty on his feet so by the time he crossed the yard, his first
interpretation of what was going on was just firming up in his
mind. And that, as Angus explained to Finbar, was when
everything went black.

The explanation came in the consulting room at Slagfield

House while Finbar, with Donal in attendance, gingerly removed fragments of the spray-gun's glass reservoir from Angus's scalp. When the delicate operation was over, Finbar led Angus next door into the sitting room, sat him in one of the large leather chairs by the fireplace and, while they waited for Martha to bring a resuscitating mug of hot sweet tea, delivered a firm yet kindly homily to the dejected figure in the bandage turban.

—Angus lad, said Finbar, you have tumbled painfully onto one of the secrets of the healing trade. To practise our art a man needs four attributes: a trained hand, a thick skin, a blind eye to be cast in carefully selected directions, and an ability to duck out of the path of flying objects. You have concentrated on the first two at the expense of the more important pair. Until you can redress the balance I fear we professionals will remain unable to accept you onto our team.

—Aye, muttered Angus sadly.

And that was all he did mutter. Not one further word, though he sat there for another twenty minutes sipping his tea and offering the doctors an occasional shamefaced smile.

Three days later Donal got a message to call on Angus after the evening surgery. The High Street shop front was shuttered and Donal went down the side alley which led to the deep freeze room and the wooden stairway to Angus's bachelor flat. Angus, still turbaned in bandages, answered the knock and, as a greeting, thrust a blood stained package into Donal's hand.

—An offering for the doctor's kitchen, he said. A few wee slices of liver. Tell him that I've taken to heart what he said.

Donal started to thank him but Angus put a finger to his lips to command silence and led him back down the outside stairs to the little yard behind the shop.

In the centre of the yard the smouldering remains of a bonfire still generated thin trails of smoke.

—I wanted you to see it, said Angus. The funeral pyre of my

ambitions. Evra piece of equipment, evra manual I ever had, even my hand tailored vigilante uniform all gone and finally cremated.

> *The soger frae the wars returns*
> *The sailor frae the main*
> *Bit I hae parted frae my love*
> *Never to meet again, my dear,*
> *Never to meet again.*

—Maybe you could tell the doctor.

Then he squeezed Donal's hand with the solemnity of someone bidding farewell to a relative after a family funeral. The moment would have been more moving if he hadn't chosen the hand that contained the soggy package.

Later while Finbar and Donal were eating the liver, lightly grilled, Donal asked whether he'd really witnessed a cure or just a temporary remission.

—I doubt he'll relapse, said Finbar. Men who reach the age of Angus and myself without being wed are more conscious than others of that cliché about loving and losing. With luck he'll write off the past and be grateful he enjoyed it. But we'll have to keep an eye an him for a month or two and try to steer him clear of any enthusiasms that might disrupt the harmony of our humble community.

The telephone rang in the hall.

—I'll get it, said Donal.

The caller was the desk sergeant at Slagthorpe police station. Donal made a few notes on the pad beside the phone, then returned to finish off his liver.

—Got to go, he said. Some fool tried to pacify a mad dog they'd admitted to the animal shelter in Mafeking Road and got nasty bites on both arms.

—Mafeking road? Animal shelter? That's a new one on me, said Finbar.

—And me, said Donal. Only opened this afternoon according to the sergeant. Owned by a mad Scot wearing a turban.

Donal, still standing, gobbled down a last mouthful of liver and laid his knife and fork on the empty plate.

—He's the one who got bitten.

Something Organically Wrong

When I was a boy, a visit to the cinema was a comforting experience, the nearest I could get to a return to the womb. The Slagthorpe Gaumont was a large warm palace, reassuringly protected by a wide-shouldered commissionaire with a waxed moustache and braid on his cap. He and his liveried flunkies led us from a dirty and depressing world and ushered us into cosy darkness where nymphs with torches lighted our way to red plush seats.

This afternoon, during a nostalgic mooch round the town, I revisited the Gaumont for the first time since my return. The pre-war gilt was tarnished. The commissionaire and his flunkies had been replaced by a fat lady in a cardigan who interrupted her knitting to sell me my ticket. The pile on the seats had worn bare and, saddest of all, below the screen was an empty pit. Could it be from this dark void that Herbert Moorcroft once rose, in twice-nightly colourful splendour, at the keyboard of the Mighty Wurlitzer?

Whatever happened to the cinema organists? It seems that one night, while I was busy growing up, they descended into their pits, switched off their coloured lights and walked out into the night never to be seen again.

Herbert Moorcroft was part of my youth. An old-time professional with no liking for fancy frills, he, ascended decorously to the strains of Here We Are Again and worked his way methodically through his medley of Popular Tunes of the Moment while the glass panels of his instrument ran through their routine colour range – red, gold, green, blue, purple and back to red again. At the end of his programme, Herbert descended sedately, waving to us coyly with one hand while his other hand and both feet hammered out Here's to the Next Time.

Herbert was an integral part of the Gaumont syndrome – reliable, comforting and, above all, predictable. It was a sad day when he left – promoted to manage a new super-cinema in Slagcaster.

Herbert was succeeded by Cliff Hepinstall. Cliff was one of the new men – flashy where Herbert had been sedate, flamboyant rather than reliable and bursting with what the Slagthorpe Echo called *an inborn flair for showmanship*. In the Cliff era, a night at the flicks took on a new dimension. The films grew no less predictable but the Musical Interlude flowered into a dramatic occasion. It always got off to a flying start because Cliff had a well-earned reputation as a chaser and occasional catcher of local women. So when his performance started, as it always did, with a slide flashed on the screen, *And now for your entertainment - Cliff Hepinstall and his electric organ* we responded with ribaldry and cheers.

Cliff had somehow managed to boost the lift-off power of the Mighty Wurlitzer so he emerged from the pit with the sort of acceleration that, in the old days, would have catapulted Herbert Moorcroft into the front row of the circle. His ascension was not only swift but deafening. As he shot out of the ground, his feet thundered out flashy arpeggios on the pedals, whilst his hands ran up and down the keyboards creating decorated runs.

When Cliff was at the Mighty Wurlitzer we didn't just sit and listen as we did with Herbert Moorcroft. Cliff demanded participation. The words of the songs appeared on the screen, scratched onto smoked glass slides, and we were all expected to sing. If we didn't Cliff would stop in mid-bar and cajole us, then repeat the same line again and again until he got a satisfactory response. Even when we joined in wholeheartedly, he would slip in an occasional slide spiced with the witticism *Sing up, it won't burst your elastic.*

In the Cliff era, Herbert's sedate musical interlude evolved into a cabaret act. Towards the end of his recital, a slide on the screen would announce *A Pause for Imitations.* Then Cliff would manipulate the stops and keys of the Mighty Wurlitzer to give us trains, bagpipes, aeroplanes and ships' sirens before ending with his creative triumph, a flushing lavatory.

Cliff also had an eye for colour. Not for him Herbert's routine run through the spectrum. If we had a selection of Irish Airs, the Wurlitzer would glow green, and we grew weary of songs dragged into the programme by their titles: Deep Purple, Golden Earrings, and that Red, Red Robin that kept bob, bob bobbin along.

In contrast to his dramatic entrance, Cliff always finished with a soft sell. As he ended his programme, the organ glowed red and started a slow descent, like a misshapen sun sinking below the horizon. Then Cliff stood up, gave us a deep bow and turned to the keyboard to strike up Mood Indigo. The colour of the Wurlitzer took on a hue that taxed its colour-mixing power to the limit and to, thunderous applause, Cliff descended to ground level where, if you sat in the circle, you could see him switch off the lights and make a quick grab for the nearest usherette.

One night, as we watched this dramatic descent, a dreadful thing happened. Maybe Cliff's accelerated entrances had overtaxed the Wurlitzer mechanism, or maybe it was sabotaged by the boyfriend of an usherette. Whatever the cause, as Cliff struck up the first few bars of Mood Indigo, the entire organ, and Cliff, disappeared abruptly, as if a hangman had opened his trap. There were thirty seconds of cacophony then silence, until a quick-thinking projectionist slipped on a record of Victor Sylvester.

It proved a critical moment in my adolescence. I was in one of the two-seaters in the back row making unexpected progress with a new girl friend. I had already achieved what would now be level four on the post-Kinsey International Petting Scale and had elicited the promise of a post-cinema stroll through the notorious Fairy Dell in the Corporation Gardens where, 'twas said, the trees were more sinned against than sinning.

Unfortunately, the new girl friend had just started as trainee reporter on the Echo and was as keen as mustard on her job. As Cliff and the Mighty Wurlitzer crashed out of sight, she leapt from my embrace, readjusted her clothing, and left me in a state of dejected detumescence.

She dashed to the organ pit where she found Cliff, covered in blood and broken glass and lying in a pool of light that rapidly changed from red to gold to green to blue to purple. A stretcher party, closely followed by my girl friend, carried him to an ambulance which whisked him off to the Memorial whence my inamorata sent intermittent despatches to the Echo.

After two days of *Surgeons are fighting for his life*, she told us that *Mr Hepinstall's condition is as comfortable as can be expected*. The Echo's picture of Cliff lying in a hospital bed with two black eyes, his head swathed in bandages, one arm in a splint, and a plaster-encased leg suspended from a pulley, suggested that her expectations of comfort were none too high.

Sadly Cliff's condition never became comfortable enough for a return to the keyboard. Like Herbert before him, he abandoned the Wurlitzer and turned to cinema management. My girl friend, equally wisely, gave up journalism and married a publican.

The Gaumont was never the same again.

This afternoon, as I gazed at that black and dusty void beneath the screen, I wondered if it had ever happened … Herbert Moorcroft, Cliff Hepinstall and all those Will Hay films.

Was it really so long ago or had I lived for a time on a different planet?

Visit us with thy Salvation

The best known member of Slagthorpe's medical community is our Member of Parliament, Brigadier Digby Knutsford, MP, OBE, TD, LMSSA, RAMC. (LMSSA is the medical qualification bestowed by the Apothecaries Hall of Dublin, the degree of last resort for those who fail to qualify elsewhere. Rumour has it that the Dublin Licentiate lies within the gift of the examiner to whom the candidate presents his credentials. In the Digby's day the qualifying credentials were two cases of Chateau Lafitte.)*

In the ten years the Brigadier has represented Slagthorpe in the Mother of Parliaments, he has earned a reputation for economy of political expression. He has made only two appearances in Hansard

Brigadier Digby Knutsford (Slagthorpe): Never!

and

Brigadier Digby Knutsford (Slagthorpe): Pshaw!

though he once provoked a ministerial statement from the Chancellor of the Exchequer:

Mister Speaker, I distinctly heard the gallant and honourable member for Slagthorpe shout Bollocks.

---

*For historical reasons that had nothing to do with quality or competence, the LMSSA degree enabled its possessor to appear on the General Medical Council's Register of peer-approved doctors. In 1972 the GMC dealt a grievous blow to medical humorists by blocking this side entrance to the profession.

Digby compensates for his inactivity at national level by taking an intense interest in local affairs and sublimates his medical and administrative drives by organising elaborate exercises for the Slagthorpe Civil Defence force. Other communities may have disbanded their CD forces in deference to government wishes but Brigadier Digby pays scant attention to the wishes of government … particularly one packed with Conservative lefties.

Every second month at 1000 hours on a Sunday morning it is assumed that a mufti-megaton hydrogen bomb has exploded in the region of the String Vest Manufactory and, at 1010 hours precisely, three busloads of amateur actors elaborately made up as casualties leave the Town Hall to be scattered about the borough.

Attached to the casualties' lapels are neatly written labels describing their injuries in the official nomenclature prescribed in *The Slagthorpe Civil Defence Medical Manual, compiled and edited by Brigadier Digby Knutsford, MP, OBE, TD, LMSSA, RAMC*. The injuries have little to do with the effects of atomic conflagration but are nostalgic echoes of the brigadier's experience during World War II. Thanks to an administrative oversight, his Field Ambulance spent the first three years of the war at Tunbridge Wells where it treated only simulated patients, real ones choosing wisely to attend the local hospital. Then in late 1942 Digby and his men were issued with tropical kit, inoculated against yellow fever, and posted to a sub-tropical region on the outskirts of Shepton Mallet.

Though aware of their error, the RAMC's top wallahs maintained the proud tradition of the Corps: *Never Surrender. Never explain.* When the organisers of the Second Front asked for medical operational plans, the wallahs covered their mistake by deleting Digby's unit from the Order of Battle. Thus, while most of the army's doctors were dashing off to France, chasing up through Italy, sheltering from North African sandstorms, or trekking through the Burmese jungle, Digby was in Shepton Mallet organising exercises with mock patients and earning regular promotion, there being no other candidates on the home front.

With so much time upon his hands he became a dedicated student of RAMC manuals published between the wars and an enthusiastic promoter of first-aid competitions. That's why the nuclear holocaust assumed to emanate from the String Vest Manufactory of a Sunday morning causes no radiation sickness nor flash burns. Instead Slagthorpe is beset by epidemics of Trench Foot and Sand fly Fever and a good half of the injured suffer from Gunshot Wound of Right Thigh designed to determine which team can apply the quickest and neatest Thomas' splint.*

On the mornings of Operation Slagthorpe Salvation, the action starts when Digby gets a signal that the casualties are in position and announces *Gentlemen, we are now active red*. A fleet of ambulances, manned by enthusiastic first aid teams, whizzes off to retrieve the injured and carry them to the Civil Defence Medical Centre, set up in the Slagthorpe Billiard Hall where volunteers have covered the tables with loose planks laid over dustsheets to protect the integrity of cloth and cushion. When casualties arrive each is placed on a planked-over table to await medical aid. The aid comes in the shape of Brigadier Digby who approaches the table, stands at the non-baulk end, reads the casualty label, pontificates about the treatment already given in the field, and castigates any team that has lined up its patient with the label in baulk.

Then, watched by a clutch of impressionable first aid workers, Digby makes exciting surgical decisions. The women of indeterminate age who spend the mornings brewing gargantuan quantities of hot sweet tea, find it hard to conceal their adoration, as with delicate surgeon's fingers, he writes dramatically on the

*The Thomas' splint is a leg-length iron frame designed to immobilise a shattered limb. The bandages that hold it in place need to be applied carefully. This makes its application a favourite item in first-aid competitions where marks are awarded for speed and neatness rather than effectiveness.

labels: Amputation of left leg, Splenectomy, Craniotomy, and occasionally, to stimulate even more breathless wonder, removal of shrapnel from heart.

A week ago last Sunday the brigadier's exercise, as always, brought Slagthorpe's traffic to a halt. Stuck in the jam was an open-top Morgan sports car piloted by Reggie Scott-Huffingham, an impatient young man with a king-size libido who was on his way home from a Saturday night's wantonizing. Confronted by a gummed up High Street he made a quick U-turn, took a short cut through a builder's yard, and accelerated along Slagheaton Lane.

Too late he discovered that this too was blocked by one of the brigadier's ambulances. He applied his brakes harshly just as his wheels struck a patch of oil on the road. The Morgan slewed violently and rolled over through 360 degrees before parking itself neatly beside the kerb. The first 90 degrees of the roll slung Reggie from the cockpit. In mid-flight he knocked his head against a lamp post, then landed on the pavement where he lay unconscious.

The incident passed unnoticed by the nearby first-aid persons whose concentration was focused on applying a Thomas' splint to a victim of nuclear warfare. Five minutes later, when they found Reggie, they commented favourably on his make-up and his acting, threw him roughly onto a stretcher, bundled him into their ambulance alongside their other two catches, and rattled off to the Billiard Hall.

Brigadier Digby was having one of his more adventurous mornings. With nonchalant aplomb, he had already performed a dozen craniotomies, seventeen amputations, and a liver repair despite taking time off to give a short lecture on Purposeful Physical Training for Stretcher Bearers. The tea-ladies were as enraptured as ever and waited eagerly while the team that had collected Reggie laid out its bag of casualties on the planked-over tables.

Digby went straight for the one with the Thomas' splint like a guided missile homing in on its target.

—Aha, he cried, that knot is at least one inch off centre. We'll be having your names for idle treatment.

Then he turned to Reggie and his face grew pale.

—Good God, he said. Who's responsible for this?

The team leader quaked and the tea brewers smirked.

—How many times have I got to repeat it? *We fight disease with proper documentation.* This man has no label.

—We thought you were trying to catch us out, said the team leader sheepishly. We reckon he's a head injury with concussion.

Digby looked closely at Reggie.

—Make-up's damn good. Acting's not bad either. Pity he's making a basic mistake. What is it?

The team leader looked nonplussed.

—Look at his breathing, man. No unconscious man ever breathed like that.

The tea brewers giggled in sycophantic chorus.

—Did you examine him for other injuries?

—Er, no, sir.

—Well, you'd better do it now, hadn't you?

The team leader hauled up Reggie's right trouser leg and revealed a bloody mess.

—Strewth. I reckon that's a complicated fracture of the right tibia.

The pull on the trouser caused blood to pulse from the wound. The first aid team panicked. The tea brewers shrieked with alarm. And Reggie groaned

All turned to the gallant brigadier for help … just as he hit the deck.

Brigadier Digby Knutsford, MP, OBE, TD, LMSSA, RAMC, has one tiny chink in his armour.

He faints at the sight of blood.

The Entrepreneurial Gas Man

When the history of postgraduate education comes to be writ, two or three burnished pages will need to be reserved for the exploits of Anastasias Satterthwaite, anaesthetist, patron of the performing arts, and Grand Master of the Ancient and Antediluvian Order of Upholstery Stuffers.

Andy, as he is always known in the town, was born in a nursing home midway up Slag Hill and is a true Slagthorpian: proud, intelligent, opinionated and, in all matters municipal and political, essentially dishonest. He is the grandson of the legendary Sir Wilfred Satterthwaite, the Master Upholstery Stuffer who founded Slagthorpe's Haberdashery Emporium, and the only son of Alderman Percy Satterthwaite JP, present owner of the Emporium.

Alderman Percy, who keeps not just a finger but both thumbs in local pies, was the inaugural chairman of the Slagshire Regional Hospital Board, an appointment that might explain why Andy was appointed a consultant anaesthetist at the Slagthorpe Memorial on the strength of a licentiate bestowed by Dublin's Apothecaries' Hall and six years' experience as Medical Officer to the South Slagshire Electricity Board. (Of which, by chance, his father was a non-executive director.)

Soon after Andy's arrival in the anaesthetic department, the Memorial's senior surgeon, Lionel Tetchy, likened his impact on the Memorial's operating theatres to that of North Sea gas on

Slagthorpe's gas cookers – guaranteed to make any procedure not only hazardous but potentially explosive.

Yet Andy, thanks to some enthusiastic coaching from his flighty French registrar, Suzette Gassenaire, managed to hang on to his job. She showed him how a few simple techniques could reduce anaesthesia to bag-squeezing and crossword-puzzling; he reciprocated by showing her how Ongoing Registrar Education could extend to acrobatic frolicking on the back seat of his Ford Cortina.

Andy also discovered that a man who practises on his own midden has certain advantages. One day he had to anaesthetise the notorious blonde and brittle Maye Smerthwaite, post-war toast of the Slagthorpe Golf Club. As he inserted a syringe into a vein on the back of her hand, Maye looked up.

—Excuse me, love, she asked, but did I hear that nurse call you Doctor Satterthwaite?

—You did.

—Don't tell me you're Percy Satterthwaite's lad.

—I am.

Maye sighed

—If only I'd played my cards right, I could have been your mother …

And with those words she slid into the welcoming arms of anaesthesia.

Two weeks later Andy's father quadrupled his allowance and he and Suzette were able to enrich their professional relationship on the more commodious upholstery of a Jaguar.

Andy's new-found affluence bolstered his confidence but did little to ease the lot of Lionel Tetchy's patients, who continued to wake up blue, vomiting, and with loosened incisors. The Memorial's medical committee could do little to help because the patients *did* wake up – even if, as Lionel pointed out, they usually did so just as he was about to open the peritoneum.

Then one bright morning, much to the relief of Lionel – and

more so of his patients – the postgraduate education bandwagon rolled into town. The Slagshire Regional Hospital Board announced it was building a Postgraduate Centre in Slagcaster and wrote to all hospitals within its fiefdom soliciting nominations for the post of Postgraduate Tutor. Within 24 hours of receipt of the letter, members of the Memorial's medical committee, conditioned as they are to read the small print before the large, called an emergency meeting and unanimously nominated Andy as their candidate. So eager were they to get him out of the hospital that they despatched a motorcycling hospital porter to Slagcaster to hand the signed record of their decision directly to the Regional Board secretary.

At the same time Lionel Tetchy, who had agreed to make a personal approach to the Regional Board, invited the chairman, Sir Willoughby Wright-Ponce, to dinner at the Slagcaster Conservative Club. After the first decanter of Chateau Haut Brion had flowed contentedly through their oesophageal sphincters, and the sommelier had placed the second decanter on the table, Lionel extolled the contribution Sir Willoughby could make to the health of the region by putting Andy in a full time job that kept him away from patients.

Half way down the second decanter he made bantering reference to a copy he possessed of a bill that the Hotel Crillon in Paris had submitted when Sir Willoughby and his Lady had taken a short break in that delightful city and which, thanks no doubt to a secretarial error, had been paid from NHS coffers.

At the next Board meeting, the chairman told his fellow members he had heard persuasive local argument in favour of appointing young Satterthwaite and, because supporters of the other candidates were less practised than Slagthorpians in the art of chicanery, the board was happy to endorse Sir Willoughby's recommendation.

Andy accepted the job with enthusiasm. He soon discovered that most GPs who turned up for postgraduate lectures were less interested in enlightenment than in the signatures of attendance that won them extra payment. Listening to the lecture was a penance they endured to ensure that their quarterly cheques were adequately nourished. He also realised that the success of his centre would be judged by the size of the audiences it attracted. So why not give the punters something they could enjoy while they earned their educational loot? His centre, he decided, would concentrate more on entertainment than information and he would become less a tutor than an impresario.

While other centres organised symposia on *Ongoing Psychodynamics at the Doctor-patient Interface*, Andy set about turning himself into the Lew Grade of the postgraduate world. He discovered there were only a dozen or so doctors in the Britain who could give lectures that were both entertaining and instructive. He signed them up on handsome retainers to do a couple of turns a year in Slagcaster and presented each performance as a sort of cabaret after a slap-up dinner paid for by a pharmaceutical company.

Andy was also the first tutor to get a stripper recognised under the regulation that governs the distribution of postgraduate largesse. In theory recognition is given only to sessions that can be shown to be educational but Andy had spotted that the keepers of the academic purse strings endorsed events purely on their title which, in the unworldly terrain they inhabited, was assumed to indicate the content. They approved the evening with the stripper because Andy entitled it *Excitatory Patterns in Visual Pathways*.

Demand for attendance at Andy's courses became so great that he was soon able to sell tickets and two years later he could boast that people had to wait longer for his season tickets than for those at Manchester United.

During those years he'd added a cinema to the centre to accommodate his *Refresher Courses on Forensic Psychiatry* which featured many of the great crime movies: Hitchcock and Raymond Chandler seasons and repeats of James Cagney's and George

Raft's finest performances. He followed this with *Essentials of Forensic Medicine* which allowed him to broaden the range to include routine who-dunnits or any film involving a cop or a crime. The success of these educational ventures led him to establish his celebrated and oft-repeated course, *Analysing the Complexities of Interpersonal Relationships* which allowed him to show the entire oeuvre of Frank Capra, his favourite Hepburn and Tracey movies, and eventually any movie that might fill the armchair seats he had installed in the cinema.

The success of the cinema courses encouraged him to expand the postgraduate library, particularly the Forensic section. Forensic Psychiatry offered books by such as Dashiell Hammett, Raymond Chandler, James M Cain, and Simenon while the General Forensic section offered the works of Ngaio Marsh, Dorothy Sayers, John Dickson Carr ... indeed any writer who could extend a doctor's knowledge of forensic theory and practice.

The library also developed an innovatory Interpersonal Relationships Section which those seeking information created for themselves. They just had to fill in a form nominating a book that they thought would enhance their understanding of the human condition and the library would acquire it. Their choices ranged from Trollope novels and the plays of Anton Chekhov to the Kama Sutra and Lady Chatterley's Lover.

Though the library proved a valuable adjunct, Andy never forgot that the appeal of the centre depended on its live performances. And like any good impresario, he didn't neglect family entertainment. One of his most successful innovations was the introduction of a Family Season Ticket which entitled the holder to discounted tickets for up to four close relatives at special gala evenings.

He kicked off his first season of Gala Evenings with a concert by the Slagthorpe All-Voice Choir, *Synchronous and Combined Laryngeal Exercises*, and An Evening with Ken Dodd, *The Creative Hinterland of Mania*. The demand for tickets for Ken Dodd was so great that he had to transfer the meeting to the Temperance Hall. Later gala performances included a series of concerts by the Slagheaton Colliery Silver Band, *The Aetiology of Emphysema*, and a step up the cultural ladder with a sell-out recital by Yehudi Menuhin, *Improving the performance of your catgut*.

As news of Andy's success spread through the demi-monde of show business, an engagement at the Slagshire Regional Post-graduate Centre became an attractive booking for international entertainers visiting Britain to do the Clubs Circuit. Demand for tickets for Special Gala Evenings like Sing Along with Tony Bennett, *An Unusual Case of Cardiac Displacement in Northern California*, and An Evening with Raquel Welch, *Whither Morphology?*, was so great that Andy had to stage them in the Slagshire Woolgatherers Covered Market (seating capacity 10,000).

Andy's enterprise has brought great benefit to his postgraduate domain, now more a complex than a centre. Not only does it have a lecture theatre and library but a bar, a restaurant, a comfortable cinema, squash and tennis courts, two swimming pools, and a ballroom which can be let for weddings and municipal functions.

Slagshire's legendary Postgraduate Tutor still enjoys thinking up educational titles for his meetings though he no longer needs to do so. Two years ago he cut the Slagshire Educational Complex free from its NHS apron strings and now runs it as a non-profit business. All money left after he has paid his own outrageous salary is used to support postgraduate activities across the Region.

Andy has never forgotten the debt he owes to Lionel Tetchy and his co-conspirators who recognised that he might be better at keeping audiences awake than at keeping patients asleep. And he is proud of the role he has played in medical education

When, at the behest of his father, the Ancient and Antediluvian Order of Upholstery Stuffers honoured Andy's enterprise with its Grand Mastership, he referred in his inaugural address to Ministry of Health statistics which show that Slagshire GPs take a much greater interest in postgraduate education than doctors in other parts of the country.

—Our doctors, he said, prefer an holistic to a narrow specialist approach and are proud of this great county's reputation for pragmatism. No longer do they look on their postgraduate centre as a fount of useless information but more as country club where they can engage in educational and health-giving activities, often at the same time.

And if that isn't worth a burnished page or two in the history of postgraduate education, I'd like to know what is.

God rest ye Merry

It started with an unusual request during the evening surgery in Slagfield House. Only a handful of people turned up, most having been put off by the frost and the forecast of snow – it was the sort of evening you needed to be really fit to venture out to see the doctor.

The last person in the waiting room was a distinguished old boy with rubicund cheeks and elegant grey hair who, each time Donal opened the door to call the next patient, had been sitting quietly in the corner reading a paperback. Now it was his turn. He rose briskly to his feet and revealed that when standing he was a good six inches shorter than he looked sitting down, say about five foot seven in his brown suede boots. He tucked his book into his pocket, switched on a genial smile and, as he strode into the consulting room, gave Donal a big wink and an *Evening, doctor*.

The wink suggested Donal should recognise him but he must have shown that he couldn't because, as he turned to the filing cabinet to get out the notes, the old boy anticipated the question he was about to ask.

—Snitterton. Albert, Edward, Nathaniel.

—Snitterton ... Donal repeated the name as he searched for the card and then, just as he found it, he remembered.

—Charlie, he said.

—That's it doctor. You got it. The stage name. Charlie Chuckles. I were a friend of your Dad's, *old* Doctor Donovan.

—You used to come my birthday parties and do conjuring tricks. Dressed up as a Chinaman.

—Right again, doc. Ching Ling Soo. The Mysteries of the East brought skilfully and tastefully to your own front room. Children's parties our specialty. Those were the days.

Donal looked at the card in his hand. Albert Edward Nathaniel Snitterton had not been a drain on the NHS. Over the past twelve years he had visited his doctor twice, each time to have his ears syringed. As Donal hesitated wondering which name to use, his patient again anticipated him.

—These days everyone calls me Charlie, he said.

—I see from this card it's your birthday in a couple of days. Congratulations.

—Eighty six, doctor. And still looking for some nice young lady who wants me for myself and not just for my body.

He gave one of the infectious chuckles with which he punctuated his act. For Charlie Chuckles was more than a party entertainer. He'd started life on the Music Halls as a boy soprano before he met up with The Two Suprendos, a father and son duo of *siffleurs*. The act was on the point of dissolving when the younger Suprendo found himself a rich widow during a summer season in Bognor. Charlie volunteered to take his place and spent nine happy years whistling his way around the halls. During those years, the elder Suprendo grew increasingly alcoholic and the partnership had to be dissolved after a catastrophic night at the Slagthorpe Hippodrome when Suprendo senior had had so much to drink that he completely lost his whistle.

The act always opened with Charlie's senior partner sitting on a park bench and, that night, while the Hippodrome orchestra sawed its way through *In a monastery garden*, the old boy started on the familiar routine:

—What magic is this we hear wafting on the evening breeze? Could it be the elegant melody of that master songster Mister Thrush?

And then he went *Phooph, phooph, phooph,* which is the sound puffs of air make when they pass whistle-less through inadequately puckered lips.

Unaware of what was happening, Suprendo senior cupped his hand to his ear.

—No, No, he said. Methinks 'tis not the harmonious thrush but the ethereal queen of the night, the stately nightingale. *Phooph, phooph, phooph.*

At which point the catcalls rose to such a crescendo that the manager rang down the curtain and the Two Suprendos were no more. It wasn't the first time the elder Suprendo had blotted his copy book but it was the last. This time the manager black listed the act and Charlie was out of a job.

He didn't take long to pick himself up – something he was to do often in his life – and he launched himself into a hotch potch of careers as manager of a Pierrot show, stand-up comic on the second class circuit, cinema pianist, cinema organist at the Slagthorpe Picture Palace (while doubling in his spare time as Ching Ling Soo) and, more recently, the life and soul of many an Alderman's Supper and Masonic Ladies Night with *A Smile and a Song of Yesteryear.*

A month or two back, Finbar had told Donal that Charlie had entered another branch of show business and was now the official organist at the Slagthorpe Crematorium. That elegant grey hair and his sense of the theatrical lent dignity to many a sorrowful occasion but, according to Finbar, the unique skill that Charlie brought to the funerals was his experience as a cinema pianist which helped him improvise suitable accompaniments as the coffins slid silently away.

He would invite the relatives to indicate the underlying theme – Anglican, Roman, Ecumenical, or Humanist – and would then develop suitable melodies. Old Comrades from the Slagheaton Fusiliers were sent off with *Onward Christian Soldiers,* Alderman Sidney Grunge, avenging angel of the magisterial bench, departed to the *Ride of the Valkyrie*, and Cynthia Clack (Contralto), Slagthorpe's First Lady of Song slid gracefully away to *We'll gather Lilacs in the Spring Again*.

Charlie gave Donal another wink.

—I knew you were back in the town, doc. We've been dealing some of your handiwork up at the Crematorium.

Another chuckle.

—Happy to say business has been a bit sharpish recently. I'm on piece work, you see. So this cold weather has been a bit of a Godsend. A bit of frost tends to sort 'em out.

Again the chuckle.

—It's good to see you Charlie. What can I do for you? Ears bunged up again?

—No thanks, doc. I'm hearing you loud and clear. Something very simple this time. So simple that I'm sorry to have to bother you with it. It's just that I've now got no-one belonging to me. They've all popped off their perches and I'm the only one left. So I wonder could you do us a favour.

He took a grubby brown envelope from his pocket.

—I'd like to leave this somewhere safe and reliable, where someone will open it when I pop my clogs. I don't want anyone peeking at it so it has to be with someone I trust. I don't want to presume but I just thought Doctor Finbar – or you, of course – might be happy to oblige. One of you is bound to be around at the time. We're not allowed to go these days without a doctor's permission.

Another Charlie chuckle.

—I'll have to ask Finbar, said Donal, but I'm sure it'll be all right.

Charlie handed the envelope across the desk. It was slim and light. The back was sealed with a large blob of sealing wax and across the front was a message written in an elegant hand: *To be opened only on the occasion of my death. Albert Edward Nathaniel Snitterton.*

Donal propped it against the ever empty inkwell.

—I'll give it to Doctor O'Flaherty after the surgery.

—Thank you very much doctor. Happy Christmas to you, and to Doctor Finbar. And try and send us a few clients in January so I can pay the Christmas bills.

Another chuckle and he was gone.

After he'd locked the surgery Donal found Finbar in the sitting room and, as he got up to pour pre-dinner drinks, Donal told him about the letter.

—A new one on me, said Finbar. Still, that's general practice. Something new every day.

Donal handed over the envelope. Finbar took a cursory glance at it then propped it on the mantelpiece.

—I'll lock it in the poison cupboard in the morning. Its the only place around here safe from the prying eyes of Martha.

He handed Donal his glass.

—You can be sure of one thing, he said. It'll contain nothing straightforward. Likely some silly trick that Charlie's up to.

And they both turned their minds to more interesting matters.

Two days later, lunchtime drinkers in the Captain's Cabin at The Admiral Byng, *Slagthorpe's premier commercial hotel*, seemed wholly unsurprised by the sight of Father Christmas sitting on his own at the end of the bar. Charlie had been there every day since he started his seasonal job in the Fairy Grotto at Satterthwaite's Haberdashery Emporium.

The lunchtime drinkers also knew it was Father Christmas's birthday because he had bought drinks all round, and a few of them had reluctantly reciprocated. Now Charlie sat alone staring at the thin layer of whisky in the bottom of his glass and preparing himself for another afternoon in Satterthwaite's basement. Through force of habit he was shaping his mind into some sort of order before he went on stage. When at last he was ready, he downed the whisky, offered a cheery Good day to the Captain's Cabin and all who sailed in her, and strode out into the Street.

Outside the air was bitterly cold and a treacherous patina of ice coated paving stones that the sun had yet to reach. But Charlie was protected against both hazards. The lunchtime whisky generated a satisfying central heating and his Santa wellies gave him a firm grip on the pavement.

He was indeed the embodiment of Christmas cheer, this perky little Santa Claus striding along beneath the High Street decorations. This year these were certainly colourful if a trifle incongruous for they consisted of illuminated starfish, buckets and spades, sailing ships and seashells, which might have little to do with Christmas but had a lot to do with the off-season hiring rates offered by the organisers of the Slagton-on-Sea autumn illuminations.

Charlie saw only the colour, not the content. For all his life his birthday had been the first harbinger of Christmas. Now it is really here, he thought, as he passed windows where electric power drills were wrapped in cotton wool and covered with silver glitter and where toast racks and fire tongs were labelled *A useful gift*.

Every shop window carried its own seasonal message:

Make Xmas Day a Colour Television Day
Light up her eyes with a sewing machine
This Xmas, Happiness is Sock-shaped

And all around him was the sound of music, powerfully amplified carols recorded on tape by the Slagthorpe All-Voice Choir and blasted from loudspeakers buried within the abdomen of the *papier mache* reindeer that the Chamber of Commerce had erected outside the Corn Exchange.

At the end of the High Street stood the drab two storey building that was Charlie's place of employment. A banner, stretched between the twin cupolas perched incongruously on the building's flat roof, carried its own seasonal message: *Don't say Xmas, Say Satterthwaite's*

As the cracked bell of Town Hall clock clunked out the news

that it was half past two, Charlie passed beneath the twin cupolas and staggered slightly when he was ejected forcefully into the store by Satterthwaite's ever-revolving door.

As he crossed the parquet of the Grand Hall, he raised his red bonnet to Miss Melody of Tooled Leather and Fancy Goods who was later to say he looked perfectly normal, if perhaps a little rosy in the face. Denise Congleton of Knitwear and Separates said much the same thing though she hinted that Charlie's greeting might have been a little saucier than usual. Fred Gomersall of The Great Outdoors has always claimed that, on that afternoon, Charlie was in such good form he even raised a smile from Joshua Oldroyd who scowls his way through every Christmas season because he has to take over Gift Wrapping and Knick Knacks and abandon his beloved Dungarees, String Vests, and Satterthwaite's Rugged Combinations for the Working Man.

A few minutes later Charlie was sitting in the basement where Joshua's counter usually stood. His impressive Elizabethan stool, on loan from Quality Reproduction, was set in an arbour formed by a trellis arch from Garden Tools sparingly camouflaged with sheets of red and green crepe paper. In front of him stretched an orderly queue of subdued and serious children who were waiting to tell him what they wanted for Christmas, hand over five shillings, and receive in return a festively wrapped item that Satterthwaite's had been unable to pass off on its paying customers during the previous twelve months.

Two forty-three was later designated as the official time at which Fate took a hand. For that was when eight year old Marlene Withershaw burst into tears. She had just unwrapped her Fairy Grotto Gift, ripping at the paper in her eagerness, and discovered that her plastic egg cup made in Hong Kong and labelled *Souvenir of a happy holiday in Slagton* was split down the middle. She turned to Charlie for consolation and laid her head upon his shoulder.

Charlie was deeply affected and, what with the whisky inside him and Satterthwaite's Christmas Musak coming over the Tannoy, he responded instinctively. Having failed to comfort Marlene with soft words and a consoling arm around her shoulders, he rose from his Elizabethan stool, took a large doll from a nearby shelf and thrust it into her arms.

—Happy Christmas, he said.

Marlene responded by flinging her arms round his neck and kissing him. Then she rushed from the grotto and up the main staircase shouting Happy Christmas to everyone around her.

Half an hour later, as the town hall clunked out three-fifteen, an urgent telephone message reached Mabel Clatterbridge, deputy manageress, in her tiny room on the first floor – Satterthwaite's prefer to call it the mezzanine – immediately beneath the port-side cupola. As soon as she'd replaced the phone, she left her office and moved towards the staircase at a speed unlikely to provoke panic. She tried to radiate an air of unconcern that wouldn't disturb the ladies ferreting among the piled up counters in Sensible Underwear.

Cyril Aspinall of Toilet Accessories met her at the head of the stairs and they descended together, matching each other's step precisely and with such dignity that it crossed Mabel's mind that they made a stately duo. As they reached the ground floor, Mabel cocked a well-trained ear.

Maybe the low rumble that fills the air when customers are in buying mood was just a touch off key but it was nothing untoward. Indeed everything was perfectly toward until they reached the stairway to the basement. A small crowd had gathered around its head. She and Mr Aspinall insinuated their way politely through the crush and, when they reached the front, were nearly swept away by a tide of children rushing up the steps. These children were laughing and cheering in a quite untraditional way and all were carrying toys – surprisingly large toys like train sets, fire engines, dressing-up dolls, even pedal cars and bicycles.

Each child who swept past wished them Happy Christmas with such enthusiasm that Mr Aspinall responded with a smile which

Mabel managed to freeze only with the severest of her looks. For now she knew she was confronting a Section IV management decision.

She had spotted two small girls labouring up the stairs, struggling to carry one of the huge teddy bears that Satterthwaite's kept not to sell but to decorate the top shelves behind the grotto. It was one of a set of six and by the time Mabel reached the foot of the stairs, now moving at an undisguised top lick, she had passed the other five on their way up.

The toy department presented a scene of devastation. Every shelf was bare, the counters empty, even the Christmas tree was gone and, as she entered, the grotto trellis, stripped of its crepe paper was being manoeuvred out through the fire exit by a serious minded lad and his practical minded father. All that was left was the Christmas Musak resonating from bare walls.

Sitting on the floor in the midst of this desolation was Charlie, legs stretched out in front of him, body leaning back, weight supported on outstretched arms while he competed with the Musak with loud guffaws of unstoppable laughter.

Mabel stretched herself to her full imperial measure of five foot six and three-quarters and emitted an outraged sibilance.

—Mister Snitterton, she hissed.

Charlie stopped laughing, looked up at her, and winked.

—Methinks, he said, that this is not the harmonious thrush but the ethereal tones of the queenly nightingale.

Then he cupped his hands to his lips and went *Phooph, phooph, phooph.*

By three forty-five, according to *The Slagthorpe Echo*, the Slagshire County Constabulary had taken control. Inspector Raymond Treadlightly, the Nureyev of the Slagthorpe Formation Dance Team, was in the basement making an assessment and, outside the main entrance Police Constable Hepinstall had parked his bicycle, removed his bicycle clips, and turned himself into a cordon. For the first time in its history Satterthwaite's had closed its doors early in the week before Christmas, and Denise Congleton later swore that, as she spread the dustsheets over the counters in Knitwear and Separates in the Grand Hall, she heard an agonised howl come from the bronze bust of the founder, the legendary Sir Wilfred.

Two hours later Donal was summoned to the police station. The police surgeon, Wee Willie McAnny, was off duty and Donal had made the mistake of picking up the phone when it rang. If he hadn't, Martha would have palmed the call off to some other doctor. She knew that while some GPs, like Wee Willie, were born to assist the police, some others, like her two, were not. Their sympathies, like those of Donal's father before him, lay instinctively with custodees rather than custodians.

Donal climbed the steps beneath the blue light with no great enthusiasm. A call from the police at this hour usually meant not just having to decide whether someone was too drunk to drive a car but having to defend that decision a few weeks later in court confronted by a driver whose insobriety had been replaced by indignation, an unfriendly magistrate who as likely as not was a member of the same golf club as the accused, and a Machiavellian lawyer who had spent the day before scouring obscure medical texts.

But this evening instead of leading Donal to the cells or an interview room, the desk sergeant took him straight to the inspector's office where they found Inspector Raymond Treadlightly gliding back and forth across the lino on his celebrated toes.

As the sergeant ushered Donal in, Raymond did an elegant reverse turn and slowly folded his arms before resting the right cheek of his bottom lightly against his desk.

—Just keeping in touch for the Area Grand Finals, he explained. This year Mavis and I have a surprise or two in store for the judges.

He then solemnised his demeanour.

—A bit of a tricky one for you this evening, doc. Respectable chap. Decent sort of background. Yet behaving in an undeniably subversive way. Thought I'd better have him checked out before we charged him and make sure he wasn't one for the eh ...

He raised his forefinger to the side of his head and twisted it back and forth to indicate a loose screw.

Then he put on his cap, picked up his swagger cane and, executing a neat double chassis with contrary body movement, opened the door and led Donal along the corridor to one of the interview rooms.

Raymond pushed back the door and revealed a heart-warming sight.

Police Constable Hepinstall, still wearing helmet and bicycle clips, sat on the edge of a table. He had wrapped a comb in Government Issue lavatory paper and pressed it to his lips to kazoo a soulful melody not unlike that of *In a monastery garden*.

Charlie sat in a chair alongside him, eyes closed and hands cupped to his mouth, while his lips emitted the verisimilitude of the song of a thrush that Donal had once heard long ago when he went on a picnic with his parents.

As he wound himself up for the first reprise, Constable Hepinstall gathered a deep breath and swung his shoulders expressively. And in so doing spotted the visitors in the doorway. He immediately stopped blowing, got to his feet, and stood awkwardly to attention.

Charlie, abruptly deprived of his accompanist, abandoned the thrush and opened his eyes.

He looked up at Donal.

—Evening, doc, he said. And a happy Christmas.

—All we want to know, doctor, said Raymond, is whether this man is fit to be charged.

Donal didn't ask, *Which man?* Though he felt tempted.

—Can I have a word with him on my own?

—Of course. Just call us when you're through.

And Raymond and Constable Hepinstall left the room.

Thirty minutes later it was Finbar's turn to walk beneath the blue lamp. Donal had requested a second opinion and the two doctors spent some time in consultation in the interview room. It was a difficult discussion not because they disagreed but because of the distracting background noise. Charlie had moved on from birdland and was deep into farmyard animals.

Eventually, despite the intervention of morning roosters, braying donkeys, lowing cattle, and the angry woofing of Farmer Giles's collie, the doctors reached an agreed position and called a top level meeting in Raymond's office.

—Your problem, said Finbar, is that the balance of this man's mind seems to be disturbed by a profound sanity. I don't know what you want to charge him with, Raymond, but whatever you choose is not going to look good in *The Echo*. The sub-editors there have a limited collection of sobriquets and the one I see them polishing up for you is Scrooge. Not a name likely to enhance your chances in the Area Grand Final.

Raymond rose from his chair, put both hands to his forehead to indicate deep thought, and did a couple of reverse spins around his desk.

—My problem, doctor is that I'm going to have the entire Satterthwaite family breathing down my neck. You know what a mean-minded lot they are. And only last week the Chamber of Commerce demanded another crack-down on shop lifting. These are people of great influence in the town.

He lowered his hands and stared hard at Finbar.

—No hope at all of you getting me off the hook?

—No hope at all, said Finbar. Much as we'd like to.

Raymond did a deliberate slow-slow-quick-quick-slow across the room. Then paused.

—What's that noise? he said.

All three listened.

A distinct rumbling noise, rising and falling in regular rhythm.

Raymond glided to the window, pushed up the sash, and looked out.

—Come and look at this, he said.

The doctors stuck their heads out alongside his into the frosty air. Assembled in the street below was a crowd of two or three hundred people, many of them with children brandishing bright new toys.

All were facing the police station and chanting:

—Jingle bells, jingle bells, we want Charlie ... Jingle bells, jingle bells, we want Charlie ... Jingle bells, jingle bells, we want Charlie...

Directly below Raymond's window Constable Hepinstall stood on the top step beneath the blue lamp. He was rocking uneasily back and forth on the balls of his feet as he confronted the crowd, having once again turned himself into a cordon.

—This could be a threat to public order, said Raymond.

He moved swiftly yet gracefully across the room, flung open the door, and bellowed down the stairs.

—Sergeant. Fetch the prisoner.

Twenty minutes later on their way back to their cars, Finbar and Donal had to thread their way through a huge crowd packed into the High Street. All traffic had come to a halt and some public spirited citizen had switched off the Musak in the reindeer's abdomen. Everyone's attention was focussed on a window in the first storey of the police station where Father Christmas, spotlit by emergency lights hastily rigged in the street, led the crowd in community singing. They'd already had *Away in the manger* and *Come all ye faithful* and were now deep into *When the red, red robin comes bob, bob, bobbin' along* (with actions).

—You have to hand it to Raymond, said Finbar. After this he's going to get either a commendation or the sack.

Then, as Finbar led Donal away, the singing suddenly stopped and a frightened gasp swept through the crowd. Donal looked back. Father Christmas had collapsed over the window ledge. Raymond and Constable Hepinstall appeared alongside him and gently lifted him back into the room.

The two doctors turned and moved swiftly back towards the police station.

Later that evening a subdued Finbar went into the surgery and unlocked the poison cupboard. He took out the brown envelope Charlie had left in their care, slit it open with a spatula, removed a single sheet of paper, and read the note Charlie had written.

He smiled wryly and handed the paper to Donal.

—Instructions for his own burial service, he said. Poor old Charlie. But wasn't it great that the last sounds he heard on this earth were cheers and applause from people who'd taken him to their hearts. He wouldn't have asked for anything better than that.

He tapped the paper in Donal's hand.

—We'll make damned sure that every detail of that is implemented, he said.

Four days later the crowd that attended the crematorium was so big that the Chapel of Remembrance could accommodate only a fraction of it and the service had to be relayed by public address system to the throng outside. Finbar and Donal sat in the second row behind Raymond who was accompanied by the chief constable and the mayor. Alongside the mayor sat a scowling Alderman Satterthwaite who'd eventually been persuaded by his Public Relations manager that he should make the best of a painful job and try and scoop up some of the goodwill that spilled over from Charlie.

There were some in the crowd who feared the service might lack musicality because the crematorium had yet to appoint a replacement organist. But they needn't have worried because Finbar had ensured that Charlie would make his last exit in the way that he himself had chosen.

As the coffin glided silently towards the furnace, the double doors of the chapel were flung open and in marched the Slagheaton Colliery Silver Band in full ceremonial order blasting their way through two rousing choruses of *Blaze Away*.

Just Reward

The River Slag, having flowed glutinously through Slagthorpe, winds through the industrial devastation of the Slagshire plain before oozing into the wind-swept marsh that is its estuary.

Just north of the estuary stands a bifurcated holiday resort. The northern end, Slagton-on-Sea, is brash and vulgar, all candyfloss, bingo, Donald McGill postcards, and long queues for the ladies' lavatories. The southern end, Slagton Regis, is self consciously sedate. The gentlemen who stroll along the esplanade raise their hats to passing ladies; the Private Hotels that line its seafront terraces boast of *Separate Tables* which they adorn with starched linen and silver-plated cutlery.

No physical barrier divides the southern from the northern resort, only the social barrier that separates Hove from Brighton, St Anne's from Blackpool, St Leonard's from Hastings, and Frinton from Walton-on-the-Naze.

In Slagton Regis this November afternoon the sea is not blue but muddy grey and the breeze has a touch of east in it. The pier, the bandstand and the bowling greens impose, even in hibernation, a sense of rectitude upon the town. As does the large Victorian building that dominates the seafront and looks like a none too distant cousin of London's V&A museum.

Under the November sky the Grand Esplanade Hotel may look as if it is brooding but it certainly is not hibernating. During the summer it accommodates prosperous Slagshire families in search of sea and sand who arrive with high hopes and usually leave with new mackintoshes. During the winter it accommodates an even larger population, the permanent residents who supply the financial cement that holds its Gothic tracery together.

Most are widows of Slagshire tycoons whose husbands narrowed their lives and their coronary arteries in pursuit of the wealth that their widows now fritter away on beauty treatments, herbal laxatives, boxes of chocolates, baskets of flowers, and other morale boosters for the financially sound but socially insecure. The permanent residents also include a small platoon of retired Majors in grey flannels, sports coats, white shirts, and silk scarves, who survive at the Grand Esplanade on the crumbs that fall from the rich ladies' tables.

Within this introspective community, health dominates every conversation. And health is assumed to reside in the alimentary tract. The Grand Esplanade must be the only hotel in the country where Stewed Prunes are a permanent item on the table d'hôte. Only when the prunes and Californian Syrup of Figs have failed to do their stuff, do the residents entrust themselves to the capable – and definitely non-NHS – hands of the hotel's most popular doctor, the tall and elegant Doctor Simeon Svelte whose silver-grey hair has the same metallic sheen as his silver-grey Bentley.

For years Simeon's most rewarding patient was a lady known to her doctor as the Battleship. Mrs Myrtle Cartwright-Jones dominated the Grand Esplanade in much the way the hotel dominates Slagton Regis. Her authority, as is the way in Slagshire, derived less from class than from cash: she was by far the wealthiest permanent resident thanks to her late husband's wartime success in cornering the black market in pork pies. In those bleak yet profitable wartime days she was plain Myrtle Jones, but when her husband was summoned to what his obituary in the *Slagshire Post* called his *just reward*, Myrtle migrated to the Grand Esplanade acquiring a Cartwright and a hyphen on the way.

Doctor Svelte called her the Battleship because of the way in

which she invariably summoned him … an urgent message that
Mrs Cartwright-Jones is sinking. Myrtle usually started to sink after a
three or four day orgy of overeating and self-medication. She
would retire to bed with her bowels laden with an unhealthy
mixture of liqueur chocolates and senna pods then summon her
hairdresser and beautician. After she'd been satisfactorily coiffured
and lacquered and the beautician had filled her facial creases, as
best she could, with paste and powder, Myrtle would dismiss her
body servants, don several thousand pounds worth of jewellery,
and send for the doctor.

The only treatment she expected was that her wrist be held
tenderly for half an hour while she indulged in nostalgic
reminiscence of her medical history, her occasional encounters
with fringe members of the aristocracy, and her regular encounters
with some of the richest rogues in Harley Street.

When she grew weary of this monologue, her medical
attendant was expected to withdraw discreetly muttering caring
sounds and she would then summon her *little woman* – in truth the
distinctly unlittle Madame Blanche – who with her trusty high
colonic lavage would wash out the Battleship's colon and return
her in reasonable nick to dominate the floor at the Grand
Esplanade's *The dansant.*

One unfortunate weekend the Battleship chose to sink while
Simeon was out of town and a new hotel porter, untutored in the
nuances of permanent resident culture, summoned an NHS doctor
from Slagton-on-Sea. The GP, a mustard keen beginner in the
craft, was equally untutored in the nuances of general practice. It
never occurred to him that a stand-in's first duty is to jolly things
along until the master returns and continue all treatment unless
there is more than a reasonable doubt that it is killing the patient.

Though lacking practical experience, Doctor Mustard had
heard gossip within the trade about the antics in which Simeon
indulged and got off to a good start by holding the Battleship's
wrist in pulse-taking mode while she embarked on her monologue.

After six or seven minutes of well-acted sympathetic murmuring he grew proud of the way things were going and made the grave mistake of interrupting her. Had it been any old interruption he might have got away with it. He was, after all, young and handsome and the Battleship had already categorised him as Personable. It was the content of the intervention that was his undoing

—Mrs Cartwright-Jones, he suggested innocently, perhaps we should do something about your weight.

—My weight, she shrieked, as if he'd suggested she should strangle her grandchildren. Young man, have you read dear Doctor Svelte's notes?

Before poor Mustard could reply she dived under the bed and produced a pile of X-rays so high that, for a moment, he wondered if she might be suffering from radiation sickness.

—You've never seen anything like these before, she said, scattering mementos of innumerable barium enemas across the bedclothes.

—Dear Sir Humphrey Mainwaring said he'd never seen anything like it. He kept some of the pictures to show to the Royal College of Surgeons. I'm surprised dear Doctor Svelte didn't tell you. I'm quite unique, you know. The only woman in the world to have an extra yard of transverse colon.

Mustard who'd made a fair attempt at looking chastened now tried to radiate awe. He carried a couple of the X-ray films to the window, held them up to the light and, for a full two minutes, stared at the outline of a normal colon.

—Fascinating, he murmured, for he was learning.

But too late. Mrs Cartwright-Jones had taken invincible umbrage. She accepted the return of her x-rays with the calm of an ice maiden then deployed a combination of stare and silence to force the young doctor into a fumbling and apologetic departure. From that day forward the Battleship never expressed a fear of sinking without first checking that Dear Doctor Svelte was in town.

The young stand-in, at heart a humble fellow, accepted there were areas of medical practice he was ill equipped to enter. Simeon, he explained to his colleagues in Slagton-on-Sea was more gardener than doctor, cultivating illness with the sort of enthusiasm with which allotment holders cultivate rhubarb.

* * * * * * * *

On this bleak November afternoon when the sea is not blue but muddy grey and the breeze has a touch of east in it, two years have passed since Doctor Mustard's encounter with the Battleship. Fate plays a card and Mustard and Simeon leave their homes at the same hour to take their dogs for a walk along the Slagton Regis esplanade. A second card brings them head to head in front of the deserted bandstand. For all his deviousness, Simeon has a great affection for professional colleagues, especially those he regards less favoured than himself, so he greets young Mustard like a long lost cousin.

Once they've introduced their dogs – Simeon has a Labrador called Rupert and Mustard a mongrel called Fred – the young doctor, seeking non-doggie common ground, asks,

—How is the Battleship?

Simeon sighs a deep sigh.

—Unfortunately, dear boy, she sank. Irretrievably. Beyond salvage. The old bat who gave her colonic lavage punctured her rectum. Ended up with a pelvic abscess and got her quietus from a pulmonary embolus.

They stand in uneasy silence till young Mustard remembers that Simeon is rather proud of his nickname, *The Legacy Doctor*.

—No doubt you figured in the will?

—Ah, the will, says Simeon. Quite an impressive treasure chest. More impressive than one might have expected. I got my share, of course, though not a considerable one after the family had their whack. Still, I got the deceased's most valued possession.

—Not that tiara she wore in bed?

—'Fraid not, dear boy. Her transverse colon. Told her lawyer she knew how impressed I'd been by it and thought I'd like to keep it in a glass case over my mantelpiece. *C'est la guerre.*

Simeon pulls back on Rupert's lead to restrain impending intimacy with Fred.

—Lawyers are peculiar fellows, he says. Made the pathologists do a post-mortem to retrieve it.

—Just so you could put it over the mantelpiece?

—You jest, of course. Can't tell you officially what I did with it but Rupert spent a couple of days with a satisfied look around his chops.

He tugs at the dog's lead then nods at Mustard.

—Nice to see you, dear boy. Keep fighting the good fight.

And before young Mustard can respond, Simeon and Rupert disappear behind the overwrought ironwork of the bandstand.

EDITOR'S NOTE
A couple of pages from one of Donovan's Commonplace Books. An acerbic note above it explains that, in a mischievous moment O'Flaherty had told the Friends of the Slagthorpe Memorial that young Doctor Donovan, in his late adolescence and at university, had performed as a conjurer at parties and charity concerts.

How's Tricks?

—What I'm really after is a big finish.

—Children?

—Ten to twelve year olds. Mostly girls. A production effect was what I had in mind. Colourful but not too expensive.

—Production effect? You're in the business then?

—Of course.

Why should Donal admit it was fifteen years since he last paid his subscription to the Magic Circle? Why should he explain that he'd resolved never again to raise a magic wand in anger? Could this man ever understand what those Boy Scouts had done to his rabbit?

—Have you considered a dove pan?

—You still do dove pans?

—We'd never have earned our reputation as Slagthorpe's premier Trick'n Joke shop if it hadn't been for the quality of our dove pans.

—Doves come a bit expensive.

—Who mentioned doves? A few spring flowers, some tasteful silks, half a dozen collapsible bottles of Guinness, and a cascading two-inch ribbon. A very colourful effect. Mix a little glitter with your ribbon and you'll provoke gasps of astonishment and delight. Guaranteed. Says so on the packet.

—You've got a deal. Give me one dovepan, an assorted pack of spring flowers, four ounces of Prettiegritta, an Amazing Vanishing Dice, and one of your special offer Wundawizard Wands. How are your vanishing eggs this week?

—Fresh.

—Then I'll have a dozen. Six with yolks, five without, and one that turns into something nasty I can throw at Doctor O'Flaherty. I'll also need a few prizes.

—How about some jokes, sir? Our Whoopee Cushion with the new improved note. The broken window effect – a shattering experience. The ink on the tablecloth – very mirth provoking. Or a Doggie's Whatsit – the plastic mess on the carpet that's so realistic you can almost see it steam.

—Hardly for a children's party. Mostly girls.

—Forgive me. I got carried away. Why not try a box of our hilarious Riddle Rubbers – the handy eraser with a riddle on one side and the answer on the other? I say, I say, I say. Why do the Swiss put bells on cows?

—I don't know. Why do the Swiss put bells on cows?

—Wait for it. Wait for it. Because their horns don't work.'

—Give me a dozen. If they don't like the jokes they can use them to rub out the words they write on the walls.

—Will that be all, sir?

—I think so. It's not a gala performance. Just a Christmas party for the Friends of the Memorial. As usual when they're in trouble they send for a GP.

—Don't tell me you're a doctor, sir. Well, well, well. We don't get many members of your profession in this shop. But seeing as you are here, I'm sure you'll be very interested in my back.

—I'm afraid I have a surgery to catch.

—On a Tuesday it was. I bent over a new consignment of Automagic Card Vanishers and got the pain. More a sort of stabbing. Right behind the braces buttons.

—Like a red hot knife, said Donal.

—Like a red hot knife, said the man.

—So I went to my GP. He gave it a quick look, handed me a couple of aspirin, and told me to rest. I was in and out of his consulting room like a fiddler's elbow. Not like the days when doctors *were* doctors.

—And guides, philosophers, and friends, said Donal.

—And guides, philosophers, and friends, said the man.

—So next day you demanded to see a specialist.

—How did you guess? But a fat lot of good it did me. I went up to the hospital and had my full examination, my X-rays, my physiotherapy, and my infra red. And after four weeks I was no better. So I saw the specialist again. And what do you think he did?

—Handed you a couple of aspirin and told you to rest.

—You're telepathic. How about a pack of mind-reading cards? Then I heard about this chap in Slagcliffe-le-Willows. Electronic diagnosis in the front room. Manipulation in the back. His daughters stretch you over a horsehair sofa and he taps your spine with his magnetic mallet.

—Sydney the Spesopractor. One overstuffed sofa and two understuffed daughters.

—That's him. And you're right about the daughters. He hooked me up to his electronic box and straight away found I had three ribs out of place. They never found that at the hospital. Four weeks they wasted and he spotted those dicey ribs in under five minutes. That alone was worth the forty-five quid

—A veritable snip, said Donal.

—A veritable snip, said the man.

—So we nipped round the back and the girls got me stretched over the old horsehair. My word you should have seen their muscles. Then along comes Sid and gives me a couple of taps with his mallet and I don't tell a lie, I could feel those ribs going back.

—Could hear them click into place, said Donal.

—Click, click, said the man. And when I got up the pain was gone.

—You're joking, said Donal.

—I'm not, said the man. It was gone. Vanished,

—As if by magic, said Donal.

—As if by... how did you guess?

Brennan on the Moor

The village of Ostlethwaite-cum-Hardy lies in an isolated valley at the north-west tip of the Slagshire Moors: a cluster of farmhouses and stone cottages, a church, a vicarage, a general store, a pub, and a horse trough dedicated to the memory of three Ostlethwaite men mown down in Flanders in the first world war. An added plaque commemorates a fourth man lost on active service in the Home Guard in 1941 when he pierced his foot while doing arms drill with a pitchfork and succumbed to gas gangrene.

Ostlethwaite is the centre of a community whose members live in farmhouses scattered across moors where sheep munch their way through their life-long lunch. The village is some three thousand feet above sea level and over ninety miles from the sea. Yet if you enter The Ruptured Packhorse on the third Friday of any month, you will find it packed with men wearing yachting caps and reefer jackets and sporting navy blue ties emblazoned with the pennant of the Ostlethwaite Yacht Club.

These are no foreign invaders from far off Slagcaster. Nor escapist day trippers from the industrial smoke and dust of the Slag Valley. These are all locals. The Ostlethwaite Yacht Club has but two rules.

One: All members must live in the village or on the moor.

Two: Any member who owns or hires a boat, or gives succour to any person who owns or hires a boat, faces immediate and ceremonial expulsion.

The yacht club's monthly drink-in is an inerasable date on the village calendar. Nathaniel Burghwallis, landlord of The Ruptured Packhorse, is the club's honorary purser and at his own expense has had the club crest poker-worked into the ceiling above the bar: a pint of ale foaming over a rusty anchor supported by the motto *Per ardua ad aqua*. Only once has hush descended on the roistering that fills the bar on third Fridays. That was when a parsimonious newcomer demanded to know the advantages of joining the club.

Nathaniel's quick response averted an ugly scene.

—Once you're a member, he said, leaning across the bar, you earn the privilege, if you so desire, of being buried at sea.

The club's founder, and its present commodore, is the local GP, William Patrick Brennan, who arrived in the village soon after the second world war during which he spent four years as a prisoner of the Japanese. In the years he struggled to survive while working on the Burma-Siam railway, Bill kept his brain alive by making detailed plans of what he would do if he ever got away. Within two years of returning home, he found exactly what he wanted and established himself in Ostlethwaite as a kind, conscientious, and reasonably skilled GP.

Only then did he set to work on the second part of his plan. Before the war he had tried to read every word written by McMullen, Maurice Griffiths, Eric Hiscock, and other yachting writers. Soon after he moved to Ostlethwaite he started to build a small cruising yacht in his back garden with the intention of towing it one day to a triumphal launch on the Slag Estuary.

During his first summer he laid the keel and planked the lower third of the hull and, to preserve his handiwork from the rigours of the Slagshire winter, covered it with a low open-ended barn. The following summer he became so engrossed in the internecine affairs of the inhabitants of Ostlethwaite Moor that he had little time for boat building and managed to add only a few planks. By his third summer his engrossment in general practice was complete and his enthusiasm for boat building waned to the point of extinction. So he founded the Ostlethwaite Yacht Club.

Finbar suggested that Donal should meet Bill as part of his education in the art of general practice. So today, on his afternoon off, Donal navigated the moor's network of dusty roads and farm tracks at the wheel of his latest love, his new MG TC. Well, not exactly new. Two weeks before, it had stood unloved in the yard behind Stan Glover's filling station but this afternoon it roared along the hillside dazzling the sheep with reflected sunlight from its re-sprayed paint and lovingly polished chrome. Donal's only doubt about his new found love was the name that, in a moment of pretension, he had painted along the side of the bonnet: *Anna Livia Plurabelle*.

From the window of his cottage in Ostlethwaite, Bill Brennan monitored the progress of the cloud of dust that zigzagged down the far slope of the valley to the track at its foot before starting on another zigzag up the slope towards the village. So when Anna Livia Plurabelle swept up the lane, Bill was already standing at the cottage gate. He watched Donal park his car on the balding grass in front of the shack that serves as village hall and village surgery. And, when Donal crossed the road, Bill grasped his hand and kept a firm grip on it while he inspected young Donovan from tousled hair to trouser turn-ups, like a senior officer greeting a new subaltern.

—I never met your father, he said, but Finbar tells me you are the very image of him.

He relaxed his grip

—Welcome to the back of beyond. You picked a fine sunny day for it.

Putting his arm around Donal's shoulder, he ushered him across the garden to a couple of chairs parked in the shade of a gnarled yew. Between them was a table on which stood a large pot of freshly-brewed tea, two huge mugs, and a plate piled high with sandwiches. While Donal washed the dust from his throat with tea and filled his belly with sandwiches, the pair of them indulged in the ritual exchanges that occur when GPs meet. They swapped accounts of the bizarre antics that some of their patients had been up to, the bizarre antics in which more than some of their colleagues had indulged, and reached consensual agreement on the irredeemable stupidity of the local Executive Council.

Bill, it seemed, rarely ventured away from the moor and he talked of the strange things he found had happened to the world on the few times he re-entered it. Only when Donal felt secure enough to venture onto what might be sensitive ground did he mention the boathouse. Could he perhaps have a look at it?

—Of course, of course, said Bill, but tis no great sight, I fear.

He led his guest down through the orchard to a derelict barn where rotting planks and timbers lay buried beneath greenery that sprouted in all directions through rusty gaps in the corrugated sheeting.

—I keep her there just in case one day I feel inclined to start building her again. Of course, if I did ... and finished ... I'd be drummed out of the Yacht Club. I would have to tow my darling to the sea, point her away from the land and head for the horizon.

—Do you think you ever will?

—Some questions should never be asked, young man. And, if asked, should never be answered. For the time being, I prefer being a commodore to being a sailor.

He looked at Donal's feet.

—I see Finbar warned you to put on sensible boots. Hang on there for a moment.

He loped off to the cottage porch and returned carrying a well-worn pair of walking boots. He leaned against one of the apple trees while he pulled them on and did up the laces. Then, shoes in hand, he led Donal around the cottage to a concrete slab on which stood the wartime jeep in which he visits his patients. He threw his shoes into the back of the jeep.

—Jump aboard young man and I'll show you why being a

commodore is more rewarding than being a sailor.

Donal looked back at the cottage

—Don't you have to leave a message? How do they contact you when you're not at home?

—We have a simple arrangement. Cissie Cook runs our local exchange from her corner house in the village street. One plug-in board in her front room covers every phone and call box on the moor. If someone wants me and there's no response from the cottage she sticks her head out the window to see if the jeep is anywhere in the village. If it is, she sends one of her children along to give me the message. If it isn't she crosses the road to the church and tolls the bell. Six groups of three bongs. It echoes right across the moor and she repeats it every ten minutes till I phone in.

—Does the vicar mind?

—Mind? He loves it. If he sees Cissie approaching, he dashes into the belfry ahead of her so he can pull on the rope. Like a kid playing with one of his toys. Now jump aboard.

Bill started the engine, engaged the four-wheel drive, and they set off along a stony track down the slope of a shallow valley that lay behind the village. Ahead of them was Crag Tor, a tall pinnacle that, like most of the rocky outbreaks on the moor, was clothed in grass and heather save at its very peak where the rock broke though.

When the track petered out near the base of the pinnacle, they left the jeep and clambered across scree until they reached a narrow path that zigzagged upwards through heather. After half an hour of scrambling climb, Donal realised that the sandwiches had been a bad idea and showed genuine heroism in keeping pace with the lean figure ahead. As the slope grew steeper he found himself clinging to tufts of grass and heather ahead of him and was virtually crawling when he reached the rock platform that forms the summit. He hauled himself over the edge and lay for a moment or two on the flat rock recapturing control of his lungs. Then he stood and turned to look at what had been behind him while he climbed.

All around was open moor scarred only by two crevasse-like valleys, their bases lined with conifers. The barren contours were broken in places by walls of loose stones, most of them near the half dozen farmhouses dotted across the moor. Bill handed Donal a pair of binoculars and got him to focus on a small gap in the hills to the south-east. After much focusing and re-focusing he caught a shaky glimpse of the new Slag Valley arterial road where lorries and cars shuttled urgently twixt Slagcliffe-le-Willows, Slagthorpe, and Slagheaton.

—If you don't want to join 'em, beat 'em, said Bill.

Donal handed back the binoculars.

—I prefer what I can see just with my eyes, he said.

He sat on the rock. Alongside him, Bill squatted on his hunkers like a Bedouin … or a man who had spent four years as a slave.

—A lot of the folk who should know better think it's a lonely life up here. An old medical school chum even said he pitied me. Sat where you're sitting now and told me I'd cut myself off from civilisation. Warned me that my reason would grow blunt if it weren't challenged by people of similar intellect … he actually used the phrase, God help him, people of similar intellect.

—He sounds like a psychiatrist.

—Psychiatrist be dammed. He's a bloody orthopaedic surgeon. All that sawing and chiselling is making him blind.

Donal grinned. For a moment he closed his eyes and turned his face to the sun. Then he stretched out flat on his back and watched a pair of buzzards tracing indolent circles above the moor.

Bill still hadn't made his peace with the orthopod.

—A practising doctor cut off from civilisation, can you believe it? What an ignorant bugger he is. My patients are every bit as civilised as his … or yours. And my closest friends up here aren't exactly dimwits: the ones back in the cottage … Chekhov, Thurber, Joyce, Perelman, Yeats … if you want the full list you can look on the shelves when we get back. And every one of them on top form whenever I turn to them.

—It's the same with the music makers. Schnabel, Schwarzkopf, the Quartetto Italiano. They glide into the cottage the moment I drop the needle into the groove … Mozart, Haydn, Beethoven, Mahler, bursting to oblige a man should he tire of his own company. I wish I were a person of … what was it? … similar intellect to them.

The sun was warm on Donal's face and he found himself drifting towards sleep. He woke with a start when a shadow fell across his face. Bill was standing over him.

—I get the feeling, young Donovan, you could be developing a taste for this. Lying there like a tripper on a beach. I'll have to detoxify you next winter. Get you back when a nor'easter sweeps across the moor and the rain travels horizontally down the village street. For now, I'd best get you back on solid ground.

—This is solid enough for me, said Donal. He looked up and saw that the buzzards were now circling directly above them as if trying to fathom what they were up to.

Donal rose reluctantly to his feet. He moved to the rim of the ledge and looked apprehensively at the narrow path they would have to travel down. Beyond the valley was a raised plateau on which someone had placed a scale model of Ostlethwaite-cum-Hardy. He could see a boy running across a field behind the church, a black dog bouncing around him. The dog was barking but the sound didn't reach him. A silent movie.

—Can you hear the church bell up here?

—Unfortunately yes. The first time I climbed up I thought I'd found sanctuary. The second time Cissie tolled me down.

Donal took a last look back across the moor. Bill watched him.

—Can't take it with you, I'm sorry to say. We'd best get on the move before this romantic air sozzles our brains. You'll find it easier if you face inwards, at least at the start. It's more comforting to look at where you've been than where you're going. I'll be ahead of you.

They spent an hour edging their way down the path. Donal

found it hard going and, as they made the final scramble across the scree, he feared that the aching muscles in his calves would seize with cramp. It was a moment of minor triumph when he hauled himself aboard the jeep. Bill climbed in alongside him and they sat for a moment regaining their breath.

—Always more hazardous coming down than going up, said Bill. And more tiring. But I hope you enjoyed it. Finbar said you would. He's one of the few who understands why I stay up here. He doesn't write me off an escapist.

He put the key into the ignition slot.

— One lesson you'll learn young Donovan is that a GP never escapes. My patients here on the moor can weave as rich tangled patterns as patients anywhere: they're just as instructive, just as rewarding, and, at times, just as frustrating as the friends who sit on my shelves.

He started the engine and they set off on the bumpy trek home. Back at the cottage, they sprawled in armchairs sipping their way though a bottle of La Tache while Schwarzkopf sang them the Four Last Songs of Richard Strauss and Karl Bohm and the Berlin Philharmonic entertained them with a Mozart serenade.

Eventually, Donal sat in the open cockpit of Anna Livia offering thanks but reluctant to leave.

—Let me know if you ever think of retiring, he said.

—Don't get carried away, said Bill. This sort of practice wouldn't suit a young man like you. Apart from anything else you'd need to take a vow of poverty. The list of patients is tiny and, for all the incentives the NHS offers rural fogies like me, I earn much less than people like Finbar and yourself. To make money up here you'd need to turn criminal.

—Criminal?

—When I was student, there was a Dublin street ballad we used to sing when we'd had a few jars. Brennan on the Moor. About a highwayman, Ireland's answer to Dick Turpin. Robbed the rich, gave to the poor, got himself hanged. Traditional stuff.

I've often thought that, if times got really bad, I could drive down to the arterial road, hold up a coach load or two of solid citizens and make off with their wallets.

—Why bother? You could just finish the boat and sail off over the horizon.

—Now, Now. I'm talking only about practical ideas. Robbery it would have to be. The song always goes down well at the Yacht Club. Let me give you a few bars.

And he set off with the flourish of a barroom baritone

It's of a famous highwayman a story I will tell;
His name was Willie Brennan, and in Ireland he did dwell;
And on the Kilworth mountains he commenced his wild career.
Where many a wealthy gentleman before him shook with fear.
Brennan on the moor, Brennan on the moor,
A brave undaunted robber was bold Brennan on the moor.

—Only as a last resort, I think. For the time being I'll keep on robbing the minds of the folk who sit on my shelves. Good luck to you now and drive carefully. Get Finbar to bring you along one Friday to the Yacht Club. I'm allowed to have two guests. *Droit de Commodore.*

As Anna Livia Plurabelle wound her way up the moorland track, one image refused to erase itself from Donal's mind. It wasn't the world as seen from Crag Tor, nor the buzzards circling overhead, nor the rotting timbers in the barn: it was the object, unmentioned by Bill, that he had seen mounted in a glass-covered frame above the cottage fireplace – a Japanese sword snapped in half.

Fire Power

The big wheel in Slagthorpe's fire brigade is Walter McWhirter, known to us all as McWhirter the Water Squirter. During the twenty years he spent as a humble hoseman, Walter developed unusual notions about fire fighting and on the proud day when the Slagshire County Fire Officer crowned him with the fire chief's helmet and handed over the ceremonial axe of office, Walter enunciated the dictum which has ever since stood between Slagthorpe and consummation by eternal flames:

—A battle against fire is like any other battle and your fire fighter must be trained like any other fighter. I promise you that from this day forward the name McWhirter's Squirters will strike terror in the heart of every fire.

Battle training at the Slagthorpe fire station involves little running up and down ladders or jumping into sheets. McWhirter's men spend most of their time on the drill square moving to the right in column of three or in the station house polishing their boots. Specialist training in hosemanship, water squirting, and kiss of life by numbers is relegated to one hour each evening and Walter's sturdy lads must be the country's only firemen to advance on the flames with camouflage nets covering their helmets.

Critics suggest that the parade and kit inspection that take place on the receipt of an alarm call have reduced the unit's effectiveness but Walter has little time for critics.

—An improperly dressed fireman means an improperly dressed

fire. And an improperly dressed fire is a blot upon our island heritage.

On arrival at the scene of the flames the Slagthorpe appliances line up in an orderly rank facing the fire. Walter then mounts the bonnet of Big Bertha, the unit's oldest and largest fire engine, and gives his men two minutes worth of battle motivation: a few well chosen excerpts from Henry V followed by battle orders.

—B Company will make a direct frontal assault while C Company makes an outflanking movement on the right.

... a manoeuvre known in fire-fighting circles as McWhirter's Right Hook.

Next comes a stirring exhortation:

—And forget not, my gallant lads, that what we do today we do for England, Her Imperial Majesty and the greater honour and glory of the Slagshire County Fire Service. Keep your nozzles at the alert but hold your water till you see the whites of the flames.

He then drops his ceremonial axe and bellows: *Charge*. Whereupon B Company's warriors, with foliage waving bravely in their camouflage nets, run out their hoses and start squirting.

Despite what you might think, Walter has an enviable reputation as a fire fighter. Because most fires have a good hold by the time his men charge into action, he has developed dramatic ways of isolating the flames. His favourite is to dynamite adjacent buildings. This demolition, while unpopular with householders, gets a good deal of silent approval from the Slagshire County Council, most of whose members are builders or property developers eager to find new sites for multi-storey office blocks. As a result, Walter McWhirter was a name to conjure with at County Hall ... until last Monday when he ran head on into the Slagthorpe Memorial's senior surgeon, Lionel Tetchy.

Lionel's latest gimmick to sustain his image as the hospital's Character is to smoke in the operating theatre. He holds his king size filter tips in a sterilised forceps and flicks the ash and the butt ends into a specially designed stainless steel bowl attached to his registrar's right boot.

Last Monday, midway through an abdominal operation, when the theatre sister offered him a light from the sterilised Ronson Varaflame kept on the trolley, an officious theatre technician, who was new to the game and unversed in the traditional licence granted to hospital Characters, slipped from the theatre and telephoned a fire risk warning to Walter's HQ.

Nobody noticed. Not even when Lionel was stitching up the peritoneum and a distant voice could be heard intoning:

Now set the teeth and stretch the nostril wide,
Hold hard the breath, and bend up every spirit . . .

The first signs of trouble were two firemen with blackened faces and foliaged helmets who shuffled into the theatre clutching a stick of dynamite in each hand. Lionel, who had just inserted the last suture and was now on his third king size, gave them a long contemptuous stare.

—Members of the Hospital Management Committee, he snarled, are not permitted to enter this theatre in ceremonial dress.

—You have been reported as a fire hazard, said the better camouflaged fireman. We have orders to isolate you, by demolition if necessary.

Without a word Lionel marched up to them, seized the dynamite from their hands and walked into the surgeon's room. There he opened the window and flung out the explosive sticks.

Three of them landed harmlessly on the management committee's private lawn but the fourth scored a direct hit on Big Bertha, fortunately inhabited only by old hoses and Walter's Tupperware box of coleslaw sandwiches. The force of the impact detonated the dynamite and there was an almighty explosion. As the smoke subsided and rusty pieces of Big Bertha embedded themselves in the hallowed lawn, Walter ran from the coal shed in which he'd taken cover and waved his fist angrily at the surgeon's window.

—Philistine, he cried, with tears running down his cheeks. Hooligan. Vandal. The Slagshire County Fire Officer shall hear of this.

Lionel removed the fire extinguisher from the wall of the surgeon's room, took careful aim through the window and gave Walter the full benefit.

—Some people are born to squirt, he called. And others are born to be squirted. You, Walter McWhirter, have been sailing too long under false colours. Good day.

The Micklethwaite Inheritance

No Slagthorpian would consider himself decently buried unless the obsequies were arranged by Jeremiah Micklethwaite and Sons (1874), Builders, Joiners, and Undertakers.

Right up to the 1950s, if you lived near a Micklethwaite building site you would occasionally hear the foreman blow three blasts on a whistle. The workers would then down tools and line up to be driven away on a horse drawn waggon or, in later years, a sand-spattered lorry. Thirty minutes later, faces scrubbed, eyes downcast, and dressed in smart morning suits, the same men would walk slowly by, solemn pall-bearers alongside a hearse or marshals of the sombre procession that followed. An hour later they would be back on the building site in muddy boots and ragged trousers, shouting cheerful obscenities at one another and whistling at all young women who dared pass by.

The post war housing boom, the growth of casual labour, and the coming of the Lump destroyed that duality of employment. The building side of the business is still firmly based in Slagthorpe but the needs of the bereaved are now serviced from a string of shop-front parlours dotted along the Slag valley from the Junction to Slagworth village.

Charon Micklethwaite, present managing director of Micklethwaite Funerals, acknowledges that the secret of the business's success lies in the family genes. Charon is a tall man and has a long thin face, doleful and immobile. Deep furrows droop from each corner of his mouth and from the outer corners of each eye. His lips are incapable of a smile, his eyes incapable of a twinkle. His classical Micklethwaite face is, in short, set in a state of perpetual mourning. He last grinned when he was fourteen and since then his facial structure has grown so rigid, it could be fashioned from *lignum vitae*.

This Micklethwaite face has proved to be the Micklethwaite fortune. Bereavement can provoke a desire for traditional ritual and mourners in the Slag valley have learned that a Micklethwaite face at a funeral proclaims far better than they can themselves the grief they feel for their loved ones.

The Micklethwaite empire that we know today is largely the creation of Uncle Jeremiah the Eighth, whom Charon succeeded. Faced with the challenges of post-war Britain, Jeremiah replaced the horse-drawn hearse with a purring limousine and converted a shed in a corner of the builders' yard into an embalming room. He also created a Chapel of Rest in the old building manager's office, a sanctum previously hallowed by the passage of used fivers to members of the council's planning committee.

The post war building boom – augmented by discreet municipal liaison transferred from the building manager's office to the private dining room at the *Everything Flambé* – generated a spectacular expansion in the building side of the business and loosened its connection with the smaller yet profitable undertaking trade. By 1954, the year when Jeremiah the Eighth set out on his own last journey – silk-lined oiled teak, hand-worked brass handles – Micklethwaite's had split into two businesses. Micklethwaite Homes looked after building and property development; Micklethwaite Funerals offered a less flamboyant yet more profitable service than it had of yore.

Jeremiah's post-war modernisation of the funeral business went far beyond the limousine, the embalming room and the Chapel of Rest. These were but outward signs of a deeper philosophical change. In 1948 when Slagthorpe's intelligentsia borrowed Evelyn

Waugh's *The Loved One* from the Boots Lending Library and sniggered at the burial practices of Southern California, some of the less bizarre of those practices were being quietly imported into Micklethwaite's.

Micklethwaite Funerals was no longer run by undertakers but by funeral directors and those who had inherited the Micklethwaite face became bereavement counsellors. (This title was also conferred upon the chief carpenter who, thanks to a lifetime of physiognomic conditioning, had developed a pseudo-Micklethwaite facies.)

The most solid evidence of change was the conversion of the former Ladies' lavatory into a Counselling Suite – with no loss of amenity because the Gents was refurbished as a Unisex Facility. (Jeremiah was as ever ahead of his time). The new Suite put the punters more at ease while the bereavement counsellors dropped words like *grief therapy* or *closure* into the conversation – words which they'd been taught would facilitate the sale of more expensive coffins or, as they preferred to call them, caskets.

Along with grief therapy came a better class of funeral. The Chapel of Rest was refurbished as an Ecumenical Room of Meditation and the harmonium was replaced by an electronic organ. This instrument had no keyboard, just a panel of buttons which offered a choice of Britain's best loved hymns or consoling melodies from Ivor Novello. To her great relief, Great Aunt Cissie Micklethwaite was able to retire and no longer had to trundle down the High Street on her tricycle to vamp consoling chords for the bereaved.

Thanks to his uncle's enterprise Charon Micklethwaite now runs a highly profitable business and, if you judged him only by his face, you would guess he was Micklethwaite through and through. But you would guess wrong. For buried in his chromosomes is a romantic gene acquired in 1928 when his father, Jeremiah the Seventh, then aged 71, decided to marry an 18-year old Greek waitress at the Slagthorpe Kardomah. She was, said Jeremiah, the only person who knew how he liked his tea.

Sadly for poor old Jeremiah, the effort of conceiving Charon induced a catastrophic stroke from which he never recovered. He died while his son was but twenty weeks into his uterine life. The distaff side of the Micklethwaite family saw it as a Judgement. The young widow managed – just – to tolerate the Micklethwaite clan until Charon's birth but, three weeks into the puerperium, she fled to California with a handsome bequest from her husband and the assistant manager at the Kardomah. She left everything else behind, including Charon.

Her son has no memory of her and was brought up as a *de facto* orphan by his Slagthorpe aunts and uncles. In his late adolescence he went to California in search of his mother but California is a big state and, despite fraternal assistance from the US National Association of Funeral Directors and Embalmers, he found no trace of her. The only memento he has is his forename. She chose it when she spotted the Micklethwaite facies in her newborn babe and knew that Destiny had marked him as the family's next ferryman.

When Charon's uncle, Jeremiah the Eighth, died, as the Echo put it, *without official issue*, Charon took over the firm. He enjoys the business and has enhanced its reputation, running it with a kindly efficiency that appeals to Micklethwaite's customers and endears him to all who work with him. His staff refer to him as the Quiet Man and he has few friends outside the business apart from Doctor O'Flaherty. They got to know one another during a bleak mid-winter when a virulent respiratory infection cut a swathe through the Mount Ararat Twilight Home and they kept meeting in the way of business. It was therefore no surprise that he should turn to Finbar when he needed advice about a problem that troubled him deeply.

The romantic gene on Charon's chromosomes was, it seemed, aglow with passionate intensity … inflamed by the presence of young Wendy Bickerstaff who had joined Micklethwaite's as typist, tea girl, and deputy assistant embalmer. Charon's problem was that his depressing mien was getting between him and the object of his desire. Whenever he tried to declare his love, Wendy took one look at his face and assumed he was about to admonish her for a spelling mistake, putting sugar in his tea, or being too heavy handed with the formalin. Four times he tried to declare himself and four times Wendy interrupted him with an apology before dashing tearfully from the room.

After much discussion, Finbar prescribed a pragmatic solution. Charon, he suggested, should invite the object of his desire to Slagthorpe's vernal festival: the annual Masked Ball of the Slagthorpe and District Pigeon Fanciers Association. If Charon's words came from behind an artificial mask rather than his natural one, said Finbar, Wendy would listen to what he had to say.

Unfortunately, Finbar's advice came a little late and when Charon went for a fitting at Percy Haddock's Dressing Up Shop, *Slagthorpe's finest carnival costumier*, he found that, though Percy was well stocked with masks, the demands of The Pigeon Fanciers had left him with only one outfit in Charon's size. The desperate Charon was prepared to try anything yet few would have given much for his chances when, on the evening of the Ball, he and Wendy rolled up to the entrance of the Arcadia Banqueting Suite, she as Little Bo Peep and he as Mephistopheles, sitting side by side in the front of a Daimler hearse.

Yet unbeknownst to Charon, but definitely knownst to Doctor O'Flaherty, Wendy had already fallen in love with her boss: hence the tears when he spoke to her harshly. That evening, as they walked beneath the single string of fairy lights that the cheeseparing Arcadia manager had draped over the entrance, Wendy knew she was crossing a significant threshold. When Charon offered his stuttering invitation to the ball he hadn't noticed, because he'd been too busy trying to keep his face turned away from her, that his words had set her all a-flutter. She hadn't had a proper night's sleep since but now her time had come. This was the evening she was sure – for she was a great reader of Barbara Cartland – when he would crush her in his arms both savagely and tenderly and, even more paradoxically, combine a naked animal passion with a deep respect.

Yet, after two quicksteps, one slow foxtrot, a Palais Glide, and a Hokey Cokey, Wendy was beginning to harbour doubts. Charon had tripped over his tail in the quicksteps and the Mephistophelean mask seemed to inhibit him even more than his natural one. Fate, however, was about to take a hand and did so soon after Doctor O'Flaherty disappeared into the janitor's office during a slow waltz. Suddenly all the lights went out and, as a frightened Wendy clutched Charon tightly, he tore off his false mask and, inspired by the knowledge that now his face was free yet his beloved couldn't see it, he heard himself pour out words that Wendy had often read but thought she would never hear. At 3 a.m. that morning, in the flat above the Embalming Room there was, as Finbar put it, a consummation devoutly to be wished.

The following year Wendy and Charon were unable to attend the Pigeon Fanciers' do. The reason lay in his cot in the flat above the Embalming Room where the newly weds were camping out while waiting to move into the new house Micklethwaite's Homes was building on Higher Drive. One morning when Finbar and Donal visited the office to sign a couple of cremation certificates, Charon invited them upstairs for a cup of tea. While they waited for the kettle to boil, Wendy insisted that they tip toe into the bedroom where Jeremiah the Tenth lay gurgling in his cot. As he looked at the baby Donal spotted early evidence of the Micklethwaite inheritance.

Later, after Finbar and Donal had each had a cup of tea and a new-baked Maid of Honour, they clambered back into the Morris Cowley.

Finbar turned the key in the ignition and the engine growled.

—Did you notice, doctor, that when I tickled that babe's tum the Micklethwaite facies crumpled into a smile. There's life for you. After generations of suppression, humanity can still break through.

Donal didn't like to point out that the smile came only after Jeremiah the Tenth had farted. Still it was a hopeful sign.

Egbert's Dream

The Third and present Lord Slag, grandson of the First Lord who gave us the Memorial, is rarely seen in the town. He lives in Lucerne and divides his time between divorce petitions in Nevada, paternity suits in the South of France, and regular appearances in the social column of the Sunday Express. In contrast, his younger brother, Egbert Slag, is a down-to-earth, hardworking fellow who, up to a year ago, staggered through life, weighed down by two great burdens.

The first was that, at a young and impetuous age, he developed a vocation to become a general practitioner. He'd barely recovered from the strain of qualifying and doing his house-jobs, when the second burden was laid squarely upon his shoulders. His father died and, under an eccentric will, settled all his money on his elder son but left the family seat, Slag Manor, to Egbert who, though he loved the house, had no income to maintain it.

Slag Manor lies to the south of the town half-embraced by a polluted U-bend in the Slag river. When Egbert moved in, it was a gaunt grey building, turreted and sprawling, set at the centre of a litter-strewn park. By day it was a desolate place but when the sun went down it could, according to a local balladeer, summon up a gothic charm.

Oh, carry me back to the Manor Park
Where the misty moonlight steals

O'er the river at night
Casting shimmering light
On the rusty bicycle wheels

Egbert set up a single-handed practice in a ground floor corner of the West Wing and, despite the gloomy surroundings, his practice flourished – not because Slagthorpians have any sense of loyalty to the family that exploited their smoky town, but because Egbert is a kind, considerate, and conscientious doctor. Yet, as the years went by, Egbert, as is the destiny of kind, considerate, and conscientious doctors, crept nearer to bankruptcy. The park around his house grew more and more ill-kempt, his family's clothes grew more and more threadbare and Egbert himself grew wearier and wearier. Until the night he dreamed his Dream.

Egbert's Dream was a wide-screen, 3D, multi-coloured effort, provoked by a supper of pickled herring, a bottle of Spanish Burgundy, and the reading before retiring of the whole of Kubla Khan and a chapter from Duke of Bedford's autobiography. The following morning, he leaped from his bed, rang a cousin in a merchant bank, and launched the scheme that has since restored him to solvency and Slag Manor to somewhat gaudy grandeur. It has also transformed Egbert's surgery into one of those well-equipped, well-staffed, natural-wood and Formica affairs that draw orgasmic cries from forward thinking members of the Royal College of General Practitioners.

The brilliance of the Dream lay in its simplicity. Egbert decided to throw open his stately surgery to the public.

The immediate benefits were considerable. Patients who were at first discomfited to find that they had to pay five bob at the main gate in order to get to the surgery, coughed up cheerfully when they discovered that, on their way up the drive, they could dally at the children's zoo, the model village, the boating lake, and the vintage stethoscope museum. Indeed, Egbert's first delighted finding was that the profit on candy-floss alone more than covered his receptionist's salary.

The real profits, however, came from the coach loads of solemn citizens who, thanks to those highly educational television programmes on the BBC, had become dedicated medical voyeurs. Their all-in package included not just a trip around the grounds and the stately home but a conducted tour of the surgery where they could see real patients sitting in a real waiting room and a real doctor signing real certificates. Slagthorpians with heart-warming human stories to tell made a point of visiting their doctor at the week-end when they could be sure of a large receptive audience from which they could evoke tears or laughter and occasional bursts of applause.

Egbert soon discovered that he could score heavily over television by presenting minor surgery not only "live" but in three dimension and full natural colour. Even the most seasoned of voyeurs were prepared to pay extra to enter the Your Life in His Hands pavilion to watch Egbert skilfully remove a verruca or a sebaceous cyst, and he quickly found that he could stimulate the fringe profits by adding an incision of a pulp infection[*] to the programme.

Anyone who fainted as the incision was made was carried into the waiting room, inspected by Egbert and, as soon as he or she recovered, signed up as an NHS temporary resident for whose treatment Egbert received an additional NHS payment.

This summer Egbert capped the Duke of Bedford's *Love In* by holding a *Suffer In* and next year intends to invite a number of distinguished surgeons to appear as guest stars in the Your Life in His Hands pavilion. Slagthorpe's very own Lionel Tetchy has promised to put on an exhilarating performance in which he will combine a cholecystectomy with a shouting match with the theatre

---

[*]An abscess in the fleshy pulp at the tip of a finger. A common form of infection in pre-antibiotic days that grew less common in the late 1950s.

sister and Egbert hopes to line up a Caesarean section for the August Bank Holiday with the hope of making a tidy side profit from a competition to name the baby.

Today Egbert is a happy man. The house that he loves is in a reasonable state of repair. He has beaten off the bogey of financial disaster and, although he has more than his fair share of exhibitionists on his list, he can afford to practise a reasonable and satisfying standard of medicine.

Could Egbert's Dream indicate the next step forward for those imaginative GPs who have already installed fruit machines in their waiting rooms?

Child's Play

The blame, if blame there has to be, rests with the twinkle in Mrs Bamforth's eye. Finbar is susceptible to twinkle and particularly susceptible when it dances defiance in eyes confronting trouble. Last Tuesday evening when Mrs B came to the surgery she was certainly confronting trouble. Not big trouble compared to some she had brought to the doctor over the past 25 years ... but still trouble.

Mrs Bamforth first met Finbar when he delivered her only child. Just over 40 she was when her daughter was born. Needed special attention at her age, the hospital said, yet she'd gone into labour a week early while buying trimmings for the cot in Slagthorpe market. They shipped her off to the Memorial in an ambulance and parked her in a corner of Casualty.

—You've got lots of time, said the nurse. As its your first. Takes a long time, the first. We'll get you up to the labour ward later.

Then the nurse went off to do something important. Finbar, who'd been visiting one of his patients, came strolling down the corridor just when she felt the head bursting through. Never seen him before in her life. Took one look at her, whipped off his jacket, shouted for help, and delivered the baby before anyone else arrived. Her daughter Mary. He'd looked after them both ever since.

It was to do with Mary that she came to the surgery on Tuesday evening. Well, not so much Mary as her granddaughter Lucy. Mary was in the Memorial. Came off her scooter and broke her leg. So six-year old Lucy had moved in with Mrs Bamforth at her little council flat in Inkerman Crescent where she'd been since her husband died. Just round the corner from where Mary and Lucy moved when Mary's chap went off with that hussy from the lipstick counter at Satterthwaite's. Living so near kept the family together. Mrs B did a lot of baby sitting and, during school holidays, Lucy spent the day with her Gran while her mum was at work at the glue factory.

Mrs Bamforth's Tuesday crisis was provoked by Lucy's birthday or at least by the birthday party that Lucy's mother had arranged for next Saturday in the Temperance Hall. That afternoon the Temperance caretaker had rung to tell her the hall couldn't be used. Flooded. Burst water main.

—Serves them right, said Mrs B to Finbar. All that singing *My drink is water clear*. Well they'd got their water now. Right up to their you-know-wheres.

There was no space for a party at her flat. Nor at Mary's. Nor, it seemed, anywhere else. She'd tried the council and the Women's Institute. She'd even tried the vicar though they never went to church, but no one could find her a place. Not at four days notice. It would break Lucy's heart if she had to cancel the party what with all her friends invited and the excitement mounting as they ticked off the days. So what did Finbar think she should do?

That's when the twinkle did its stuff. After the surgery, Finbar gave me my instructions. Next Saturday I was to stage a children's party here in Slagfield House.

—Should be right up your street, he said.

I know not why. The only party I ever helped organise was for a girlfriend when we were both medical students. Her twenty first. Our biggest worry then was security. How to protect against intrusion by gatecrashers or police. Our best hope was that both would arrive at the same time.

On Saturday I would face a different threat. Not to my safety but to my reputation. GPs who want their practices to thrive, need to be known to be *good with children*. The party had to be a roaring success if the Slagfield House practice were to hold its position in the parental assessment league – an influential rating that is never written down but whispered in queues at the grocers or over cups of tea in front rooms.

I tried to allay my anxiety by tackling the problem in a systematic way. I drew up a chart of objectives, organisation, and methods. I even bought a book of instructions. *Pre-planning*, said the book, *is the secret of a successful party*. (I had no time to consider what post-planning might be.) And I pre-planned to some purpose.

Treat it as a military operation, said the book. So I did and, when D-day dawned sunnily over Slagfield House, it dawned on a garden transformed into what the book called *a well planned party area*. With help from Mrs Bamforth I had marked out tracks for three-legged, sack, and potato races, filled our pink paddling pool, borrowed from the Young Wives League, with water that sparkled in the sunshine, and concealed expensive Treasure Trail trophies in the shrubbery.

Meanwhile, Martha had bustled round the kitchen with unaccustomed energy, buttering rolls, cutting sandwiches, frying sausages, de-moulding psychedelic blancmanges, and stacking the refrigerator with bricks of ice-cream and a kaleidoscopic collection of fruit drinks. By 14.00 hours on D-day, Slagfield House was equipped and provisioned to withstand the most rigorous assault.

Then the district midwife called Finbar away to a confinement. At a stroke we lost the only member of our team who could assume the mental age of our guests. A setback but not a catastrophe. I'd been warned by the book that I would suffer setbacks and I had confidence in the master plan.

The enemy started to infiltrate our position round about 15.30 hours. They looked innocent enough in their billowing party frocks, silk ribbons, lace stockings, and best shoes. Tired-eyed parents, veterans of tough campaigns fought over their own territory, dumped their charges on our doorstep and scurried away smiling mysterious smiles.

—Poor fools, I thought. D-day holds no fears for the man who pre-plans.

By 15.45 we had the enemy at our mercy, cornered in the surgery waiting room. All presents had been opened and cooed over, and the wrapping paper neatly stowed away. Admittedly, four toys were already broken but a wise general knows he will suffer early casualties in his best planned campaign. We were ready to move into Phase One. I flung open the French windows to reveal the pre-planned paradise that lay outside. There was a sizzling flash of lightning, a cataclysmic clap of thunder, and rain descended with a ferocity whose like I'd seen only once before when it knocked over Dorothy Lamour in *Typhoon* and swept her across the silver screen.

Half the children, frightened by the lightning, burst into tears, and demanded to be taken home. The other half dashed through the doors, danced merrily in the rain and then, mustering like the Gadarene swine, plunged into the paddling pool. Within fifteen seconds Phase One had crumbled to tearful and bedraggled disaster.

For a moment I almost lost control. Then I marshalled my reserve forces from the kitchen, every towel from the airing cupboard, and a bizarre collection of discarded child wear that Martha had put aside for the Brownies' Jumble sale. By 16.10 hours Martha, Mrs B and I had dried and re-clothed the Gadarene and were ready to move to Phase Two: Indoor Games.

We had reckoned without the second echelon. While we were busy mopping up, the non-Gardarene had wiped away their tears and found that time hung heavily upon their hands. First they broke the pick-up arm from the record player, eliminating at a stroke musical bumps, musical chairs, musical anything. Next they cut the hired Mickey Mouse film into fifteen separate skipping ropes. Then with cool efficiency they defused our ultimate weapon by squeezing three packets of plasticine through the rear grid of the television set.

I had committed the unforgivable crime. I had underestimated the enemy.

Yet as I teetered on the brink of defeat, all those prayers the nuns used to say for me when I was a child homed in on their objective. Finbar returned from delivering the baby. He took one look at what was happening and instantly invented the game that has since become *de rigueur* at medical children's parties ... the national health game.

First we split the enemy into three groups of NHS doctors. GPs were given ballpoint pens and a limitless supply of paper and competed to see who could write most before the bell rang for the next patient; consultants played charades among themselves; medical officers of health were sent upstairs for a short lie down. Every half hour each group changed roles and we controlled the complicated routine by threatening transgressors with the dreaded waiting list, which meant they had to stand in the hall for a long, long time.

From there on the games invented themselves: Pin the tail on the Chairman of the Regional Board, Hunt the geriatric bed, Find the Anaesthetist, Pass the buck. Our big finish was the Grand Treatment bonanza, an up-market version of Doctors and Nurses to which we contributed all the bandages, cotton wool, lint, gauze, and splints we could find in the surgery.

At 18.00 hours parents collected their children and at 18.15 Finbar and I sprawled in armchairs clutching strong drinks.

—That, said Finbar, was everything a children's party should be. Original, exciting, and educational.

As he spoke, the phone rang and I picked it up. Sally had had a lovely time, said Mrs Atherton, especially in the treatment game. She just wanted to check it was all right for a six year old to swallow five of those green tablets.

I reached for the car keys. Absolute victory, it seems, is rarely won without cost.

The tablets turned out to be Smarties.

The Age of Awareness

—Hallelujah, cried Finbar. There *is* life before death.

Sara, Arthur and Stanley raised their heads from their plates and gazed down the breakfast table. I looked up from my chair by the fire.

Finbar, at the head of the table, had torn open the post and, with spectacles on the end of his nose, was trying to decipher a roneoed newsletter. When I looked up he waved it at me.

—Here's something to warm your cockles, young Donovan. The latest encyclical from the Postgraduate Centre. Next week we are to be graced with a visit from a psychiatrist. All the way from the Great Wen. He proposes, it says here, to address us on The Age of Awareness.

—Now tell me, is that a period of history or a developmental milestone?

I didn't answer but returned to the Manchester Guardian, opened it full stretch and raised it in front of my face. I wouldn't be going to the lecture and I wasn't going to say why. The rite of passage that led me to the Age of Awareness was not up for analysis. Not by a Great Wen psychiatrist and certainly not by Finbar.

Yet the phrase nagged at me for the rest of the morning and, after the last of my pre-lunch visits, I parked Anna Livia Plurabelle on the dirt road alongside Slag Common, switched off the ignition, eased back in my seat, and tried to exorcise a childhood memory.

I think I was eleven, though I could have been twelve, when I first tried to sell my soul to the devil. I had assessed my prospects and resources and concluded that a deal with the devil was the only way I could acquire all that I wished from life … a piano accordion and the ability to play it.

I hung about for weeks with my soul on offer, even prepared to sign the contract in blood if it could be extracted painlessly. Four or five times a day I sent off telepathic messages but Mephistopheles never put in an appearance. At first I thought it might be because he knew I'd been a pupil at St Euphemia's and he was as scared of Mother St Peter as I was. Or even of the Jesuits who taught at my boarding school, though I'd once heard our fire-breathing parish priest, Fr Neil Obstat, warn my parents that Jesuits were agents of the devil.

I tried a change of content in my telepathic messages. If he were to leave the accordion under my bed together with any necessary forms for soul transfer I would sign them and return them in any way he wished. I took to nipping up to my dormitory at odd hours during the day to have a quick look under the bed. The first few times I was a-tingle with expectation but repeated disappointment dampened the tingle and I never understood why the devil was so reluctant to get his hands on an unblemished schoolboy soul when he'd taken all that trouble over dirty old Faust.

By the time I was twelve, or it could have been thirteen, I was glad I hadn't settled for a piano accordion. By then I would have signed, even pricked my finger so I could sign in blood, for the ability to run as fast as Cartwright, the school's Victor Ludorum. But try as I might to conjure up the devil, he never appeared, not even for a laugh.

I suspect that, at the time, I wasn't so much under the influence of Goethe as of the cone-hatted magicians and mysterious Orientals who wandered the pages of the Hotspur and the Wizard dealing with baddies in short sharp magical ways and transmogrifying weakling goodies into strong, Cartwright-like, accordion-playing heroes.

They were the successors to the fairy godmothers who, six or seven years before, had disguised themselves as witches and gone round offering woodcutters three wishes which the silly old fools always went and wasted.

I can remember round the age of six, or it could have been seven, being irritated to the point of despair by the lack of imagination in the woodcutting trade. I would need not three wishes but only one because, quick as a flash and before the good fairy could renege on the deal, my first wish would be that all my future wishes would come true. Yet fairy godmothers, it seemed, never put anything on offer to precocious kids like me but wasted their magical powers on those old boneheads in the woodshed.

God knows I tried. I lay awake at nights waiting for a wish-offering being to materialise; I took to walking in Slagden woods hoping to find an elephant with a thorn in its foot or an ugly but transmutable toad in some form of distress. I visited the junk shops round Slagthorpe market and gave a surreptitious polish to every brass article I found in the desperate hope of conjuring up a genie. But I conjured up nothing but frustration.

I suspect it was when I realised I would never get anything out of the goodies that I decided to put my soul on offer to the arch baddie. No wonder I felt cheated when he too rejected me.

By the time I was thirteen, or it could have been fourteen, hormonal changes resuscitated my interest in fantasy. I fell in love with Red Riding Hood. Before any psychiatrist shouts *Eureka* I should explain that I actually fell in love with the golden-haired girl who was playing Little Red Riding Hood in the pantomime at the Slagthorpe Hippodrome. For a whole week I attended every matinee and evening performance and hung around the stage door afterwards hoping for a glimpse of my Beatrice. I imagined she'd be swept off in a Rolls-Royce to the dazzling new *Roadhouse* that had just opened on the Great Slagshire Highway. (Shirley Temple was getting a lot of publicity at the time.)

Only on Friday night did I discover that I'd been waiting

outside the wrong door, an exit used only by the chorus of woodcutters (again) and elves. The doorman told me that the principals left from the other side of the building. I dashed round just in time to catch a glimpse of my beloved. I almost didn't recognise her because she looked distinctly older off than on but such was my infatuation I wasn't going to let a difference in age stand between us.

I looked for the Rolls but couldn't see it and as she walked away I did a quick Sexton Blake and trailed her to the bus stop. I waited in the shadows until she got onto a Trackless – which is what Slagthorpians call a trolley bus – that was headed for the streets behind the cattle market which my mother never let me ride through on my bike. I kept her under observation from the back seat.

When she got off at the stop outside Arkwright's junk shop I followed her, flitting Sexton-like from shadow to shadow up a narrow street, until she let herself in to a tall semi-detached with a sign in the front window: ROOMS. I hung around waiting for a light to go on in a window and for a tantalising silhouette to appear on a blind, as it did at the pictures. But all the upstairs windows remained dark and, after half an hour, I dragged myself home.

I didn't sleep at all that night and early next morning was back on observation outside Arkwright's. She came down the narrow street about midday. I trailed her onto another Trackless, got on after her and, with a courage I've never known since, plonked myself in the seat beside her.

For three stops I gazed unflinchingly ahead and then I turned to her and explosively declared my passion in a mixture of rehearsed poetic phrase and stumbling improvisation.

For a moment she stared at me with soft grey eyes. Then she spoke.

—Fuck off, she said.

I had reached the Age of Awareness.

Executive Health

This morning's contingent of breakfast guests at Slagfield House had wiped their plates clean, picked up their carrier bags, and left for the benches in the Corporation Gardens. Finbar looked up from the Manchester Guardian propped against the teapot on the breakfast table.

—Productivity. That's the copper-bottomed, OK word of the moment, he said. The papers are full of it. There's so much talk about Profit and Effort you'd think they were playing full-back for Manchester United.

He gulped down all that remained in his large breakfast teacup.

—In our line most of the emphasis seems to be on Effort. The only creative approach to Profit came from the genius who invented group therapy. What a gift to psychiatry that was. Multiple fees for each session and a chance for a fella to catch up on his reading while his patients treat one other. That's the sort of thing that should get one of these Queen's Enterprise Awards.

He grabbed his napkin, wiped the egg stains from round his mouth, and got up from the table.

—I'll leave you to finish the newspapers while I get on with the fight against disease. Don't forget you have to pick up that new steriliser from Slagcaster. I'm beginning to miss the background bubbling in the surgery.

For all of five hours I would have backed Finbar's notion that group therapy sat at the top of the medical enterprise league. Then

I rediscovered Archie Bland. I remembered him as a tall, urbane young man with long fair hair, a lock of which would flop engagingly onto his forehead; a subacute-on-chronic medical student who eventually qualified by becoming a close personal friend of every one of the examiners. It was much the same Archie, though now fraying at the edges, that I ran into this afternoon in Slagshire's cathedral city.

To be accurate it was Archie who ran in to me. I'd collected the steriliser from the medical supplies store and was tootling gently past Slag Minster when, right in front of the statue of St Cuthbert de Slag, Archie ran his glittering new Rolls into the back of Anna Livia Plurabelle. He was travelling slowly and our bumpers exchanged no more than a gentle kiss but Archie's immediate reaction, before he recognized me, was to leap from his car and stuff £5 notes into my top pocket.

—No need to involve the insurance, old boy. Plays the devil with the No Claims Bonus.

When recognition dawned, he greeted me effusively and I appreciated the grace with which he didn't ask for his money back. Instead he whisked me off to the Cathedral Bar, *Customers please note we have no connection with the building next door,* where he treated me to a couple of large scotches and an account of his rise to the very pinnacle of affluence.

—It all sprang from one bright idea. Mine, of course. But every Royce needs his Rolls. Or is it the other way round? I found mine at the Slagcaster Conservative Club. A fellow called Reggie Beauregard I'd known at school. He'd just been left a cool two million by a doting godmother and, after we'd had a drop of the *gazpacho* and a morsel of the *Poulet Basquaise,* floated down on a couple of decanters of Bonnes Mares 1911, he decided to stake my idea.

Archie opened a gold cigarette case lined with Balkan Sobranie and flashed it in my direction. I raised a hand in polite refusal and instead of lighting one for himself he slid the case back into his pocket

—Though I say it myself, it was a pretty smart idea. The Bland and Beauregard Top Executive Health Farm. Out in the middle of Ostlethwaite Moor. A rambling old mansion that Reggie tarted up. Sank a well in the garden and up came Ostlethwaite Spa Water. You can buy a bottle here at the bar. But that's only a side line. The powerhouse of the business is the health farm where we provide high-pressure executives with a regular check-up. A complete 5,000 mile service with a strip down and re-lubrication of the decision-making apparatus. The car analogy was Reggie's. It goes down well with the clients.

—But what does it mean?

—Quite simple, dear boy. When they arrive, I give them a going over with the old stethoscope, patella hammer, blood pressure machine, and flashing lights; then they spend half an hour chatting up a pretty girl while she does their ECG and EEG. A nurse in a short skirt takes a drop or two of blood, then they piss into a beaker before chasing another little raver round her X-ray apparatus. After that we lock them up. Miles away from the madding whatsit, up there on the lonely moor (his tone for a moment waxed poetic) where all that is heard is the mating cry of the Ostlethwaite Tern proclaiming its belief that one good tern deserves another. Puts them in the right mood for therapy.

—Therapy?

—Aquatherapy mainly. They drink the spa water, bathe in it hot or cold, get themselves massaged with it, they can even have it squirted up the arse. And there's Detoxification, of course. They all get that. We feed them nothing but fruit juice for a week and send them home feeling virtuous. We can't lose. No outgoings on food and we make them sleep on hard beds between blankets so we save on the laundry. They love it.

—They actually pay for this?

—Our fees, dear boy, are astronomical. Nobody feels that this sort of thing does them any good unless they're paying through the nose for it. There's a useful masochistic streak in wealthy businessmen. Make them uncomfortable and cut them off from the little luxuries that make their lives worth living and they just *know* it must be doing them good. And of course the fees include colour therapy and Versak.

—What the hell is Versak?

—That's our exclusive line. You've heard of Muzak – relayed background music? We relay personalized verse to each inmate. I work out the detailed prescription for the Versak and the colour therapy at my first examination. I see you, for instance, as an eau-de-nil type. That means you'd get a pale green room and a diet of mint drinks. On the Versak we'd give you Henry IV, Part I in the morning, Hiawatha in the afternoon, and Moments with Ella Wheeler Wilcox in the evening. After a week of that you'd find a return to work as refreshing as a holiday in Barbados.

—Don't any of them revolt?

—Of course they do. Indeed, we hope they do. We have another company that runs a farmhouse restaurant just a healthy stroll across the valley. The only place for miles. Plenty of booze and decent grub and the prices unashamedly exorbitant. We pretend not to notice when they sneak out for a meal. Most of them do. I'm told starvation can be rather unpleasant

Archie looked at his watch.

—Must toddle along now. I'm giving a lecture to the Slagshire Institute of Directors. *How Detox can help you increase your market share* or some similar bollocks. Keep up the good fight, dear boy.

I watched him go with the same wonder – or was it envy? – that I knew when we were medical students. Could Britain be facing a new outbreak of medical enterprise? Archie isn't the only doctor impervious to moral reservation and there must be a few more crumbling mansions up on the Slagshire moors. We're lucky that, every Archie needs his Reggie. Or is it the other way round?

Requiem for a GP

At one end of the Slag Valley, tucked up a geological cul-de-sac, lies the colliery village of Slagworth: streets of back-to-back houses, half a dozen corner shops, the Miners' Welfare, and a cemetery – all created at the turn of the century by the old Slag Valley Colliery Company, determined to possess its workers before, during, and after use.

The village straggles down the slope of the valley. At its lower end is the pit, Slagworth Main, and at the top, overlooking the cemetery, stands the Doctor's House, an Edwardian villa of smoke-blackened stone. For forty years until last Wednesday, it was the home of Doctor Fergus McConnachie who claimed that his status as *confirmed bachelor* derived from as genuine an act of faith as *confirmed Christian*. He might also have claimed, had the phrase been available at the time, to have been the vocational trainer of Doctor Finbar Aloysius O'Flaherty, singer, poet, intellectual punch up artist and highly successful general practitioner.

Fergus, a ruddy bearded Highlander who owned no nether garment save the kilt, spent the whole of his GP career striding the sloping streets of Slagworth ... until last Wednesday. Then, in the middle of his evening surgery, he infarcted the main branch of his left coronary artery and, in an electrical storm of fibrillation, shuffled off his mortal accoutrements.

Today was the day of Fergus's funeral and for an hour or two this afternoon Finbar entrusted the care of our patients to a friendly neighbouring practice. He wanted Donal's presence in the car and the pair of them sat silent in the Morris Cowley while Finbar navigated jerkily along the fifteen miles of industrial devastation that form the Slag Valley. Near the head of the valley they turned onto a metalled but unfenced road that ran up the hill past old factory sheds and scrap metal dumps then an occasional barn and farmhouse before swinging right across the blackened hillside and entering Slagworth from above.

At the fringe of the village, they came to a tall laurel hedge with a gap at its centre. Finbar turned the Morris Cowley through the gap and onto a gravel patch in front of the tall stone house where, more than twenty years before, he had lived for the eighteen months he worked as Fergus's assistant.

He parked the car but, instead of climbing the steps to the heavy door with its brass Day Bell and Night Bell, he led Donal down a pathway that ran between the house and a line of dusty poplars. Beyond the house the path opened onto a garden, a patch of tough grass bordered by hardy shrubs and the few rock plants sturdy enough to survive Slagworth's noxious atmosphere.

Finbar walked to the centre of the grass and stood silent for a moment, gazing down over the village rooftops towards the sprawl of Slagworth Main. The spinning wheels at the heads of the derricks accelerated and slowed as the pit cages dropped into the shaft below. Cloudy mixtures of smoke and steam billowed from the machine sheds and coal cleaning lines. A tank engine shuttled back and forth in the marshalling yard, prodding and tugging at strings of wagons heaped with new-cut coal. Cast-iron tubs, heavy with silt and mud, swung lazily from cables that carried them from the pithead along a string of pylons up the side of the valley to an artificial peak where each tub, with a cathartic heave, dumped its contents onto a mountain of sludge that dwarfed the village.

Finbar's attention wasn't focussed on Mammon's gift to the valley but on something much closer: the glimpses of granite and marble that showed above the privet at the garden edge. He turned to Donal.

—Every doctor's house, he said, should overlook a cemetery, if only to give us a regular reminder of our ultimate achievement.

He walked over to the wicket gate that separated the doctor's garden from the village burial ground.

—I am, of course, quoting Fergus. He always claimed the only treasurable aspect of this house was that it overlooked the cemetery. He'd stand at the dining-room window and say: Come here, laddie, and you'll see what we achieve, even when we're at our best. All we can offer the punters is a little palliative treatment for the fatal disease we're all born with.

Finbar bent to unlatch the wicket gate and, as he and Donal walked between the gravestones, he confessed he was replaying a ritual. During the eighteen months he'd been Fergus's amanuensis, his boss would insist that just before lunch, whatever the weather, the pair of them should walk down the hill along this path.

—Lets take a stroll amid my mistakes, he would say, and, as we walked along chatting about the happenings of the morning, he would pass on ideas about medicine more practical than the stuff they dished out at medical school. Every now and then, he would pause in front of a gravestone and tell me why the bones beneath it might have lingered a little longer on this earth if the village doctor had been less of an idiot. And, as we strolled, he would weave the names on the headstones into a social history of the village.

—This is where I first heard about Ernie Bucknell. Monday to Friday he wore a stiff collar and worked in the Slagthorpe Council office. But on Saturday nights he toured the working men's clubs as an all-in wrestler. He'd climb in the ring in a black mask and wearing black tights under his bathing trunks because, on Saturday nights, Ernie transmuted into the Slagheaton Phantom.

—His opponent was always a clean-limbed local lad and the Phantom's job was to get the boos going. At the start of the bout when they went to shake hands, Ernie would grab his opponent's fingers and bend them back. Then as his victim screamed with pain he would force the lad's arm up behind his back in a painful hold from which the only escape was an athletic somersault. The somersault won thunderous applause and set the scene for a conflict between Good and Evil.

—Booing the Phantom brought great joy to the audience and Ernie's job was to ensure that joy was unconfined. He punched the lad in the kidneys while the referee looked theatrically the other way, knocked him senseless with a swing of a galvanised bucket that happened to be handy, kicked him as he lay on the ground, laid out the referee when he tried to intervene, indeed broke every rule that would have been in the book if a book existed. At the end of the first round, the young lad lay motionless on the canvas and the referee started to count him out until, at the very last second, he was saved by the bell.

—Then, in the one-minute break, came a one-minute physiological miracle. The young lad recovered his marbles. As the bell went for the second round, he leaped from his corner and fought back in clean muscular style, bouncing athletically off the ropes, lifting the Phantom high over his head and spinning him round before flinging him across the ring, pinning him to the floor and twisting his arms, legs, or neck until he squealed. The booing now changed to cheers which waxed hysterical when the Phantom finally surrendered, pleading to the referee in cringing submission.

—Then, while the hero pranced round the ring acknowledging the cheers, Ernie sidled off to the lavatory and put on his overcoat and cap. He slipped his mask into his coat pocket, collected a ten bob note from the chairman of the committee, and set off for the next club on his bicycle. That's Ernie over there. The one with the glass dome over the artificial lilies, just to the right of the Celtic Cross.

Finbar and Donal strolled another ten yards along the path between the graves.

—Now here lies Mavis Tate, aged eighteen. Not the one with the marble chippings and the cherubs. Mavis is the standard-issue wooden cross to the right. No cherubs for her. Died of septicaemia after an illegal abortion. An only child and a lonely child. *Mother died in childbirth*, it said in her notes. She was raised by her Dad. That's him next door to her, on the far side. The small granite slab. He got here a month ahead of her. Before she'd screwed up the courage to tell him she was pregnant. That's his second grave. Before they could bury him here they had to dig him out from under the black stuff.

The granite slab bore a five line inscription:

Albert George Tate
Aged 39
Killed Slagworth Main Colliery
10 November 1937
The price of coal

—Sometimes we paused for Fergus to demonstrate the evidence for his Inverse Law of Epigraph: the more unctuous the inscription, the more unscrupulous the rogue who lies beneath. He brought great gravity to his reading of the scroll that two angels hold perpetually unfurled above the bones of Alderman Stanley Bickerthwaite JP ... and great relish to itemising Big Stan's impressive record of municipal corruption.

—Most days we'd stop and gossip with Albert Smethurst, an ex-miner whom the council appointed cemetery keeper. He'd made his name as the virtuoso of the Slagworth allotments and he garnished this sombre terrain with colourful shrubs and flowers. People came for miles to gaze upon his floral clock down there in front of the war memorial. I'm told he still creates what Fergus called floral posters in the centre of the circle where the hearses stop to unload – banks of bedding plants arranged to spell out uplifting messages: *God is Love, We know not the day nor the hour*, or *Rovers for the Cup*.

—Albert raises the plants in a greenhouse he built over there behind the laurel hedge. In my day he also used it to grow pound

upon pound of tomatoes. Often he'd hand us a brown paper bag.
The finest tomatoes in the county, Fergus would say as we carried
them into the kitchen. Could it be that Albert has access to a mulch
denied to the rest of us? And the housekeeper Annie would twitter
Oh don't be disgusting, doctor and then she'd tell me to make sure I
washed them under the tap before I ate them.

—Talking of Annie, we'd best go back to the house and pay
our respects before they bring Fergus home.

Last Thursday morning Fergus was moved to the Chapel of
Rest at Jeremiah Micklethwaite and Sons in Slagthorpe. Today the
hearse was to carry the coffin straight to the cemetery but as it
climbed the hill to Slagworth the driver found the road blocked by
a group of miners in best suits standing outside the pit gates. Their
leader brought it to a halt by raising an imperious hand. Ignoring
the protests of Charon Micklethwaite, the miners unloaded the
coffin onto their shoulders and carried it up the hill to the village,
then through the silent crowd that packed the main street until they
reached the Doctor's House. There Annie and Fergus's GP partner
Karim Ikthar stood on the steps alongside Finbar, Donal, and
Fergus's two surviving sisters

The sisters and Annie, and Karim and Finbar, were ushered
into positions immediately behind the coffin, ahead of a clutch of
union officials and parish councillors. They persuaded a reluctant
Donal to join them before the silent cortege moved off around the
house, across the garden and down the path where Fergus and
Finbar used to take their lunchtime stroll.

The cemetery was packed with people. The crowd overflowed
into the surrounding lanes and was noisy with gossip until the
coffin appeared at the wicket gate. Then someone shouted, silence
descended, and a wave of movement swept across the side of the
hill as men and boys removed their caps and hats. The Slagworth
Colliery Band, drawn up in full dress uniform around the War
Memorial, struck up *Abide with me*. The crowd stayed silent till the
second chorus when everyone joined in with the solemn vigour

they displayed when they followed a Slagshire team to a Final at Wembley

The miners carrying the coffin threaded their way, with difficulty, through the crowd until they reached the place where Albert Smethurst, now an old man, stood hatless and moist-eyed alongside the muddy hole he'd dug for his friend the doctor. While Albert's sons gently arranged the slings that would lower the coffin into the ground, old Hellfire Williams, a former check-weighman at Slagworth Main and jobbing Methodist preacher, reminded the crowd that one day each of them would have to follow their doctor into a more just world so they'd best behave themselves in the meantime.

The Smethurst *boys* – they were both in their 50s – lowered the coffin gently to its settling place and, as they removed the slings, two members of the Slagworth Youth Club in best Sunday clothes – Eddie Witherdale (10) whose plastered down hair made him look as though he'd come straight from a swim in the river and Edna Scowcroft (8) whose freshly permed ringlets gave her a look of Shirley Temple – stepped forward awkwardly and showered the coffin with armfuls of chrysanthemum heads clipped from Albert's finest blooms.

Then as Hellfire invited Annie to scatter the first trowel of earth upon the coffin, the band struck up again and its sonorous version of *Jerusalem* echoed across the valley drowning the disquieting sound of clods of earth thudding onto the coffin.

Once again the congregation in the cemetery and in the lanes outside raised their voices in a solemn reprise of the chorus. Down in the valley the derrick wheels stood still and a wail from the pit hooter signalled the end of Fergus McConnachie's shift.

Suddenly the music was over and, as women stepped forward to arrange the wreaths – ostensibly to ensure that no inch of fresh-turned earth remained exposed but really to read the cards and assess the generosity of the tributes – the crowd started to shuffle away. Annie had to go back to the house to entertain Fergus's sisters who had travelled down from Scotland. She invited Finbar and Donal to join them but Finbar declined. He and Annie embraced and she hurried back up the hill. The doctors' progress was slower because men with soft voices and broad shoulders pressed through the crowd to shake Finbar's hand and to exchange muttered greetings. It took them maybe half an hour to make it back to the wicket gate, with Donal feeling more and more of an outsider.

As they drove back to Slagthorpe along the industrial runnel of the Slag valley, Finbar sat silent behind the wheel of the Morris Cowley, for once ignoring the antics of other road users who were put upon this earth to plague him.

Donal reflected on the way Slagworth bade farewell to its GP. What did a man have to do to earn that kind of respect? Certainly not big things; they were celebrated with honours and decorations and commemorated by Abbey Choirs. A bare headed crowd, a brass band, and an honest declaration of love were earned by lesser things: an accumulation of small acts of sympathy and kindness and occasional understanding, that the bestower didn't remember because they were rarely offered consciously.

Only when they were back in the drive at Slagfield House and he'd switched off the ignition, did Finbar speak.

—Mining communities, he said, know how to bury their own. They've had too much practice.

Then he turned in his seat to face Donal.

—Tell me doctor, on the day when they turn off the juice, what more could a man desire than being planted contentedly amid his mistakes?

A Night Out

—There's a section in Roget's Thesaurus that reads: *sensual, carnal, gross, beastly, hoggish, overindulgent, licentious, and debauched*. It's the best description I've ever read of a hospital party.

Finbar had his elbows on the table and a large mug of Gaelic coffee cupped reverently in his hands as if it were a chalice to be raised before a congregation.

—Did you know that Roget was one of us? A certificated stethoscope carrier? I hope his medicine was better than his Thesaurus. Never found a decent word in it. Designed for folk who want to substitute one cliché for another.

Donal was impressed by the ease with which Finbar got his tongue twice around thesaurus considering his likely level of blood alcohol.

For the moment, having dealt with Roget as perfunctorily as he had dealt with Ian Smith and Rhodesia, John Profumo and Miss Keeler, and the reasons Sean O'Casey should never have left Ireland, Finbar had satisfied his appetite for dogmatic assertion. He allowed his gaze to wander round the empty restaurant where the cane chairs were stacked on the tables, the *Closed* sign hung in the window, and the only evidence of life beyond dessert came from the sibilant espresso machine.

The muscles round Finbar's eyes corrugated as he sought to penetrate mists of memory. For this was the blessed Feast of Saint Patrick, an evening when every Irishman feels under obligation to conjure visions from the past. By a long-standing tradition, established in the days of Doctor Donovan the First, the health of all patients in the practice had been entrusted to a neighbouring partnership of friendly Scots and Finbar and Donal were having their Night Out.

For two months there had been discussion of how it should be spent. In the early days the discussion had been expansive, embracing a Louis Kentner recital at the Slagcaster Opera House, Arthur Askey and Richard Murdoch at the Winter Gardens in Slagton Regis, even an expedition to the world that lay beyond the Junction with mention of hotel rooms, the Festival Hall, the West End stage. But as the day grew nearer, and initiative was hobbled by inertia, they settled for the same Night Out the Slagfield House practice had every St Patrick's day: a slap-up dinner at Slagthorpe's *La Dolce Mavourneen*, supervised by the establishment's owner, chef, and only waiter, Luigi O'Flanagan.

It seemed the right place to honour St Patrick. True, Luigi's connection with the Emerald Isle was only forty years old, established when his Dublin-born father jumped ship in Naples and two week's later jumped Naples leaving a sample of his DNA behind. But you can't deny an O apostrophe in a name and Luigi's genetic inheritance included an understanding of the behaviour of people like Doctor O'Flaherty. Every December when Luigi bought his next year's Boots Desk Diary he turned reflexly to March 17 and entered an evening booking for Doctor Finbar.

Tonight he had, once again, done them proud, serving wholesome portions of the house specialties *Taglietelli Brian Boru* and *Osso Bucco con bacon and cabbage*. He had also, once again, burrowed deep and dangerously into his cellar.

Finbar replaced the mug of coffee on the table. The thought of Doctor Roget had conjured a vision from the mist. Did Dear Doctor Donovan know, he wondered, that he Finbar had first come to Slagthorpe as a medical registrar at the Slagthorpe Memorial? And if he had not done so and thereby made the acquaintance of

Dear Doctor Donovan Senior, as kind and generous and saintly a man as an impecunious registrar could ever meet, the pair of them would not be sitting here this moment?

The questions were clearly rhetorical but Donal nodded his head slowly to affirm he was in the presence of sapience. He was no longer surprised that Finbar could wrap his tongue around thesaurus. The O'Flaherty cerebration engine had slipped into cruise control: no longer did his blood alcohol threaten befuddlement, it was now the fuel of garrulity.

—Though I say it myself, without over-blowing my trumpet – and, for God's sake, if you don't blow the old trumpet yourself who the hell will blow it for you? – I measured up well to the challenge of working in an English hospital. I may have been the only Paddy at the Memorial yet I was there but couple of months when the residents awarded me the only honour that lay within their gift. They invited me to organise a party.

He raised the sacred coffee mug once more and sank his upper lip deep into the mixture the better to suck the fusion of John Jameson and dark espresso through the layer of cream. He replaced the vessel on the altar and wiped his lips with the handkerchief that sprouted from his top pocket, a broad swathe of green silk decorated this evening not with horses' heads but with golden harps.

—The Memorial's RSO … he had a double-barrelled name that now escapes me … was off to be a consultant somewhere in the back of beyond. He was a kindly fellow and the residents wanted to give him a send-off worthy of the man. Yours truly was unanimous choice as party organiser.

—The Finbar of those days may have been young in tooth but he had survived enough residents' parties to understand that the object of the exercise is catharsis … a release of the tension that accrues when young men and women spend too little time asleep and too much time coping with events beyond their comprehension. I also knew what was likely to emerge once booze anaesthetised the cortical areas that have to do with decorum. So the only way to protect the Memorial's patients ... indeed to preserve the fabric of the building ... was to get the boys and girls off the premises early in the evening.

—In what I thought was an imaginative move, I booked two rows of stalls at the Slagthorpe Hippodrome to see Slagshire's favourite comedian Sid Smuttie in his touring revue *Fig Leaves and Apple Sauce*. It wasn't exactly high culture but it would keep the lads away from the bottle for a couple of hours ... and low culture has its own appeal if you seek it low enough.

—You couldn't really seek much lower than Sid Smuttie. In those days, there were still lingerings of wartime austerity and you could tell the sort of show you were in for at the Hippodrome from the look of the girls legs in the opening chorus. If they wore stockings, you knew you were in for a classy evening; if they wore stocking paint, you knew you were in for routine tat. In Sid's shows the stocking paint was streaky – never washed off, just occasionally patched.

—Apart from the chorus of girls of all ages ... their only common denominators were long legs and an ambition to become dancers ... Sid's company was built around his multinational extended family: a young Hungarian stripper who was Sid's girl friend, an older Polish stripper who was said to be Sid's mother, a Welsh tenor who always sang loud and sharp and lived with the older stripper, and a busty contralto who doubled as a sword-swallower and lived with a fluffy little woman who did an unpredictable act with a troupe of savage untrainable dogs.

—The maestro of this ill-tuned orchestra was the alcoholic Sid whose instinct for innuendo helped him create a twice nightly symphony of sex, smut, and sentiment guaranteed to fill Slagshire's lower grade music halls to just above break-even point. In short the show suited my purpose exactly and the evening would likely have been a triumphant success if I'd spared myself one moment of indiscretion. Yet, unfortunate man that I am, those are the very moments I find most difficult to resist. The day before the party, some would-be wit among the residents asked *What dress?* and I, with unfortunate acerbity, answered *clerical*.

—From such felicities grow outrageous fantasies. Twenty-four hours later when I entered the residents' dining room for the ritual start-up drinks I found it abuzz with curates and priests plus a bishop or two in purple dickies and gaiters. All I could do was nip back to my room, put on my interview suit, and turn round my collar like everyone else.

—One hour and four firkins of ale later the Memorial's entire resident staff, save for the three who had lost in the draw and were left behind to minister to the afflicted, set out for the Hippodrome. We caused a bit of a stir because it isn't every night in the High Street you see staggering curates attempting four-part harmony of half remembered rugby songs, vicars whistling at girls in the cinema queues, bishops climbing lamp-posts, or a fully-clad RC monsignor taking his ease in the municipal horse trough.

—Yet our effect on passers-by had nothing on our impact at the Hippodrome. When Sid Smuttie made his entrance he very nearly dried when he saw the front two rows filled with clerics. He was even more shaken by their response to his first semi-soiled story. Old pro that he was, he paused for but a second before, with boisterous encouragement from the front rows, he slipped into the grubby routine he usually reserved for smoking concerts at the Slagthorpe Chamber of Commerce.

—The evening began to take off in a way no show at the Hippodrome had done for years. The unaccustomed sound of cheering from the audience brought members of Sid's extended family to the wings to see what new catastrophe had struck them. It took them some time to appreciate that the noise was a fusion of cries of encouragement instead of the usual disparagement. Once they caught on, the enthusiasm that flowed across the footlights warmed their world-weary faces, melted their drawn expressions of insecurity, and even provoked tentative smiles. It was a compelling demonstration of the effectiveness of group therapy and the health-giving properties of mutual support. For health, as we all know – save perhaps for the benighted Doctor Roget – is a synonym for happiness.

—I was proud of my doctors that night. Though near to incoherence, they retained their powers of healing. The Welsh tenor could not have won greater applause had he sung on key. The sword swallower had to give the first encore ever demanded of her and obliged by ingesting the bottom three feet of a crozier handed up from the stalls. Sid found himself rekindling ambitions that had faded with his youth. And his mother found herself dreaming of a retirement bungalow in Peacehaven.

—There was magic abroad in the theatre that evening. My troops had escaped from the trenches and for just one night ...

> *Everyone's voice was suddenly lifted;*
> *And beauty came like the setting sun ...*

—Yet, at the very moment we caught a glimpse of the higher planes of ecstasy, blind Reality came clumping on in his heavy boots.

—As always, he chose his moment well, right in the middle of the Artistic Tableau: *Miss America strips for action.* The young Hungarian, performing with an abandon Sid had never witnessed, either on or off stage, had divested herself of a handful of stars and most of her stripes when a couple of vicars and a very damp monsignor clambered on stage determined to render assistance.

—'Twas clear they were motivated by the most noble of our profession's aspirations, the urge to minister to a fellow being in her hour of need, but some insensate philistine in the wings rang down the safety curtain and, despite the frenzied pleading of Sid and cacophonous protest from the auditorium, the curtain stayed down.

—The insensate philistine turned out to be the Hippodrome's general manager Reg Trundle, the only person insulated that night from the electricity that crackled round the theatre. But then poor Reg had a problem with his job thanks to being a member of an exclusive Calvinist sect. He used to square his conscience during Sid Smuttie shows by wearing earplugs during the performance and removing his spectacles before looking at the stage.

—He also drew great solace from the fact that on normal nights Hippodrome audiences reacted to the presence of evil with unsmiling seemliness. What outraged him that night was not the behaviour in the front stalls – what else could you expect from decadent high churchmen and papists? – but seeing members of a Hippodrome audience actually enjoying themselves.

—Reg it was who flicked the switch that lowered the safety curtain. Reg it was who immobilised the electric motor that controlled it. And Reg it was who stood in the box office refunding admission money to all non-clerical members of the audience while inwardly rejoicing that on this one night at the Hippodrome he had done God's work.

—Which all goes to show that the fellow upstairs *does* work in mysterious ways, and that people like Reg, who are strictly downstairs, find the sight of health in others extremely discomfiting.

Finbar dabbed the outer canthus of each eye with the green and gold silk, then raised the coffee mug in both hands and sipped from its rim.

—I heard only the other day that the lad who dressed as a monsignor had handed in his stethoscope and was running courses on strength through self discovery in Southern California. A great loss to the craft.

He replaced the mug on the table, traced a pattern with his finger among the crumbs that littered the white linen cloth, then gazed restlessly around the restaurant. His eyes settled on the strings of beads that curtained the doorway between dining room and kitchen. The sight spurred him to bellow,

— Luigi.

Luigi scuttled anxiously through the beads, polishing a wine glass on a napkin.

—Si, dottore.

He nodded towards the hissing machine.

—You like more of the Gallic?

Finbar shook his head.

—No, no. I am replete. I just want to ask you a question.

Luigi shuffled towards them, polishing the glass.

—Luigi machree, tell me what you would do if two smart fellows like us came in here one evening, ate and drank as much as we have done, and then told you they had no money.

Luigi burst into noisy laughter.

—No pay, dottore, no pay. You know very well what I would do. They no pay, I give them a good Irish boot up de arse.

Finbar rose from his seat, moved unsteadily away from the table, then bent over.

—Take for two, he said.

Showing the Flag

Live the Dream winks the neon sign across the road from my hotel room. I've been living it now for four days and can no longer distinguish fantasy from reality. The dream was a gift from Sandy McWhirter, son of Slagthorpe's dynamic fire chief, McWhirter the Water Squirter.

Sandy was never comfortable with his father's martial approach to life nor the turbulent household it created so, when the time came for him to choose a career, he was determined to find one that would ensure an amiable existence. He was a bright lad and did well enough at Slagthorpe Grammar for the headmaster to badger his parents into sending him to medical school. Sandy enjoyed his first years as a medical student but, when he reached the stage where he could no longer con his way through the exams with a good memory and a glib tongue, he decided that medicine was incompatible with his ambition.

Thanks to the snippets of anatomy and pathology – not to mention the Latin phrases – he'd picked up in medical school, he found work as a freelance copywriter offering his services to advertising agencies and drug firms who sought to sell their products to doctors. One of the drug firms, Slagshire Pharmaceuticals, was so impressed by his work that it offered him a full-time job. He wasn't keen on working in an office – he preferred to write at home – but the salary was tempting and he decided to give it a whirl.

Sandy's imperturbable good nature made him a popular figure round the office and so beguiled his boss that he sought to turn it to profitable ends. He persuaded his protégé to abandon copywriting and join the company's team of sales reps who visit GPs in their surgeries and try to cajole them into prescribing the products of Slagshire Pharmaceuticals.

The timing was just right for Sandy. He was about to set up home in a cottage on Slagworth Moor with a lass who had taken his fancy. He didn't enjoy office life and the new job would allow him, once again, to work from home with an occasional visit to head office for a briefing or training session.

Things worked out even better than he'd hoped. He and his Slagshire lass achieved contentment and, though he was not the best of salesman, the GPs he visited liked him, even trusted him. Sandy's diffident approach to selling drove his sales manager to stuttering fits of rage but Slagshire Pharmaceuticals were happy with his work because of the goodwill he created.

I am one of the GPs who succumbed to Sandy's charm. I enjoy his visits to the surgery because, once he has done his duty by his bosses, he fills me in on the medical gossip circulating round the county. And it makes a refreshing break in the middle of a depressing surgery to have a cheerful healthy person walk into your consulting room.*

---

*Today the pharmaceutical industry is a collection of similar companies operating in similar ways. In the 1960s the business of making and selling drugs was just beginning to become an industry. The companies grew from disparate roots. Dye-makers discovered that the waste products piled in their yards had useful biological activity; patent medicines companies started to investigate biological mechanisms that might yield prescription drugs, chemical companies diversified into pharmaceuticals, companies with no experience of chemicals were attracted by a new profitable market.
Today the marketing of pharmaceuticals is a competitive hard-nosed business. In Sandy's day, thanks to the diversity and insecurity of the companies, the selling was more amiable and more responsible. Like Donovan, many GPs enjoyed the visit of an affable drug rep, who didn't try the hard sell and was prepared to admit his company's product was no better than others.

Just two weeks ago Sandy walked in and asked if I'd like a trip to America. Just like that. His bosses were inviting a handful of British GPs to be their guests at the annual meeting of the American Endocrinological Something-or-other where the Slagshire Pharmaceuticals version of the Pill would play a starring role. His sales director had asked him to nominate the two GPs in his area most interested in research. Sandy couldn't think of one but saw a chance to repay Finbar for the kindness he had shown Sandy's Gran when she took to her bed for the last time.

—Just wondered if you and Finbar would like to go, doc. Only five days, he added as if expecting a refusal.

Poor ingenuous lad. He had no idea he was offering me a ticket to enter a fantasy that dominated my war-time adolescence. Back then my only windows on the world that lay beyond the barbed wire on the beaches were the screens at the Gaumont, Regal, Ritz, and Picture Palace. Twice since the war I'd crossed the Channel and trodden streets where men and women died to win my right to be there. But America remained unattainable, a fantasy flickering on a cinema screen. I could scarce contain my excitement while I waited for Finbar to accept Sandy's invitation on our behalf.

For four days now our patients have been at the mercy of the new Slagthorpe deputising service and we've been rubbernecking our way through Dreamland. It came as a bit of a surprise to find it really does exist – cars like horizontal juke-boxes, boys on bicycles throwing newspapers onto lawns, bell boys in pillbox hats, elevator clerks in white gloves. Only this time the picture's not in black and white but in full natural colour with stereophonic sound.

We're in Chicago. The Edgewater Beach Hotel. One time haunt, says the brochure, of Al Capone. The barman translates that as meaning that Al, like most of Chicago's glitterati, dropped in occasionally for a meal. He also says the place ain't what it used to be. When the city routed Lake Shore Dive between the hotel and its waterfront, the Edgewater Beach fell out of fashion and slipped downmarket.

Hosting this conference, says the barman, is its bid for survival. Should have seen it in the 30s and 40s, he tells us. But seeing it now is good enough for me. It serves quite nicely as the place where Fred Astaire whirled Ginger across the marble floor, where Edward G Robinson and his henchmen strode towards the elevator, where the Marx bothers destabilized the dignity of Margaret Dumont.

I slipped easily into the culture on our first morning. At breakfast, the waiter asked,

—How would you like your eggs, bud?

With a nonchalance engendered by those hours in the Gaumont, I replied,

—Sunny side up.

—Eggs up, he said and made a note.

—And how would you like your bacon?

Wham. He had me on the floor in the first round. What arcane choice was he offering? Then I remembered the word on which the British empire was built.

—Medium, I said.

He made another note and went away satisfied. I've still to discover the extremes between which I steered my course

Yesterday Finbar and I honoured our side of Sandy's Faustian deal and went to the conference. For six hours we were members of an audience of at least a thousand which sat in a darkened ballroom where men with voices free of inflection stood behind lecterns and read at us from pages of impenetrable prose. While they read, a screen above their heads confronted us with slides packed with the sort of mathematical data I was pleased to wash from my brain once I got my School Certificate.

Finbar and I made heroic efforts to stay awake but we needn't have bothered. Our hosts from the American partners of Slagshire Pharmaceuticals seemed delighted just to have us there. It soon became clear that they too understood little of what was said but assumed that we understood it all. They weren't keen to reveal their ignorance so they talked only briefly about the meeting and took us out to dinner.

This morning our hosts packed us into a coach with the other British doctors and ferried us around the city on a guided tour. This afternoon Finbar and I camped beside the hotel pool to while away the hours before the Conference Gala dinner. As we lay on cushioned loungers, shaded by umbrellas, we sipped, as elegantly as a man can sip when his oesophagus is near to horizontal, at Glenside Specials. These, in the patois of the menu, are *Rich old Scottish whisky, lovingly blended by ancient crofters on the banks of Loch Lomond, poured caressingly over crushed ice, and lightly laced with pure Ohio spring water*.

At first we were on the defensive. The early English summer being what it is, we were shamefully pale, while all around us cavorted bronzed American men and even more bronzed American women. But after two or three Glenside Specials we felt the need to assert ourselves.

We couldn't hope to compete with the crew-cut characters performing spectacular leaps, somersaults, twists, and turns from the high board. Then Finbar spotted, at the far side of the pool, what we thought was a shuffle-board court – a smooth concrete surface with a triangle marked in white paint at each end. Both triangles were divided into sections, each containing a number, and I had a vague notion that the shuffleboard game consisted of knocking discs into these sections in a Brobdingnagian version of shove-ha'penny.

There, we decided, was the place to establish our identity. We walked over to the pool manager's office.

—Could we have the shuffle-board kit? I asked.

—Sorry bud. The sticks are all broken.

—Not to worry, just let us have a few shuffles.

—Shuffles?

—That's what we call them in the old country, I explained.

—Suit yourself. How many would you like?

—Twelve of course, snapped Finbar. As you've broken the sticks, we'll have to play Royal Shuffles.

—Royal Shuffles. Oh, my.

He handed over a dozen fibre discs and, after we'd thanked him in a shamefully patronising way, we each had another Glenside Special to fortify us on our way to the court.

We were soon engrossed in an entertaining game of our own devising. The basic play involved kicking the discs across the court and trying, by skilful cannoning, to get as many discs as possible into scoring sections. We elaborated the rules as we went along, encouraged by regular sips of Glenside Special.

A pleasant half-hour passed before we noticed we had an audience. Strapping American males in bathing trunks had gathered discreetly at a distance, watching us intently. The pool manager wandered among them whetting their interest with knowledgeable murmurs of *Royal Shuffles*.

Finbar sidled up to me in mid-court.

—If I know Americans, he whispered, they're trying to work out the rules. Next they'll start practising and before we know where we are, they'll challenge us and beat us at our own game. There's only one thing to do.

Halfway through his next turn he paused dramatically.

—My God, he cried, I think I've set a treble bob major.

I examined the court carefully.

—I do believe you have.

I raised my voice a decibel or two.

—There's no doubt about it. You'll have to go for a West Wittering Eagle.

Finbar shrugged yet managed to give the impression of repressed excitement.

He retired to one corner, placed his shuffle with exaggerated care, then turned his back on the court. He took a long deep breath and held it in statuesque concentration. After maybe thirty seconds, he exploded, leaping in the air and giving his disc a fierce back heel into the middle of the triangle. Shuffles shot in all directions.

I waited till the last one settled. Then I walked slowly across the court, examining the position of each disc. I lingered for a time beside the last one before walking over to Finbar and shaking him by the hand.

—That, I said, is the finest West Wittering I've seen since W.G. eagled the Duke of Rutland at Hampton Court.

From that moment the mood of our audience changed. No longer did they puzzle over rules that were clearly too complicated to be absorbed at one session. They relaxed and drank in a sight which they knew in their hearts was revealed to few men: two Royal Shufflers performing at the peak of their powers.

As the Glenside Specials homed in on our cortical cells, we filled the air with impressive cries:

—Stand aside for a Tolpuddle Triple.

—One more for a Shepherd's Bush Empire.

Bursts of applause began to greet our more impressive manoeuvres and our audience was soon as enthusiastic and generous as only American audiences can be.

National identity had been defined on both sides. When we reached the limit of our invention, Finbar and I retired to opposite sides of the court and bowed to one another three times. Then we gathered up our shuffles and returned to our poolside table, amid enthusiastic applause. Men and women came up and shook us by the hand. Half a dozen children asked us for our autographs.

As a final gesture we called the waiter and reinforced our identity by ordering a large pot of tea.

When we got it, it was iced.

Gratuitous Health Care

The dream is over. Time to wake up. I write this on a Boeing 707 on the way to Heathrow. Three minutes ago the distinguished gent in the row in front of us – a Fellow of the Royal College of Physicians, a Doctor of Philosophy, and a revered member of British medicine's intellectual elite – called over the stewardess.

—Terribly stuffy in here, he said. Would you mind opening a window?

Finbar, leaning towards me, whispered,

—Knowledge, unlike wisdom, comes in compartments.

Earlier this evening while I sat in the airport's Lone Ranger Bar-B-Q waiting for my Chef's Special: *a corn fed, hickory barbecued, tender and succulent, prize-winning T-bone*, a thought struck me.

Indeed three thoughts struck me at the same time. The first was to wonder how my steak could have won a prize while it was still on the menu. The second was a memory of the New Yorker cartoon in which an angry diner asks a man in white apron and tall hat, *Are you the chef that this steak is a la?* The third was an imaginative idea for improving the service we offer patients in NHS hospitals.

Thanks to the generosity of our hosts, I've spent the past few days observing high bourgeois restaurant behaviour. Americans have imported many European customs and I enjoy the way they take some of our staler traditions and revitalise them with energy and enthusiasm. Occasionally, however, they treat the import with far too much deference. I've been disturbed, for instance, by the respect restaurant goers bestow upon the maitre d'hotel, or as they prefer to call him, the maytruh dee.

In the USA, this personage commands servility and outrageous tips in return for dubious favours. Patrons assume he knows which are the best tables in his domain and, in return for cash, he will escort you to one of them. You may spend the whole of your meal wondering what's so great about sitting behind a pillar, or directly beneath the down draught of the air conditioning, or with your knees separated by the leg of the table, but you are expected to draw sustenance from the envious stares of neighbours whose bribes you topped in your bid for precedence.

When the House Full notices go up, the maytruh assumes imperial power. In response to ostentatious dollar waving at the restaurant entrance, he will conjure up cosy tables for two which have (additional tip) romantic lighting or are (mammoth additional tip) discreetly placed for extramarital adventure.

In fashionable places, the demand for favours so exceeds supply that a successful maytruh dee can extort not only bribes but extremes of flattery. His subjects debase themselves in his presence in the hope of getting a smile or – what bliss – an exchange of words. The words themselves have little value. The reward is the envy that glows in the eyes of those who witness their bestowal.

I find it irksome that a man can command such grovelling respect when his only duty, apart from pocketing dollar bills, is to wander among the peasants engaging in light banter at a level of condescension determined by the size of the tip. The vassals, the lower tippers, have to make do with the enquiry, *Everything all right, here?* Yet if, in response, one of them impertinently suggests that everything is all wrong, the enquirer seems capable of little action save bullying his deputies.

Which talk of bullied underlings brings me back to the NHS. My third thought in the Lone Ranger Bar-B-Q was that we should re-import the post of maytruh dee, refurbish it in European style, and establish it in our hospitals in the form of a maitre or maitresse d'hospice. Shortly before patients were admitted, some of the money due to be spent on their care would be handed to them to dispense as gratuities. They could spend it how and when they chose; any left over when they were discharged would go back whence it came.

Consider the advantages. Patients would have the means to command the respect that they deserve. The maitre d'hospice would greet them at the hospital entrance and conduct them with impressive ceremony to their ward. Crinkled notes handed over *en route* might secure that nice little bed by the window, or one with a good view of the television set, or (for a more generous consideration) one well out of the television's range. A surreptitious coin slipped to the ward clerk on arrival would ensure that clothes were neatly folded and not thrown in a cupboard or that grandma would be allowed to keep her teeth.

At last hospitals would have a way to distribute revenue in the way that patients chose – a goal that politicians claim to seek but seem determined not to find. What's more, the revenue would be distributed widely because the gratuity system would extend far beyond the maitre d'hospice and the ward clerk. Tipping, once allowed, would soon, as it always does, become de rigueur.

Patients would leave coins under their pudding plates, or in their saucers, and suddenly the business of dishing up hospital grub would generate enthusiasm. Nurses would have coins pressed into their palm after they'd rendered cheerful or sustaining service. Those with initiative would develop Specialities of the House: Nurse Dugdale's Sweet n'Dry, *The blanket bath that makes a new patient of anybody.*

Specialised services like the Sweet n'Dry, or meals flambéed at your bedside, would guarantee crinkle rather than coin. Porters would no longer sit scowling in their lodges but would scurry around the hospitals bearing messages and gifts, walking dogs, and feeding parking meters.

Doctors would not be denied largesse. Anaesthetists who'd

earned the reputation for preserving teeth and for inducing little post-operative nausea would find pound notes pinned to the patient's gown. General surgeons who treated tissue with respect and didn't leave painful haematomata would receive a post-operative pourboire as would proctologists who handled the sigmoidoscope* as if it were a gentle explorer rather than an aggressive instrument of war. Housemen who taught themselves how to give painless injections or to take blood painlessly from patients' veins would have coins pressed into their palms.

The gratuity system would, in short, reward enthusiasm, consideration, and skill as effectively as it would penalise casualness, indifference, and ineptitude. Pavlovian manipulation by penalty or reward would condition hospital staff to see things from their patients' point of view. Patients' complaints would get a sympathetic hearing. Hospitals might even end up being run for the benefit of patients' rather than for that of the staff.

The more I contemplate the notion, the more I think it could be a rip-roaring success. Yet this prospect could be its undoing. Would the NHS, conditioned as it is to backing failure, have enough imagination to run the risk of creating a success?

---

*Rigid telescope that rectal surgeons use to explore the nether regions.

EDITORS NOTE

The archive contains a handful of bound books. Most are Visiting Books listing addresses of patients to be seen, telephone calls to be made. There are three Commonplace Books, each only partially filled, and one ledger with thick board covers decorated with psychedelic shapes and colours. A label on the front cover carries the hand-written title *Phantasmagoria*.

This is where Donovan recorded what he called his daydreams, provoked by something he read in a newspaper, saw on television, heard on the radio, or overheard in a pub. A file, rubber-banded to the ledger, is filled with sheets of paper smothered with corrections, crossings out, and an occasional expletive. Donovan clearly re-wrote his daydreams many times before entering the final version in Phantasmagoria in careful "best writing".

This is a typical Phantasmagoria entry. Glued to its first page is a cutting from the Yorkshire Post.

Doctors in North Yorkshire are to have a team of "mobile clergymen" to work alongside them at accidents. Fifty clergymen of all denominations were invited to a one-day course of instruction in the technique of attending at accidents and the constructive role they can play at the scene of disasters. The course was held at the Home Defence College, Easingwood, near York.

The Great Slagheaton Disaster

The sun beat remorselessly on the corrugated roof of the Orderly Room. Outside, the adjutant's dog lay curled asleep in a patch of shade but inside, Brigadier Digby Knutsford, MP, OBE, TD, LMSSA, RAMC paced to and fro. The officer commanding the Slagshire Corps of Flying Vicars now faced what could be his finest hour. Or his most desolate. He was blind to the Roll of Honour on the wall that recorded those who had played an outstandingly constructive role at the scenes of past disasters; he was deaf to the echoing cries from the parade ground where RSM Bullshine drilled his squad of new recruits.

—Let's try it again, gentlemen, with a bit more snap this time. Blessing the Populace by numbers... by the right, Bless. Hup, two, three... down, two, three... left, two, three... right, two, three.

The brigadier's attention focused only on the loudspeaker which emitted occasional bursts of static. The die had been cast ... two of his best men ... two thousand pounds worth of equipment ... his entire stock of holy water.

The static suddenly intensified and Brigadier Digby leaped across the room and twiddled a knob. A crackly voice appeared.

—Z Vicar One to base. Z Vicar One to base. Are you receiving me? Over.

Brigadier Digby grabbed the mike.

—Hello, Z Vicar One. This is Sungod speaking. Receiving you loud and clear. Over.

—Proceeding along the West Slagshire Highway with all possible Godspeed. Caught a glimpse of Slagheaton from the last hill. A cloud of black smoke over the west side of the town. Looks a nasty one, Sungod. Over.

—Listen carefully, Trismus, said the brigadier, adopting robust man-management tones. This is the big one. That's why I've sent in my best men, the pick of the corps, the elite of the elite. When the history of this hour comes to be writ, the glory of the Flying Vicars will be writ larger than it has ever before been, er, writ. Carry your prayer books proudly, gentlemen.

The loudspeaker reverted to bursts of static and the brigadier cursed. What cruel fate had cut him off at the moment when his men were to taste some real action? He glanced at the corps plaque on the wall – a vicar rampant over a casualty couchant – and snorted.

Three years had passed since the corps' foundation and in his few honest moments Digby admitted its achievements were a touch mundane: five incidents of simple Phase One ministering at accidents, six incidents of speaking encouraging words to small boys who'd got their heads stuck between railings, and forty-seven incidents of speaking encouraging words to cats stranded up trees.

Not one real catastrophe they could get stuck into with dead and dying all over the place and well drilled blessings flying in every direction … until, at one o'clock today, as the String Vest Manufactory blew its lunchtime hooter, the hot line from Slagshire County Constabulary HQ buzzed and Digby heard the joyful news of impending disaster at the Slagheaton Welfare and Working Men's Club. The mammoth new Black Pudding Griller had gone critical.

Even as a breathless chief inspector gave the news, Digby heard an almighty explosion echoing down the line and knew that glory was there for the grasping. He turned instinctively to his most experienced team – the Rev Enoch Trismus, perpetual curate at St Mary's and All Slag, and hellfire preacher Father Neil Obstat, Slagthorpe's RC parish priest – his top pair who regularly won trophies at the divisional competition. Their mission was to establish contact, relay a rapid situation report, and start preliminary ministering until the brigadier could send in his Second Wave.

This Second Wave, well trained in its constructive role, now waited in their Jeeps on the parade ground. Since that first desperate call Digby had heard encouraging reports of charred bodies lying all over the place so had issued the Second Wave with extra rations of Balaclava helmets and long scarves (Victims, for the use of). He had also put the Women's Auxiliary Corps of Motorised Nuns on red alert.

He now glanced at his watch for the tenth time. Thirty seconds to go to M minute. Trismus and Obstat would be at the scene by now, cataloguing the dread toll of disaster.

M minus five. Digby twiddled the tuning knobs.

M minus three, two, one. Silence. Come on now, what's keeping you?

M plus ten, plus thirty, plus fifty. Dammit, the bloody set had broken down. Then, as he aimed a kick at the amplifier, a faint voice came through.

—Z Vicar One calling Sungod. Z Vicar One calling Sungod. Over.

Digby bellowed into the microphone.

—Sungod receiving you. Present your report. Over.

—Trismus here, sir. Everything's under control. Suggest you stand down Second Wave and return nuns to store. Encouraging Words only required. Over.

—What about all those bodies? Over.

—The explosion blew the lock off the door of the bar stockroom, sir. They're lying about because … how's that you put it, Father … because they're wee-wee'd out of their minds. Over.

—But their fearful burns, man?

—Black pudding, sir. It's everywhere. All we need is Encouraging Words. Not for the men but for the club cat. The explosion drove it up a tree. Makes my fifth this month. Tally ho.

Brigadier Digby Knutsford, MP, OBE, TD, LMSSA, RAMC, grabbed the corps plaque off the wall, smashed it on the floor, and wept bitter tears over the plaster chippings.

Slagthorpe's Brazilian Bombshell

Within a month of my return to Slagthorpe, Finbar offered me a priceless gift. One evening over dinner he suggested, almost casually, that I follow in my father's footsteps and take over as honorary Medical Officer to Slagthorpe Rovers.

—Never took a liking to the game, he said. Always felt I was holding the job in trust till the right man showed up.

I wonder did he know he was offering me the only medical honour I've ever coveted. Ranked high among the golden days of my childhood are the Saturday afternoons during school holidays when I sat alongside my Dad in the front row of the directors' box at Slagvilla, Rovers' friendly home ground. On those afternoons, for the first time in my life, I experienced the peaks of exhilaration and the depths of despair, all in the space of a couple of hours.

From the moment the players trotted out of the tunnel at the start of each half, my mind had space for nothing else. Others might leave early or say it was a poor game but my attention never wavered till the referee blew the final whistle. Right up to that moment something exciting might just happen and occasionally it did. When the Rovers won I whooped for joy; the year we missed promotion by failing to score in the final game, I was inconsolable for days.

Sometimes when an injured player was helped or carried from the field, the trainer Billy Birkenshaw would look up at the directors' box and wave his sponge bag. Then my Dad would head down the stairs to the dressing room leaving me on my own. The first time that happened I was five years old and he worried I'd feel lonely. But I didn't miss him. I was too caught up in what was happening on the field.

Only once, when I was about eight, did he persuade me to go with him. I agreed only because his patient was my favourite player, *Dizzy* Eccleswick, who had twisted his knee. All I remember now is how much bigger *Dizzy* was in the dressing room than on the field. On the treatment table lay a bulky broad-shouldered man; seen from the stand Dizzy was a schoolboy, an impish mannikin who earned his nickname nipping back and forth around defenders till he made their senses reel.

On Saturday afternoons, when the referee blew the half-time whistle, my Dad would take my hand and lead me down a flight of stairs for a cup of tea in the Directors' Lounge. This was a pokey room with team photographs on the walls and only one item of furniture, an oak table laden with bottles containing most known forms of intoxicating liquor. At half time this display was rearranged to accommodate a wooden tray bearing china mugs, a bottle of milk, a bag of sugar, a teaspoon tied to the tray with a piece of string, and an aluminium tea urn. I was the only child in a room full of old men who patted me on the shoulder, congratulated my Dad on having such a fine looking lad, and talked about players and games I had heard about but never seen. When the bell rang to get the teams out for the second half two old ladies would appear and whisk the tray away as if removing a blemish from a cherished monument.

At the end of the match my Dad would say his goodbyes to the directors before they left the box then drag me swiftly past the Directors' Lounge where I could hear the clink of glass on glass, a sound my Dad once told me would continue till past midnight. Only when the Rovers were drawn away against Arsenal in the FA Cup and the two of us were entertained in the marble halls of Highbury did I experience the ambience that the Directors'

Lounge at Slagvilla was striving to emulate.

When I went away to school and university I was teased about my obsession with football. Gentlemen were expected to take an interest only in Rugby. Whenever I could I would sneak away on Saturday afternoons to local football grounds and later turn on the wireless and listen to the football results delivered with the same solemnity as the Fat Stock prices. Only one result interested me. When the Rovers won or drew, Saturday evening seemed a more inviting prospect than when they lost.

Thanks to Finbar's gift, I can now recapture a moment or two of childhood every second Saturday when the Rovers play at home. Five minutes before kick-off I take my father's old seat and glow contentedly while the Slagheaton Colliery Silver Band puffs its way through variations on *If You Knew Souza like I Knew Souza*. As the players trot out, my mind clears itself of extraneous clutter and my emotions prepare themselves for torture. I have a mug of tea at half time in the Directors Lounge which, apart from a few more team photographs on the walls, is the same as it was when I was a child. And, when the game is over I make the same swift but polite exit from the directors' box and scuttle past the Lounge. Like my father I prefer the company of the players to that of the directors, and not just because they are a lesser threat to my health.

The Rovers have always been what sports writers like to call a tough, workmanlike team and for many years kept their rightful place in the middle of the Third Division with a simple tactic: within the first half hour they would reduce the opposition to nine effective men.

Their strategy in those days was built round Chopper Hardcastle, captain and centre-half, six foot four in his football socks and a forehead flattened by repetitive heading of the ball. Chopper never indulged in those dirty fouls that draw boos from the crowd and retribution from the referee. He was far too subtle for such fooleries. He had fine-tuned the skill of letting his foot stray in a tackle and that, combined with an instinctive sense of the muscular anatomy of the lower limb, helped him to pinpoint sites where he could hobble the most twinkle-toed of inside forwards.

Chopper was also a master of the Niggle. He would irritate opposing players by nudging them, tugging their jerseys, and treading on their toes, until they burst into explosive retaliation. Then, if the referee was watching, Chopper would collapse to the ground apparently moribund and stay there till his opponent at least had his name taken and at best was sent off the field.

It said a lot for Chopper's professionalism that in the ten years he skippered the Rovers he was never once rebuked by a referee. His career ended only when he fractured his leg in an ironic accident. He fell down the steps of the Slagthorpe Memorial after visiting a Scottish international whom he'd hobbled in a cup tie the previous Saturday.

The Rovers directors expressed their appreciation for years of devoted service by making Chopper the team's manager but, with his passing as a player, the Rovers fortunes went into a decline. Opponents remained at full strength for whole games, matches were lost, receipts dropped and, at the end of the season, Rovers were lucky to escape relegation.

During the following close season Chopper the manager started to use the nous that had made Chopper the player. The first sign of his new approach was a carefully leaked story. The Slagthorpe Echo announced that *Mr Hardcastle is in South America hoping to capture a world-class player*. That threw me a bit. Only two days before, when Chopper came to the surgery to have his ears syringed, he told me that he was spending the summer in Cardiff helping his married sister with her cafe in Tiger Bay.

The Echo, however, refused to leave the story alone and, one week before the start of the new season, broke the spectacular news that Chopper had returned from Brazil with a wonder centre-forward called Bomber Bambolino for whom he had paid a *Slagshire record transfer fee*. Slagthorpe burst alive with excitement for, as luck would have it, the opening match of the season was the local derby against Slagheaton Thursday, the team always referred to by the Echo as *the strolling maestros of the Third Division*.

On the eve of *The Clash of the Titans* (© Slagthorpe Echo) I was called to Slagvilla to remove a splinter from under one of the Bomber's finger nails. It must have hurt as I tweaked it out and he delivered a spectacular curse – not in South American Portuguese but in Welsh dockside vernacular.

I looked up at Chopper who was standing beside me. He stared back stone-facedly.

—Very like the Welsh, these Brazilians, he murmured.

The following afternoon, Rovers had the biggest gate in their history. Every square inch of the ground was packed and one or two brave souls climbed onto the corrugated roof of Slagvilla's only stand. They were rewarded by a famous victory. Slagheaton Thursday had read all about the Bomber and, from the start, set three men to mark him. This left gaps for the other Rovers forwards who, if not inspired, were at least competent, and by half-time they had established a 2-0 lead.

Every time the ball went anywhere near the Bomber, the crowd grew excited. To my unsophisticated eyes he seemed a pretty humdrum player, but I was in a definite minority of one. When the Bomber's passes went astray the crowd shouted angrily at the other Rovers players for not anticipating the subtlety of the move and the thoughtful pipe-smoking Student of the Game who sits behind me muttered

—He's too bloody clever for 'em.

Once, when the Bomber tripped over the ball and it rolled fortuitously to one of his colleagues, even the directors rose to their feet to applaud.

—If only English players could control a ball like that, said Pipe-smoker

The highlight of the match came midway through the second half. As I saw it, the Bomber was getting up slowly after being felled by Thursday's centre half. Meanwhile the Rovers left back, burly

Ted Belcher, had trapped the ball in his own penalty area before striding out towards the touchline and giving the ball an almighty dig with his good left foot. The ball flew near the length of the pitch at an impressive speed, hit the semi-recumbent Bomber hard on his backside, and ricocheted into the net. The crowd erupted and the Bomber was swept round the ground in the arms of ecstatic team-mates. Pipe-smoker tapped me on the shoulder.

—That lad's cleverer with his arse than our lads are with their feet.

The goal finished the match. Thursday failed to score and the Rovers won three nil.

After that victory, the Bomber could do no wrong and Rovers, according to the Echo, *have acquired Second Division potential and look booked for a date with destiny*. Their opponents always committed at least two men to mark the wonder boy and his team-mates revelled in the freedom this gave them. They took their opportunities, grew in confidence, won nearly every game, and drew enormous crowds. The money flowed in and Chopper used it shrewdly to buy better players.

Then one afternoon I was called to the dressing room. The Bomber was laid out on the treatment table

—Sorry to trouble you, doc, said Chopper, but I think he's done a cartilage in training.

I wasted ten minutes examining a perfectly normal knee. I was about to ask Chopper why the hell he had called me when the Bomber gave me a wink. I bent my ear to his mouth.

—I know it's not too bad, he whispered, but I promised the wife, see, to be back by Christmas.

Chopper gave me a conspiratorial nod.

—These Brazilians get homesick easy, doc. I'd like to help the lad and give him an excuse to go home.

I paused for an ethical moment and then nodded in agreement. You had to hand it to Chopper. He'd judged it to a hairsbreadth. In another month, maybe a week, the Bomber myth would be exploded.

Next day the Echo produced a banner headline, TRAGIC END TO STAR'S CAREER. Yet the *tragic loss* didn't affect Rovers. They had a sprinkling of good players that Chopper had bought and, more important, they now had confidence in themselves. At the end of the season they were promoted to the Second Division and they've stayed there ever since.

The Bomber story – not the true one but the Echo one – is now enshrined in Slagthorpe pub mythology, and these days, as I sit in my privileged seat, I watch a better class of football. At least, Pipe-smoker says that I do.

Finbar Drops Out

—I always thought that fella Freud was a bit of a con artist. His work, I'm told, is a major cause of neurosis in psychiatrists. Yet I sometimes wonder …

Finbar left the sentence unfinished and tucked his chin deep into his scarf.

Anna Livia Plurabelle cruised slowly along the front at Slagton Regis on one of those dull meaningless days that can intrude on autumn. The sky was as grey as the sea and the Esplanade, which but a week before had been crowded with people behaving as if the Indian summer would last until Christmas, had the desolate air of a Sunday morning when sensible citizens lie abed coping with the effects of Saturday night. Only a handful of disconsolates idled along the front or lent on the railings gazing out to sea.

The scene matched Finbar's mood. When I got back from holiday two weeks ago I noticed an alarming change in his disposition. He seemed uneasy in conversation, sought his own company, tucked himself away in corners with his nose in a book or a newspaper, and headed for bed soon after dinner. More worryingly he had grown not so much indecisive as listless.

Today, for instance, he had raised no objection when I suggested we hand the practice over to the rota doctor and drive out for a blow by the sea. Where once he would have told me what to do with my suggestion, he quietly prepared for the expedition by wrapping himself in his old sheepskin jacket and the twelve feet of woollen scarf now wound around his neck like a python enveloping its prey. For half an hour he had sat silent beside me in the car. So silent that he took me by surprise when he piped up about Freud. The words sounded as if they'd been lying around in his brain since we left Slagfield House.

But at least, they had been spoken. I pushed my foot more firmly on the accelerator and, as we crossed the invisible boundary that separates Slagton Regis from Slagton-on-Sea, and the Esplanade became the Promenade and the shop fronts changed from haughty to brash, Finbar's mood showed signs of lightening. He turned on the Third Programme and started to hum along with Schubert; he growled at an old boy who made us stop and wait while he crossed the road in ankle-length raincoat, plastic Pixie hood and plimsolls; he offered a two fingered salute to the Slagshire Headquarters of the British Housewives' League; then, as we approached the traffic lights by the Pier Arcade, he told me to slow down and pull into a tiny car park across the road.

The cindered patch in front of *Uncle Joe's Fish n' Twopennorth* was empty save for a motor bike and sidecar. We parked alongside it and Finbar, with a show of energy I hadn't seen since my return, led the way into Uncle Joe's shack. The motor bike clearly belonged to the proprietor for we were the only customers and he was the only inhabitant.

He was wiping one of the tables in the corner and, when he looked up, his face for a moment signalled puzzlement then burst into a smile of recognition. He strode across the room and shook Finbar's hand with the enthusiasm people often show when their old GP turns up on their new territory. When Finbar explained who I was, Uncle Joe fussed over us as if we were long lost relatives. He sat us at a table by the widow then stood over us for five minutes bringing Finbar up to date on the doings of the Uncle Joe family and giving me a chuckling account of things Finbar had said and done to each of them.

Only when he ran out of anecdotes did he return to the

counter to fetch us a couple of Uncle Joe's Giant Mugs – *on the house, of course, doctor* – filled with tea that looked as if it had been brewed from mahogany. When he plonked them on the table, steam hovered over each like incense over a thurible.

And then, at last, Uncle Joe left us on our own.

—Odd isn't it, said Finbar, the way people create myths about their GPs. Nearly all of that was balderdash. They do the same for sportsmen they admire ... and teachers ... even an occasional politician. Every witty remark made in the past twenty years gets attributed to Winston Churchill.

He glanced over his shoulder. Uncle Joe was out of earshot, behind his counter and deep into the sports pages of the Mirror.

—The time has come, I think, for the big apology. I know that for the past few of weeks I've been a blot on the landscape. I must be in a mess when I start talking about Freud. Maybe I'm just going through the menopause. And yet ... and yet ... and yet ...

Once again he ducked out of finishing the sentence. Instead he blew across the top of his tea in the hope of getting the temperature down to drinking level. Uncle Joe's Giant Mugs are double lined like thermos flasks and have a message printed round the rim, *Hot to the last drop!!!!.* Finbar tested the temperature with the tip of his little finger and rapidly withdrew it.

—I suspect you never knew I was a pillar of the Alternative Society. Didn't know myself till I saw a programme on the telly while you were away. The Local News. Previewing, may God forgive them, the Slagthorpe Alternative Festival.

—I assumed it would be the usual nonsense. Grow Your Own Rhubarb ... I left my Heart in Sagittarius ... Cometh the Hour, Cometh the Flower ... that sort of rubbish. Then on came this doll explaining her deep emotional need to drop out. The most ravishing creature they'd had on the box for years. As she gazed at the camera with soft grey eyes and chattered on about flinging off the shackles of sexual inhibition, I developed a compelling urge to opt out of bourgeois society.

—Before the week was out, and while you were poncing around on your holiday in Greece, I was on my way to my first Love-in with the high moral fervour of a libidinous rattlesnake.

Finbar tried to take a sip from the Giant Mug but his lips were driven back by the heat and he wiped them vigorously with the back of his hand.

—First, of course, I had to have the gear. I got Martha to run up an Indian-style paternity shirt from an old floral curtain … and for God's sake don't tell her why I wanted it. I told her it was a present for a patient … Then I spent an embarrassing half hour in our new boo-tique. Would you credit that? A man's boo-tique in Slagthorpe, the ancestral home of Mens' Outfitters. You can find it down the alley behind the Cycle Shop. Swinging Sid's, *The Swinger who put Burtons out of business.*

—In the event, Sid turned out to be a patient. Molly Brisket's boy. Nice young lad and he gave me his personal attention. Fitted me with a pair of trousers so tight that future generations of anatomists will regard that muscle that tightens the scrotum as a purely vestigial ornament.

—Come Saturday afternoon, as the dawn of Aquarius drew nigh, I got into my alternative togs and … I hope you don't mind … fished out a few strings of beads from your grandmother's trunk in the attic. It hasn't been opened for years.

—I hung the beads round my neck, combed my hair forward to cover that embarrassing bare patch on my right temple, tied the cat's bell round my wrist, and set off to resolve my erotic fantasies. On the way I borrowed a couple of chrysanthemums from the window boxes outside the Town Hall and stuffed them into my belt.

A tentative sip from the mug. This time he was able to swallow, if only with a grimace.

—I'll admit that when I arrived my first reaction was one of disappointment. But then there may be more encouraging settings for a cultural revolution than the Municipal Recreation Ground, especially when the wind is coming in from the gasworks end.

—And Slagthorpe's cultural dropouts were not exactly a bacchanalian bunch. True, they had one or two risqué slogans on their T-shirts but they tended to sit around in uneasy groups, staring sheepishly at one another while they racked their brains for alternative remarks. Their only defiant blow against authority was to ignore the municipal warnings to Keep off the Grass – a purely symbolic revolt because, as you know, the last blade of grass disappeared from the Municipal Recreation Ground sometime during the first world war.

—It was more a revivalist meeting than an orgy, possibly because, in the middle of the congregation was an earnest balding fellow up on a stage chanting soul poetry to the accompaniment of a soul orchestra. At least that's what they called themselves on the placard. Three fellas with mouth organs, seven unisex persons with long hair, bands round their foreheads and brand new guitars, young Ernie Chapatti, whose dad runs the Star of India, with six days growth of stubble round his chops and his uncle's ill-tuned sitar and, adding incongruous but much needed body to the sound, the lead tuba from the Slagheaton Colliery Silver Band.

—With that competition Baldy had to beef up his chanting till it became more of a bellow … a bit like the MC at the all-in wrestling in the Corn Exchange.

> Fall in love with a middle class society
> And your life will flow out of you
> Into a puddle
> Where well-integrated citizens
> Can come and dance
> In their Wellington boots.

—I didn't see Baldy stoking much in the way of orgiastic fire so I set out on a bit of a reconnaissance and my spirits began to rise. Away from the self-conscious bunch around the stage, lay a surfeit of promising talent strewn across the dusty soil, a fair number already indulging in shameless alternative activity.

—After some deliberation I settled for a nymphet of promising nubility stretched out between the tramlines on one of the municipal tennis courts. She had long blond hair, or maybe it was a wig, a flower-bedecked straw hat with a broad brim which she'd pulled down over her face to shade it from the sun, a short black mini-skirt, and a T-shirt that inquired, *Are you being served?*.

—I settled nonchalantly beside her and trying to add a catarrhal timbre to my voice I said, God forgive me, *Hi, goddess. Care to tune in to a little soul talk?*

—Goddess raised a lazy arm to lift the hat from her face, then turned towards me to reveal the all-too-familiar features of Mavis Pilkington and her even more familiar acne, subject of much protracted discussion in my Friday evening surgeries.

—O-o-o-h, doctor, she said, brightly. Fancy seeing you here. That last ointment you gave me was fab and I've kept my promise. I've given up squeezing them.

—The conversation, I sensed, had taken a non-erotic turn. I found myself wondering what view the General Medical Council might take of a doctor tuning in with one of his patients. I hastily offered Mavis a chrysanthemum from my belt and accepted a rather scruffy dahlia in return.

—That was when I discovered she had a companion. A large hairy lad encased in black leather that bristled with metal studs. He raised himself slowly on one elbow, and looked me carefully up and down before delivering the only soul message I was to receive from the Alternative Culture.

—Get stuffed, cradle-snatcher, he said.

—It was a moment of revelation. In just ten seconds I'd been deflowered. A year ago I might have picked a fight but that afternoon I slunk away in embarrassment. Not just embarrassed but middle-aged and hurt. I tell you no lie but on the way home I seriously considered dropping in at the Darby and Joan for a hand of Solo.

Finbar tried another sip from the Giant Mug then stared at the surface of the murky fluid.

—Another of milestone, I suppose. You start your life playing the engaging young lad. Next you're the lusty adventurer who carries his years lightly. Then you wake up one morning and discover you've grown into a dirty old man.

He gazed out the window at the empty promenade. The room was silent save for the sizzle from the deep fryer.

After a moment of indecision Finbar shook his head and smiled

—Still it has its consolations. I doubt I'll be seeing the Pilkington girl again. And I never really coped with the poor kid's acne.

—Cheers.

He raised the Giant Mug flamboyantly as if it were a pint of Guinness and only when he filled his mouth with a scalding draught did he realise it wasn't.

As Finbar cursed and sputtered and Joe came scurrying from the counter I sat contented in my place. The salutation *Cheers* had proclaimed the exorcism of Finbar's demon. I leave it to Freudians to analyse the abreaction.

EDITOR'S NOTE
A handwritten page from a Donovan diary.

Bush Telegraph

I sat in the corner seat of a British Rail compartment reading the latest S. J. Perelman in a determinedly unprovocative way. I indulged in none of the antics of a Perelman addict; no sudden peals of laughter no rolling on the floor frothing mildly at the mouth, no jabbing the book under the nose of my neighbour to point out the source of my hilarity. I just sat there in my only respectable suit radiating the polite decorum which Doctor Endymion Gasconade, Slagthorpe GP, alderman, JP, BMA councillor, Fellow of the Royal College of General Practitioners and member of all those you-name-it-I'm-on-it medical committees assures us will once again make Britain great.

And yet. And yet ... and yet. The flatulent owl who sat opposite kept peering round the side of his Daily Telegraph and scrutinizing me through horn-rimmed spectacles. I looked down to check that my flies were done up. They were. But my flickering glance had made him bold. He leaned forward.

—Excuse me, he asked in a deep lugubrious voice. Are you aware that you're wearing no shirt?

He glanced at the blue label over his right shoulder.

—This *is* a first class compartment.

—It's quite all right, I whispered back. The new Oxfam campaign. Make every second Sunday a shirtless day. We send the laundry money to the underdeveloped.

—How commendable, he boomed and retired behind his Telegraph.

How the hell had it happened? I was on my way up to the Smoke for an afternoon meeting at BMA House. And I was a person of some importance. The official representative of the Slagthorpe Division of the BMA nominated by a unanimous vote at our divisional meeting. True there were only two members present but they were unanimous.

Finbar and I had turned up at the Memorial's library expecting one of those meetings where pharmaceutical reps lay on a hot buffet and hand out free pocket calculators. We had drawers full of calculators but it was Martha's night off and a free hot meal was an attractive alternative to half an hour in Stanley Hetherington's Chips with Everything: *They come to sneer but stay to scoff.*

When we got to the library the librarian told us that the free food and calculators meeting had been last week. This week the BMA wanted us to choose a representative for an emergency meeting on the recurring decimal of medical politics ... reform of the Association's constitution. It could have been the mention of constitution – though it was more likely the absence of free grub – that persuaded Slagthorpe's BMA members that they could spend a more rewarding evening at home.

We were about to leave when the division's secretary rang to say he'd done in his back and would be grateful if someone else could take the chair and perform the usual shoe-in of Endymion Gasconade as our representative. Finbar, who normally has a deep aversion to the BMA and all who sail in her, was happy to oblige. He quickly summoned me to order, proposed the vote, and declared me elected by acclamation. Within a week the postman had delivered two huge bundles of unreadable BMA documents.

It's not every BMA representative who gets a unanimous vote and, conscious of the honour, I really made an effort on the big day: clean socks, polished shoes, brushed hair. I even polished my glasses for the first time this year and put on the clean underpants that mothers tell their sons will be the first things a hospital will examine if they are knocked down by a bus. I also lashed out on a grey pinstriped executive three-piece that Finbar immediately designated my BMA suit. I had to catch the five a.m. train from the Junction and, never having knowingly worn a waistcoat before, I tried it on when I got out of my bath. What with the rush to drink my breakfast tea and pack my overnight bag while the taxi was waiting at the door, I must have thrown on the rest of the clobber without remembering there was nothing beneath the waistcoat.

The flatulent owl lowered his paper and gave me an appreciative smile.

What the hell would I do when I got there? Shirt shops don't open on Sundays. I could turn up my raincoat collar while I registered at the small hotel I'd chosen because it was close to Tavistock Square. But what about the meeting? Perhaps I could manage with the top half of my new Marks & Spencer's floral pyjamas. Combined with the grey pinstripe it could give me the look of those literary gents they interview on Late Night Line-Up. But I had no tie. Maybe I could set a new fashion with a casually knotted dressing gown cord.

—What's all this, then? asked a gruff voice.

The ticket collector stood in the doorway.

—Show us yet ticket, lad.

He couldn't conceal his disappointment when I handed him a first class ticket, and he made a swift survey to see if I'd slashed any seats.

—It's the Oxfam campaign, boomed the flatulent owl. Shirtless Sunday.

The ticket collector beamed.

—I do apologize, sir, he said. I'd clean forgot. And may the good Lord smile on your efforts, sir.

—Thank you, I replied politely. We will fight the good fight.

The curtains, in my hotel bedroom, might solve the problem. If they were kept furled by those bands of cloth with a ring at each end; if the bands were not too gaudy; if I could remove the rings from one of them, I could knot it round the collar of the floral pyjamas If. If. If. The odds against were too high. They'd probably give me a room with Venetian blinds.

The flatulent owl brushed past me on his way out of the compartment and gave me one of his slow, encouraging smiles.

Perhaps the hotel porter could lend me one of his spares. But I didn't fancy my chances of getting the right collar size. Cyril, chief honcho in Classic Shirts and Quality Neckwear at Satterthwaite's Haberdashery Emporium, says I have a difficult neck. Maybe one of the hotel waiters. But a detachable dicky and a greasy black tie would hardly enhance the BMA pinstripe. Not in one who was unanimously elected ... and by acclamation.

The flatulent owl brushed past on his return. Again I got the reassuring smile and, as he sat down, I saw with horror that he, too, was shirtless. Grey chest hairs sprouted between the lapels of his electric blue mohair.

—Better late than never, he said. Especially when it's in a good cause.

Fashion, they say, is fickle. But the desire to help others is near to universal. Six hours and two trips to the dining car later, when our train halted in its London terminus, the ticket collector appeared on the platform outside our compartment and, with a flourish, flung open the door. He wore no shirt. Nor did the porters scattered along the platform. Nor did my bowler-hatted fellow travellers who, as they streamed towards the exit, nodded fraternally as I descended from my carriage.

The receptionist who greeted me at my small Bloomsbury hotel had also shed his shirt, as had most of the representatives at the meeting. The others who'd been too busy to watch television or listen to the radio wore the shamefaced looks of men who'd turned up in lounge suits to a dinner-jacketed party.

I hope Oxfam was grateful. I was.

A Race Apart

Jersey islanders are proud of their Festival of Flowers and the caballeros of Pamplona wax eloquent about their Running of the Bulls. Yet the citizens of Slagthorpe will tell you that, if you seek colour, panache, and unconstrained indulgence, you need to go no further than the town's annual Tribute to the Noble Horse.

On the first Saturday of every April the sooty scrub of Slag Common is carefully camouflaged, if never successfully concealed, behind a facade of fairground booths, sideshows, dodgems, coconut shies, and candy-floss machines and the honest burghers of our gloomy town embark on a 24-hour orgy that leans heavily on the consumption of pork pies and brown ale, topped off with the debauchery of all-night Bingo.

The excuse for this uninhibited merriment is the running of the Slagthorpe Amateur Handicap Plate which for nearly 200 years has successfully evaded the clutches of both Jockey Club and National Hunt Committee. The seeds of the event were sown in the late eighteenth century when a young Slagshire blood, who fancied the wife of a local nobleman, challenged her husband to a bareback race across Slag Common.

Unbeknownst to both contestants, the prize in this race *passionelle* was, as the Corporation brochure puts it, *having it away contentedly* with the local baker. The night before the competition, the practical-minded lovers carefully reinforced every hedge on the common with solid slabs of English oak. During the race both contestants fell and broke their necks and the erstwhile lovers settled down to the notional contentment of a solid Slagshire marriage.

This scandalous affair is now commemorated by a race in which a collection of horse-like animals compete over one lap of the Common. The only condition of entry is that each rider must be an amateur who has lived for five years within a three-mile radius of the Corporation refuse dump which, for historical reasons long forgotten, is defined as the sporting centre of the town. The prize is the celebrated Slagthorpe Loaf which, by a tradition designed to echo the origins of the event, must be prepared by a local baker. These days that means the local branch of the Slagshire Co-operative Wholesale Society which for the past five years has presented the winner with a sliced loaf specially wrapped in decorative waxed paper.

An ingenuous stranger might ask why a race for such an insignificant prize should cause such a stir in the town. The answer lies in the betting. Despite an elaborate handicapping system organized officially by the Slagthorpe Corporation, an unofficial committee of native Slagthorpians, meeting before the event, decides who will win. The main reason for whipping up the tourist trade is to keep the odds on the course equably divided while the local money goes surreptitiously onto the designated winner. So the Carnival, which the Corporation's brochure describes as *One of Britain's great traditional sporting occasions*, is regarded locally as a legitimate supplement to a true Slagthorpian's income.

This year's local selection was a pensioned-off hunter called Fearsome Fred which Slagthorpe's Welsh vet, Glyn Beerie-Jones had acquired from an arthritic landed gent in the Quorn country. Throughout the winter Fred's coat was allowed to grow long and shaggy to disguise his class, and he was given intensive and secretive training on a lonely beach to the south of Slagton Regis.

The clandestine committee had every confidence in Fred and felt that the only possible threat came from a mare called Miss

Cegenation entered by a former Slagheaton butcher who'd made his fortune in the black market during the war and was notoriously lacking in local loyalty. Miss Cegenation was rumoured to be the result of a *crise d'amour* on the North Slagshire Moors when a thoroughbred stallion broke free from a famous stud and indulged in an uninhibited five-hour romp amongst the mares who hauled the Corporation refuse carts.

When the committee called in Doctor Finbar Aloysius O'Flaherty to advise on the genetic possibilities, he was unable to predict which side of the family would most influence Miss Cegenation's performance but came up with one of his characteristic wheezes. He suggested that the best way to cope with the Miss Cegenation problem was to nominate Glyn Beerie-Jones as her jockey. Glyn was happy to oblige and, because he is regarded locally as Slagthorpe's answer to Lester Piggott, had no difficulty in selling his services to the black marketeer.

On the great day, Glyn brought Miss Cegenation to the starting line to join the field – a bizarre collection of hacks, ponies, carthorses, and one strange animal that could have been a mutated Great Dane. The sideshows and gaily coloured booths had once again persuaded our visitors that this was not a serious occasion and all the local money had been safely placed on Fearsome Fred at relatively healthy odds.

Our gallant MP, Brigadier Digby Knutsford MP, OBE, TD, LMSSA, RAMC, started the race and the motley collection of horseflesh lumbered off into the country to cheers and laughter from the visitors and stony-faced silence from the natives. Eight minutes later, anxious eyes focused on the far end of the finishing straight beheld a piteous sight. Miss Cegenation and Fearsome Fred led the field but the mare was some 20 lengths ahead of Fred and this despite the fact that she was travelling sideways as Glyn lay back in the saddle pulling so hard on one rein that his mount was staring him in the eyes. With two furlongs to go the situation was no better and we'd all resigned ourselves to witnessing the ultimate debasement of a great tradition, when Glyn was suddenly touched by greatness.

A man of unpretentious intellectual power, he said later that for one blinding second he was aware of metaphysical inspiration. One hundred yards from the finishing post, when his strength appeared to have been taxed beyond its limit and Miss Cegenation seemed certain to win in a sideways walk, our heroic Welsh vet flung himself from the saddle. The cheers of the crowd, suddenly reinforced by local voices, turned to a mighty roar and two minutes later, as Fearsome Fred staggered past the post, the roar took on a Te Deum-like quality.

Glyn was carried from the course on a stretcher and taken by ambulance to the Slagthorpe Memorial where, according to the Echo, doctors were soon *fighting for his life.* It later emerged hat he'd broken an ankle and the following morning *a hospital spokesman described Mr Beerie-Jones's condition as Comfortable* (© Slagthorpe Echo).

Later that day when the Mayor later visited our hero in the orthopaedic ward, he spoke for the whole community when he declared:

—Never was bone broken in more noble cause.

Glyn now walks easily with neither limp nor crutch. This afternoon, at an unpretentious ceremony, he received the Freedom of the Borough and next year Slagthorpe hopes to weave yet another colourful thread into the rich tapestry of British Sporting Tradition.

Avuncular Advice

Finbar Aloysius O'Flaherty MRCP, MB, BCh, BOA

Slagfield House, Netherway Lane, Slagthorpe

Dear Alphonsus,

It is one of the regrets of my life that I don't know you better. But your mother, kind sister though she is to me, has spent most of your life trying to keep you away from my influence. I've no doubt she did it for the best.

She's just written to pass on the good news that you have outwitted the examiners. I'm delighted to hear it. She has also passed on, and this must have cost her dear, your request for your uncle's advice on how to build a career in hospital medicine. So here goes.

You've already made the most important move by being born a man. Next you must acquire what we doctors call Authority.

I've just seen a perfect example. An hour ago an old chum popped up on my television set. When we were students, few would trust him with the price of a drink, let alone the address of a girlfriend. Yet there he was on my screen telling us why every twelve year old girl should or shouldn't be on the Pill. I forget which it was but he was very convincing.

Authority like that doesn't come cheap and you'll have to buy it by playing along with the system. Hospital jobs are less easy to come by than they once were but, if you get the protection of a well-ordered brotherhood around you, you'll find you can still progress through medicine without too much trauma – provided you keep your eyes down, your nose clean, and your thoughts and your flies buttoned up in public.

A good move is to get a job at one of those hospitals that call themselves Centres of Excellence. Before you apply, find out what sort of person they're after: a brain, a scrum half, a freemason, or even the statutory black or woman they're prepared to appoint in these permissive times. Most likely they'll be after a decent chap known to one of the consultants or recommended to him by another decent chap at another decent place. That's the job to go for, using all the arse-crawling ploys you acquired at medical school.

Once you're through the door, you yourself will have become a decent chap and will remain one for evermore if you can cultivate a reputation for being *sound* and avoid the dreaded *too clever by half* or even worse *too big for his boots*. (That last remark is usually made by those who are too small for theirs).

A Centre of Excellence will also give you plenty of practice at the job because your boss is likely to be busy elsewhere; not necessarily ringing up the till in private practice but attending meetings where he can extend his acquaintance with men of influence and power. When Ian Aird was professor of surgery at the Royal Postgraduate Hospital, he used to travel a lot. When asked who did his work when he was away, he always replied: The same people as do it when I'm here.

A centre of excellence will also afford you chances – in the corridors and wards, or over the coffee cups – to exchange well-turned witticisms or deep insightful remarks with some of medicine's most powerful patrons. You need to impress them, depending on which way you're aiming your career, with your modesty, your common sense, your zeal, or even your healthy irreverence (expressed, of course, only within decent limits).

Don't underrate the value of these occasions because medicine's patrons have within their gift not just the best jobs but all the appurtenances that distinguish the gentlemen from the players.

If you're academically inclined, they can gain you access to research funds, consultancies to international agencies, and regular invitations to symposia in places like Florence, Tokyo, San Francisco, or Milan.

If you're keen to grub a living in private practice, they can arrange membership of dining clubs and appearances at postgraduate meetings, which get a man's name known within the trade – a much more effective way of attracting referrals of private patients than vulgar appearances in the public prints.

And if, God forgive you, you have a taste for pomp, the patrons will offer you regular leg-ups on the beanstalk that has its roots in committees and soars through the clouds to the land of gold chains, mutual votes of thanks, and even, whisper it softly, the reassuring touch of sword on shoulder.

Like all good Establishments, the system that distributes this patronage is not an organised network with a Mr Big skulking at its centre but an ill-defined scatter of well-meaning fellows, dropping a word here, a hint there, and earning each others' co-operation by lending support here, withdrawing it there. Indeed some are unaware of the power that they wield and take a naive delight in the success that seems to smile upon the decent young fellows whom they know.

Most doctors – those who enjoy their work – are amused by the antics of colleagues who play the patronage game. They mock rather than challenge and I suggest you follow their example.

You may be irritated when you see the network perpetuating mediocrity ... when you see mediocre men, with nothing to defend but their unmerited authority, use patronage to repel all intrusion by imagination, initiative or enterprise.

But, whatever you do, don't speak out. Keep reminding yourself that Authority is all. Seek not to challenge it but to acquire it. Leave the grumbling to others, get on with your work, and don't get drawn into unpleasantness. If the going gets rough, just think hard about the index-linked NHS pension that awaits you at the end of your comfortable amble.

One last thing. If you follow any of the advice I offer in this letter I will never speak to you again

Yours avuncularly,

Finbar

In December 1967, when the South African surgeon Christiaan Barnard performed the first human heart transplant in Cape Town, he was accused of jumping the gun by operating when he had no way of preventing rejection of the new heart. When his patient's condition started to deteriorate, Barnard was jetting round the world on a publicity tour, described by a consultant at his hospital as an *impetuous, flamboyant, and undignified global lap of honour.*

The fame accorded to Barnard spurred other surgeons to go ahead with operations in which science ran second place to hype. Within 48 hours of the South African operation, there were two heart transplants in the USA, quickly followed by one in India, and three in France.

Five months later, Britain's first heart transplant coincided with the *I'm Backing Britain* campaign designed to encourage Britons to buy home-produced goods. After the operation the London transplant team held a press conference at which they displayed small Union Jacks overprinted *We're Backing Britain*. Their patient died 46 days later. Britain's second heart transplant patient died after 57 hours. By then 24 patients had received new hearts but only six were alive, most having died within days or hours of the operation.

Donovan recorded his reaction to the frenzy in Phantasmagoria, his daydream book. (See p. 173)

Major Breakthrough Rides Again

The story broke late on Tuesday evening. As Richard Baker wound up the television news, he was handed a piece of paper. Adopting grave tones, he announced:

—Earlier today Doctor Finbar Aloysius O'Flaherty, a Slagthorpe general practitioner, performed the first recorded transplantation of a horse's stomach into a human being. This evening the condition of the patient, Mr Glyn Beerie-Jones, Slagthorpe's Welsh vet, was stated to be comfortable. The horse, Lonesome Fellow, had earlier broken a fetlock in the Grand

Slagshire Chase and had to be destroyed. His starting price was twenty to one.

Immediately the great engines of communication juddered into action. First off the mark, *Late Night Line-up* assembled a distinguished panel – a Fellow of the Royal College of Surgeons, a spokesman for the Patients' Association, the Bishop of Woolwich, and the secretary of the Jockey Club. Unfortunately the discussion never got off the ground. The surgeon, who'd clearly been dragged away from a good dinner picked a fight with the man from the Patients' Association and, just as Mrs Mary Whitehouse rang up to complain about the surgeon's language, the first blows were struck. The Jockey Club tried to mediate but was felled by a surgical right hook. Whereupon, with great presence of mind, the Bishop rose to his feet and offered up a prayer for Mr Beerie-Jones, the horse, and, glancing at the moribund figure at his feet, the continuing health of all members of the Jockey Club.

The following morning every newspaper carried the news on its front page but, because no reporter had been able to track down Doctor O'Flaherty or his patient, the stories consisted mainly of soulful pictures of Lonesome Fellow and snippets of equine biography.

The Royal College of Surgeons issued a statement expressing alarm that the operation had been performed by a common or garden GP. The Royal College of Physicians agreed with the surgeons. Door-stepping reporters failed to elicit any statement from the College of General Practitioners because all the members were out coping with the 'flu epidemic. The Daily Sketch made do with a quote from a College charlady who had answered the door and expressed the hope that the horse hadn't suffered – a point taken up in a hard-hitting leader in the Daily Mirror.

The medical correspondent of The Times, a notoriously solemn Scot, weighed in with a long feature headlined *A Time To Ponder*. After three quotations from Leviticus, two old Scottish proverbs, and a sidelong reference to Pontius Pilate, the writer suggested that all transplantation operations, *which are usually carried out by so-called humanists for their own personal glorification*, should be banned until the moral and ethical issues had been considered by at least two ecumenical councils.

Later, in the House of Commons, the Minister of Health claimed that the operation was a triumph for the Envy of the World.* Mr Laurie Pavitt, Labour MP for Willesden West, pointed out that the horse was a thoroughbred and asked whether it had occupied a private, an amenity, or an NHS bed. Amidst cheers from the back benches, he demanded assurances that this aristocratic animal had not been allowed to jump the normal waiting list. Mr George Wigg assured him that, throughout a long and disastrous career, Lonesome Fellow had shown himself incapable of jumping anything. (Loud laughter and snores from all parts of the House.) The BMA promised to engage in tough realistic negotiations with the Minister of Health over payments to doctors with horses on their lists.

At 7p.m. the ITA announced triumphantly that Doctor O'Flaherty had come out of hiding to appear before the ultimate national tribunal, The Frost Programme. There he would try to justify his actions to a jury consisting of Lady Dartmouth, Malcolm Muggeridge, Mick Jagger, and the entire Manchester United football team.

At 10.32 p.m. precisely Finbar sat cheerily in the chair of honour in Royal David's City.

—Tell me, Finbar, asked Frost, what emotions did you feel when you discovered you could do this operation?

—Devilment, said Finbar. You see, Charles ... I gather you always use first names on this programme ... Glyn Beerie-Jones has always been a good friend of mine and for years I've watched him drink like a fish. I thought it was high time he started to eat like a horse.

—Can you tell us, Finbar, when and where the operation took

*Twentieth century politicians' pet name for the NHS.

place,

—Certainly, Henry. At 8 o'clock on Monday night in the public bar of the Slagshire Cheese.

—In a pub?

—That's where all the best operations take place. As do the best golf rounds, fishing exploits, and love affairs. In the minds and mouths of natural drinkers. Our operation was the product of two of the most fertile and well-lubricated imaginations in the land.

—You mean that all this publicity has been over a practical joke?

—More an impractical joke. We feel that these days when everyone likes to get into the act, there is a growing shortage of acts. In a spirit of public service and increased productivity, we decided to provide a nice roomy band-waggon for everyone to jump on. Even you can't interview George Brown every night and there must be a limited supply of those visiting Nepalese jugglers. But now that I'm here, I might as well give you a few bars of The Harp that Once. . .

As Finbar rose unsteadily to his feet and burst into song, Lady Dartmouth left in a huff but Muggeridge and Manchester United showed an unexpected aptitude for four-part harmony. As Finbar explained as he wound up the programme,

—Now that Doctor Barnard has given medicine a foothold in show business, the least we can do is to make it entertaining.

The Wrong Side of the Tracks

A light wind, heavy with mist from the moors, drifts down Deanery Row and takes a playful tug at the silken gowns outside the Slagcaster Corn Exchange. For reasons buried in its archives, the British Medical Association has decided to hold its Annual Representative Meeting in our county town. The politicking will start tomorrow. Today is the day for the bolstering of egos.

This morning, the Association's dignitaries – a much used BMA word – will process to their ecumenical service at the Cathedral of St Cuthbert de Slag. All those mustered on the steps of the Corn Exchange wear academic gowns: a few have swathed themselves in doctoral colour but most have settled for black, with an occasional trimming of ermine. The country's academic costumiers have made their annual killing.

A small bespectacled boy and I watch from behind a road mender's barrow on the opposite side of the road, too embarrassed to step forward and stare shamefacedly

When it comes to gowns, splendour, it seems, has nothing to do with achievement. The chap near the head of the pack who idled his way through medical administration and got an honorary MD from the University of Manchester sprouts more exotic plumage than the chaps in the rear who earned their MBs with honest toil. One of the most resplendent robes on show goes with the least resplendent qualification, bestowed by the notorious Apothecaries' Hall in Dublin.

What would happen if a humble Slagshire private turned up in more regal silk than that worn by the BMA's top brass? Would he be allowed to walk in the procession or would he be sent to church in one of those cars with darkened windows? Thank God they haven't invited Finbar to join them. I suspect he'd have prepared himself with a trip to Percy Haddock's Dressing Up Shop, hired himself a Cardinal Richelieu outfit, and recruited Nubian slaves to carry his train.

A beadle-like character wearing a dark topper and carrying a long pole topped with the icon of Aesculapius gives the order for everyone to line up in the road. He steps smartly off the pavement then steps smartly back again. Slagshire drivers don't give way to Fancy Dans.

A sergeant of the North Slagshire Constabulary in full ceremonial fig steps out more impressively and stops the traffic with a raise of his hand. The beadle re-establishes himself in front of the traffic lights and the dignitaries line up self-consciously behind him. Endymion Gasconade, Slagthorpe GP, JP, alderman, BMA Councillor, and member of all those you-name-it-I'm-on-it medical committees, pushes himself as near to the front as he can, catches a glimpse of me, and takes an intense interest in the sky.

—They look better than t'mayor, says the bespectacled boy. He's only got a gold chain and a bowler hat.

After a long wait the traffic lights turn green and the procession steps bravely forward to tackle the angina-provoking slope of Cuthbert Hill. The sight should be a tonic for an irreverent soul like me yet I find myself beset by melancholy. How lucky they are to have a source of strength to sustain them through yet another year of points of order, amended resolutions, and thank-you-for-the-loan-of-the-hall oratory. The sermon from the Bishop of Slagcaster will set them up nicely; it would just make me more confusedly agnostic. They wouldn't believe me but I envy their confidence. They and I have grown up on opposite sides of the medical tracks.

* * * * * * * * * * *

I hadn't come to Slagcaster to mock the antics of my elders and betters. I was on a more rewarding mission. Once the ecumenical service was out of the way they were all off to a do the Lord Mayor had laid on at the Mansion House. Not your usual glass of warm white wine and bits of sausage and cheese impaled on sticks. This was a special occasion, Spanish champagne, sausage rolls, bacon and black pudding tartlets, and a lecture on *Slagcaster's contribution to British medicine*. The lecturer was to have been the County Medical Officer Doctor William Rees Evans, better known to most of us as Good Evans … an echo of his first response to any piece of news or gossip, joyful or depressing, congratulatory or critical.

Good Evans was to retire that week and the lecture was to be his last official duty. Then twenty four hours before the event Mrs Good Evans rang the Mansion House to say Willie had been stricken by a mysterious illness and would be unable to perform. The good news was that his old friend Doctor Finbar Aloysius O'Flaherty was happy to stand in and had already prepared a lecture which her husband was sure would be appropriate. The Lord Mayor and the aldermanate, who knew nothing about Finbar, were delighted to accept his generous offer. That's why I had received an invitation and a security badge that endorsed me as a *BMA Approved Guest*.

At the appointed hour, after the BMA had made its peace with God and the approved guests had had their rolls, tartlets, and half glass of fizz, we all moved into the Banqueting Hall. The Lord Mayor, aldermen, and other county worthies occupied the front seats. Alongside them and filling the four rows behind them sat the BMA top brass. Behind the BMA sat row upon row of Slagshire doctors who did know Finbar and expected a more rewarding session than we usually got from the BMA.

When Finbar stepped up to the podium, Endymion Gasconade who had sneaked himself on to the end of the front row nearly blew a gasket. This was the first he knew of the change of programme. He half got to his feet but the Manchester MD (Hon) sitting alongside him whispered an angry order for him to sit. Endymion, aware he was on an inferior rung of the feudal ladder, responded like an obedient dog.

Finbar surprised those of us who knew him by turning up neatly dressed ... well, relatively neatly dressed. He seemed unaware of the dust that had settled on the shoulders and lapels of his best suit during the two years it had hung untouched in his bedroom cupboard. Still he'd made an effort and, thanks maybe to the influence of the clean collar and neatly knotted Old Etonian tie, he embarked on his lecture in respectful and understated tones, quite unlike the hectoring we were used to in the public bar at the Slagshire Cheese.

I am, as they say in the better class of journal, grateful to the author for providing an edited text of his lecture.

Slagcaster's most significant contributions to British medicine are the same as those made every day wherever patients fall ill and doctors tend to them. Most are unrecorded acts of kindness, skill, and compassion that can be soon forgotten by some who benefit from them. And that is how it should be. Undue recognition of simple civilised behaviour can have disastrous effects upon the Ego.

The story I want to tell is of an incident in Slagcaster history that may intrigue those who take an interest in the way professionals look after themselves. The only relic of the affair is that ornate but shabby building in north east corner of the cathedral square ... the one that looks like a country cousin of London's St Pancras station. In its heyday it was known as SWA House and was the headquarters of the Slagshire Woolgatherers' Association.

In the first third of the nineteenth century woolgathering was an honourable occupation. And in 1842 a bunch of woolgatherers from hamlets scattered across the county met in a Slagcaster coffee house to form a professional association to protect their trade from *any fellowes, officialle or unofficialle, who, in anie waie, shape, or forme, thretene the dignitie of our woolgathering activitie.* The Charter was not written in Old English. Woolgatherers were notoriously bad spellers.

In its early days the SWA was an easy going and unfashionably democratic institution. The founding fathers divided the county into woolgathering divisions and representatives from each division met once a year to decide SWA policy. They also elected a council to implement their decisions. Councillors were given chains of office to impress them with the importance of their job and, by an unfortunate tradition for which the SWA was to pay heavily, all gold chain wearers were sustained by regular votes of thanks for their selfless service to their fellow woolgatherers.

Thanks to its democratic constitution the SWA was a great success. It fought off a Government takeover of woolgathering and established this wholesome activity as a respected, honoured and dignified profession. Fifty years after its foundation, a growing membership and the shrewd investment of subscriptions enabled the creation of SWA House. When the new building opened, its basilica-like proportions, its baronial dining room, high-ceilinged committee rooms and its Great Hall, with decorated ceiling and pastoral murals on its walls, imposed a sense of grandeur on even the most menial woolgatherer who entered it.

Therein lay a problem. Soon after the opening, the chain-of-office councillors found that expense-paid trips to Slagcaster, and debates on woolgathering matters of the moment, were far more enjoyable than mundane woolgathering back home. They began to increase the number of committees, sub-committees and working parties whose meetings would help them to spend more time in the comforting grandeur of Cathedral Square.

Dedicated councillors soon discovered there was so much they could do at SWA House they were left with only a day or two each month to devote to the tedious business of woolgathering. In contrast, the cheery majority – non-chain-of-office councillors – preferred a life of contented woolgathering to one of committees and working parties. For them the growing number of meetings in Slagcaster became a chore so they opted out and left them in the hands of the natural committeemen.

It thus came to pass that the most frequent visitors to SWA House spent most of their time in the company of woolgatherers of similar temperament and ambition. The perpetual votes of thanks with which they favoured one another fuelled the delusion that they were a cut above the rest, were indeed Important Woolgatherers. The more they conversed, the more they convinced themselves that mundane SWA affairs offered little scope for their unquestionable political skills. Their search for graver matters to consider led to their discovery of the National Interest.

The great advantage of the National Interest was that Important Woolgatherers who were concerned about it could travel to London and have solemn discussions with civil servants in the government department of woolgathering. Whitehall woolgatherers, they discovered, shared their enthusiasm for committees, working parties, gold chains, and the rest of it. Indeed the SWA's Important Woolgatherers found they had much more in common with their Whitehall colleagues than with their own members whom they began to refer to as The Periphery.

Peripheral woolgatherers were happy with this development. The expanding programme of London meetings, on top of the Slagcaster ones, meant that their most boring, garrulous and disputatious colleagues were away more often than they used to be and had even less time to disrupt local woolgathering.

Imagine The Periphery's dismay when one day all members received a letter from the council telling them that in future all woolgathering would be licensed by a new government department set up in conjunction with the SWA. Anyone who wanted to woolgather would not only have to pay a hefty licence fee but would have to be a paid-up member of the SWA which was now doubling its membership fee *to meet the increased demands on the association*.

The announcement sparked a revolt. Angry members wrote letters to the SWJ and called a protest meeting at SWA House. The meeting was addressed by the chairman of council.

—Let me draw your attention, he said, to the document you all received last year.

The document *Towards new frontiers in woolgathering* had 600 tightly printed pages. Few members of The Periphery had read beyond page viii. Many had used unopened copies as doorstops.

—The resolution on page 472 … paragraph roman V, little c … *that subsection seven be referred back to the SWCCS Committee* quite clearly commits your council to acceptance of government licensing. You cannot complain now that you had no notice of it.

The meeting broke up not in anger but with much murmuring within the ranks, for woolgatherers are naturally peaceful people. They returned quietly to their divisions and only at the next council meeting did the Important Woolgatherers discover that every non-important woolgatherer had resigned, abandoning the gentle trade for more profitable employment or emigrating to more favourable climes.

Most council members assumed that they faced disaster, a complete loss of subscription income. Then the Treasurer explained that a gradual liquidation of the Association's assets would allow it to survive for several more years. And the chairman of council pointed out that they had achieved the cherished goal of most professional associations – the freedom to concentrate on important matters without being distracted by troublesome members.

By prudent use of their resources, the Important Woolgatherers managed to keep the committees, the gold chains and the votes of thanks going for another seven years despite the fact there was no longer any woolgathering in Slagshire.

The only monument they left behind is that grimy building

standing in the shade of our even grimier cathedral. No longer SWA House, I fear, but the headquarters of the Slagshire Mutual Improvident Assurance Society.

Thank you Lord Mayor, for inviting me. Thank you even more for putting up with me.

Finbar left the podium to enthusiastic applause from all save those in rows, two, three, four, and five. Inhabitants of those rows clapped their hands together gently in the way of people who need to demonstrate that they are doing the decent thing. I was surprised that none of them had walked out. Then I remembered that one thing that marks out true BMA men and women is their knowledge of the intricacies of rank and protocol. To walk out while the Lord Lieutenant was still seated would have been a grievous sin – could even, perish the thought, imperil the chance of future honour.

A week later Good Evans and Finbar celebrated Willie's retirement with a weekend break at the Sparrow Hawk Inn high up on Slagworth moor. The weekend was devoted to imaginative eating and drinking with occasional interruptions for healthy walks to fill the lungs with wholesome air and to hone the edge of appetite. Among the many toasts they drank were several to the substitute Slagcaster lecture which had been Willie's retirement present to himself and devised with Finbar's help during a previous visit to the Sparrow Hawk.

According to Finbar the highlight of the celebratory weekend was the moment he told Good Evans about the phone call he'd had from Cyril Hepplewhite, general manager of the Slagshire Mutual Improvident. During BMA week a member of the Association's top brass had visited Hepplewhite to inquire about the previous history of the building. A puzzled Cyril had explained there was no previous history. The Mutual Improvident had built the offices for its own use in 1906.

The news, said Finbar, provoked a triple whammy … good 'eavens, good 'eavens, good 'eavens.

EDITOR'S NOTE
Another item from Phantasmagoria, Donovan's daydream book. (See p. 173)
Glued to the first page of this item is a cutting from the Sunday Times in
which the paper's medical correspondent proposed that society needs a new
etiquette to encourage healthy living.

> **Social Goodies**, he suggested, **should**:
>
> **meet friends for lunch at a gym or swimming pool rather than
> the pub,**
>
> **walk or cycle to the shops or work rather than using the car or
> taking public transport,**
>
> **prod house guests into vigorous walks or runs between meals.**
>
> **If someone's car is fitted with a seat belt, offer to do it up for
> them and don't take no for an answer,**
>
> **ask a sex partner beforehand about contraception and VD,**
>
> **compliment people on losing weight.**

A Healthy Lunch

Slagthorpe's avenging angel, Councillor *Big Maggie* Ramsbotham
JP, drummed her fingers on the magistrates' bench.

—Mr Droolihan, she said, are you asking the court to believe
that these incidents arose only because you went out to lunch with
Doctor O'Flaherty?

—I am indeed, ma'am, said Dermot Longinus Droolihan,
licensed victualler, unlicensed talker and resolute bachelor of this
parish.

—The good doctor and myself are dedicated to the pursuit of
happiness through physical well being. We decided that day that we
both were in need of a healthy lunch.

—And are you further asking me to believe that this luncheon
took place at the Slagthorpe Corporation Baths?

—It did indeed, ma'am. We are dedicated readers of the

Sunday Times and, sharing as we do a lifelong ambition to become Social Goodies, we resolved to follow its advice and meet for lunch at the Corporation Baths rather than the pub.

—In the shallow end of the swimming pool?

—Quite so, ma'am. We felt more comfortable there than in the gym. And we were careful to exercise full social responsibility. We left no crumbs on the diving board nor cutlery under water and we flushed all our leftovers down the gentlemen's excuse me. Doctor O'Flaherty has however asked me to apologise for his losing his grip on a *bonne bouche* when he was dive-bombed by a small boy. It disappeared through the skimmer before he could retrieve it but he trusts that neither anchovy nor olive put undue strain on the Corporation's filtration apparatus.

—The charge, I should remind you Mr Droolihan, has nothing to do with a filtration plant.

—No indeed, ma'am. I'm coming to that now. When we emerged from the Corporation Baths aglow with Goodiness, Pouilly Fuisse and the tingling effect of prolonged immersion in chlorinated water, our intention was to mount our tandem and speed home. I had left my live-in manager in charge of the bar, and guessing that he and his family would by then be sleeping off their own lunch, we intended to equip ourselves with a couple of gardening forks to prod them into a vigorous run before teatime.

—Yet as we approached our tandem which we had left chained to the railings outside the Baths we espied a blonde person of the female persuasion. No ordinary blonde person I should add but one who, if you will forgive a touch of chauvinism, ma'am, radiated a sexual appeal that would scorch a monk's cassock at 200 yards.

—As she got into her car the good doctor drew to my attention that it was fitted with one of these new-fangled seat belts. There was of course no legal necessity for her to fasten it and she was on the point of driving off with it undone. A fine opportunity there, says the doctor, for a spot of preventative medicine. A soul well worth the saving. Would you care to do the necessary, Dermot, while I dispose of the empties? So I approached the car, opened the door, and offered to do up her seat belt.

—And how did she respond?

—She pursed her petal lips, ma'am, and told me to go and fornicate myself.

—Mr Droolihan. Please confine your evidence to explaining how you came to lay your hand on this lady's person.

—The indelicacy occurred, ma'am, when I responded to the second half of the Sunday Times exhortation and refused to take no for an answer. I'll not deny that bodily contact did occur but would stress that the upshot, if ma'am will excuse the word, was not only pleasurable but made a lasting impression. And not just on me. The blonde person aforementioned, whom I now know to be the affianced of Detective Constable Snitcher, responded by flickering her eyelashes and inviting me to a party at her place that evening.

—It was in pursuance of that invitation that I presented myself that evening at what I now know to be the Snitcher household. I found it ablaze with light and its front room contained a superfluity, if ma'am will again forgive the chauvinism, of rosebuds eager for the plucking … there being a distinct shortage, if ma'am will pardon the expression, of men.

—Now, over the years I've found it is my nature, ma'am, to harbour lascivious ambitions regarding attractive persons of the female persuasion, ambitions that usually spur me to bantering conversation. That evening, however, mindful of the advice of a great national newspaper, I eschewed remarks about the weather or my considered assessment of the previous night's television programmes. Instead I selected the three most likely of what we chauvinists, ma'am, call propositions and approached each of them thus. My name's Dermot and before we progress beyond *beforehand*, could you please tell me what method of contraception you favour and whether you suffer from any venereal disease?

—The path of a social Goodie is a thorny one, ma'am. Each rosebud in turn slapped my face and, at the third slap, Detective Constable Snitcher emerged from the back room where he'd been quaffing brown ale with his colleagues on the vice squad. It was then that the alleged affray took place.

—Just hold it there for a minute, Mr Droolihan, said Councillor *Big Maggie* Ramsbotham, JP. Here we come to the most surprising element in this case. We have before us a statutory declaration sworn by Detective Constable Snitcher from his hospital bed expressing his intention of bringing no charges arising from the affray.

—Highly magnanimous of him, ma'am. Maybe 'tis a gesture of gratitude for the present I gave him yesterday of the photographs I took at the vice squad's last dinner at my establishment.

—Which leaves me to consider the remaining charge against you. That of insulting behaviour. Have you anything further to say?

—Not a whisper, ma'am, save to follow the last piece of Sunday Times advice and compliment you on losing so much weight since the night you passed out on my premises and we had so much trouble sneaking you away through the back door.

—Case dismissed, said Councillor *Big Maggie* Ramsbotham JP.

—I'm most grateful to you, ma'am, said Dermot Longinus Droolihan. What a blessing it is to be healthy.

EDITOR'S NOTE
From the edited transcript of a recording Donovan made in the Slagshire Cheese at 9.30 p.m. on May 9, 1965 when Doctor O'Flaherty addressed the Slagthorpe Young Businessmen's Association. In this except he describes the early symptoms of a syndrome that has since become all too familiar.

Right off the Top of my Head

...that's the trouble with clichés. We don't want to use 'em but we can't get away from 'em. No matter how tired you are of hearing it, the truth remains that the world *is* getting smaller. Where the hell did I put that glass? Would you mind moving that recording yoke so I can lay a hand upon it.

When I was growing up on a farm near Two Pot House, half way twixt Buttevant and Mallow in God's chosen county of Cork, my parents would spend days in prayer and preparation for a weekend trip to my aunt's all of thirty miles away. Yet, in Switzerland last summer, there I was at nine in the morning half way up an Alp crunching my muesli and, at six the same evening, was back in the surgery gazing at half an acre of flab and recording the latest thrilling instalment in the saga of Mrs Cadwallader's haemorrhoids.

The trouble with all this whizzing around is that it plays merry hell with a place's identity. Every big city in the world now has hotels that have nothing to with the place they're in but are flung out of some international concrete mixer to serve the needs of pasty faced transients, many of them men in short white raincoats and Frank Sinatra hats.

The same magazines line the shelves of gift shops in identical hotel lobbies; the same canned music tinkles in a thousand identical lifts; the same leathery prawns are flambéed in identical restaurants; the same drip-dry shirts hang in identical bathrooms and the same air-conditioning system blows the same sinus-drying draught up the nostrils of any fresh-air loving Briton who thinks a bedroom is a place for a healthy night's sleep.

I often wonder how the chaps who stay in these concrete palazzos ever remember where they are, confined in a cantonment of the same airline offices, the same car rental firms, the same travel agents, and the same expensive shops peddling the same expensive clobber. An absent-minded fella has to walk several metres, versts, or rods, poles, or perches, to find out whether he's whooping it up in Tokyo, Moscow, or San Francisco, or just spending an aberrant weekend in Slagcaster.

New age penitentiaries they are, surviving on a diet of international business conferences, symposia, workshops ... that nature of thing. Designed to get the boys out of their offices, shake hands across the sea, take a global view, get pissed together. Last year, by chance, I made the depressing discovery that all this jet-set tycoonery is just as standardised as the flambéed food, the Frank Sinatra hats, and those flat executive briefcases.

My cousin Willie was over from Boston and I took a trip to London to see him. We had a great evening at the Old Vic ... Laurence Oliver, as Martha calls him, playing a Jamaican playing Othello. I spent the night in a B & B but next day cousin Willie took me to lunch at one of the concrete filing cabinets. A long lunch it was and, after the two of us had bidden our tearful farewells in the lobby, I set off on a hunt for the room that looms large in the consciousness of a fella who has supped his share of wine.

My sense of direction was not what it might have been and I lurched through the wrong door bang into the middle of an International Business Meeting. Well, not so much a meeting ... they were all sitting around as if waiting for something to happen.

Before I could so much as beg their pardon, a long lean gent with a sinister smile and a Perry Como haircut leaped to his feet

—Gentlemen, he cried, pray be upstanding for our good friend, Mike Stancovitch.

Then he strode across the room, grabbed my arm, propelled me behind a baize-covered table, and parked me in a chair.

—Gentlemen, said Smiler barely pausing for breath, Mike really needs no introduction from me. His little finger knows more about our marketing operation than you and I will ever learn in our lifetimes. We're so glad you could make it, Mike. We are truly privileged to have you here today to share your thoughts with us.

He sat down and everybody stared at me.

—I'm terribly sorry, says I sheepishly. There's been a terrible mistake. I was just looking for the loo.

Everyone roared with laughter. A few clapped and Smiler elbowed me in the ribs.

—A great opening gag, Mike, he whispered.

I was trapped. Who were these people? Who was I supposed to be? Suddenly, pride in our heritage ebbed and flowed across my claret-soaked cerebrum. I'd show 'em. I tried to remember as much as I could of Patrick Wymark in *The Power Game** then rose slowly to my feet.

—Of course, I'm talking right off the top of my head, says I.

That seemed to go down all right.

—But I'm sure that's the way you boys would like it.

They all nodded eagerly, in unison.

—I don't have to remind you that our product licks everything else in the market and that we all have the privilege of working for an organization that is forward-looking, creative, dynamic, and above all, built on a respect for people.

There was a spontaneous burst of applause and I knew I had them. Platitudes queued up at my speech centre eager to be released into that expectant air. I began to share my thoughts in every direction.

*A television series about power politics in the boardroom.

—Let's get down to brass tacks ... forward thinking and progressive action ... purposeful planning ... the morality of pragmatism ... replace multi-lateralism with omni-lateralism.

Inanities went winging their way through an atmosphere of mounting enthusiasm. After five minutes I was quite intoxicated by it all and, fearing I might go over the top and spoil it, I wound up to my peroration.

—And let us not forget, Gentlemen, that our message is not written here ...

I plonked my right hand on my forehead.

—but here.

I laid my hand over my heart.

There was, I swear to you, a moment of deep emotional silence before a spontaneous ovation burst upon me. Men stood on their chairs and cheered and everyone started singing For he's a Jolly Good Fellow.

Suddenly the afferent impulses in my pelvic nerves dominated the inhibitory excitement in the higher centres and clamoured urgently for reflex action. If I didn't have a pee my bladder would explode. I shot from the room and headed for my original destination.

I never found out who they were or what I'd been talking about. But I know I was a big success.

As I was saying, the world is getting smaller. And I'm not sure that I like it.

Scoop

—Forty minutes of unadulterated impact. That's what we're after, doc. Forty minutes of television magic.

Jeremy Tittlemouse, fearless probing producer of Slagshire Television's *Soulsearch* gazes fearlessly and probingly across broad acres of mahogany veneer at a shadowy person who looks remarkably like me but must, at the General Medical Council's insistence, be referred to only as A Doctor.

—We're still a bit choked that Yorkshire Television outbid us for that incitement to suicide tape. We want to cap their programme with a really big idea. And that's where you come in, doc. We're offering you the chance to be part of the first programme ever to show a real person dying on the screen … live.

—We can use the Yorkshire precedent to fight off the anti mob and of course we'll make it clear we're into this for a wholly responsible reason. For religious purposes only.

—We're aiming at something that's clean, religious, and transparently on God's side. Something they'll be proud to show the next time Billy Graham plays the Albert Hall. We'll give it the full emotional impact, of course, but we won't neglect the eternal worthwhileness of the subject. We want people to see death as just another human failing.

—If we can find some nice old boy with a doting daughter and a brace of grandchildren we're straight into our warm human situation. Pre-film the family being kind to him, fetching his slippers, kissing him goodnight, that sort of rubbish. Then move in live to your actual dying. God, what impact. You've got your emotion, your grief, your significance, your role of death in contemporary society and, most important of all, you've got forty minutes of unadulterated television magic.

A Doctor stirs uneasily.

—It could be difficult, even for me, to arrange for one of my patients to die to order.

—Come now, doc. In the midst of life we are in whatsit. We won't rush you. We'll need a week or two to set the thing up. Then, once we get the word from you, we can start the pre-filming. Of course, when we get to the actual dying, we'll be on a pretty tight schedule. The one thing we can't do is over-run. And that's where I thought you could help us. We don't want to drag it out. With modern drugs and things, I'm sure you'll find it easy to give him a touch of the old euthan-you-know-what. Kind to him, kind to the family and highly convenient for us.

—It's got to be a man, I think. Don't you? I know we could milk a lot out of the mother-love bit but it's easy to go over the top with this sort of programme. Nothing worse than tearing the arse out of a good idea. Taste. That's what we're after. Taste.

—And don't worry about the technical details, doc. We'll be discreet. Won't intrude too much on the family at the final moment. We'll use a recorded death rattle so we won't need a boom microphone. And we'll keep the people in the room down to the absolute minimum … a discreet hand-held camera with its operator, the cameraman, one soundman, a couple of lighting men, the director, his assistant, my PA and myself. You can count on us to respect the dignity of the moment.

—What are your chances of getting a family to co-operate? asks A Doctor.

—Just leave the selling of the idea to us, doc. If we do our job properly … and let's face it, that's what we're here to do … the family will be swamped with gifts, wreaths, letters of sympathy, that sort of thing. We might even get the local mayor to set up a fund.

—The more I think about it the more I love the idea. With clever promotion this could be one of the great television happenings. Involve the whole nation, just like the old days. Memorial services everywhere, final credits running over a shot of the archbishop kneeling in prayer in Canterbury Cathedral, scholarships for the grandchildren, a nice bungalow for the widow. The mind boggles at the possibilities.

—And I'll make sure you get your share of the credit, doc. If we play our cards right, you could become another Chris Barnard. But we must keep our objectives clear. Forty minutes of magic. That's what we're after. Forty minutes of grab-em-by-the-heart-kick-em-in-the-balls television.

—But all made for purely religious purposes, says A Doctor.

—Of course, says Jeremy Tittlemouse.

Safe in the Arms of Morpheus

Finbar was enjoying his dream. Nothing like a chunk of gorgonzola and few glasses of Vosne-Romanée to fire up the internal projector. Tonight it was really doing its stuff. Technicolor. Wide screen. Surround sound. The full Todd-AO. And a pleasant dream too. He felt quite at home in the dock at 44 Hallam Street gazing up at the colourful crowd in the public gallery.

Lord Cohen President of the General Medical Council gazed down at him from the magisterial bench

—Doctor O'Flaherty, for the past two hours this committee has listened to your explanations with a good deal of patience. Your answers to Learned Counsel's questions would appear to have been, not to put too fine a point upon it, deliberately evasive. I must therefore put it to you directly. On the night of the twentieth of October, nineteen fifty seven, did you or did you not sleep with this woman?

The world fell silent. The ancient members of the Disciplinary Committee leaned forward, expectancy hovering above their heads.

Then Finbar spoke.

—Not a wink, your Honour.

The colourful crowd cheered, threw their hats in the air, and flung themselves from the balcony. The good Lord Cohen and his committee started to cough in unison. Their staccato coughing took on a bell-like tone. An ominous bell-like tone. Slowly Finbar recognised it, shook his head, and sought to detach himself from the embrace of Morpheus. He reached out to the phone on the bedside table and lifted the receiver. It delivered a few clipped words:

—Sorry to bother you, doc. Alan ffitch-Tucker here. The wife's not lookin' too good.

Nothing more. A click on the line and the phone started to purr. The wife really must be ill, thought Finbar, as he pulled his trousers over his pyjamas. Most men found Yvette ffitch-Tucker so stunningly attractive it was difficult to imagine her looking anything but good.

For years Major ffitch-Tucker had been secretary of the Slagthorpe golf club where he is still known as Titch, after an unfortunate Spoonerism perpetrated in an after-dinner speech by the Rector of St Ethelred's. (Henry Longhurst, the chief guest at the dinner, expressed his sympathy. One of his nightmares, he confessed, was returning from a fulsome lunch to find he had to give a live commentary on a playoff between Coles and Hunt.)

Titch had lived the traditional life, now less common than it used to be, of a genteel bachelor awaiting the death of a rich aunt. When he eventually came into his inheritance he resigned as secretary of the golf club but had so many friends around Slagthope he was reluctant to move away. He found a tenant for the inherited estate in Hertfordshire and bought himself one of the less ornate mini-mansions on Slag Hill. In between assaults on the golf courses of the British Isles he spent much of his time abroad and three years ago while wintering in Barbados had taken to himself a wife. The wedding took place in the gardens of the sprauncy hotel where Yvette was resident *chanteuse* in the cocktail bar. Yvette, the fifth daughter of a poor white family in Martinique, was then twenty-five. Titch was sixty-seven.

Once they were married Yvette gave up the day job and, when they arrived in Slagthorpe after their honeymoon, her mischievous charm and her sexual precocity soon made her the toast of the Golf Club. She clearly hadn't been attracted to Titch by his sexual allure but, as the chairman of Slagthorpe Rovers put it one evening in the Dormy Bar, she might not score often at home but she had the best away record in the league.

And now she wasn't *lookin' too good*. Finbar backed the battered old Morris Cowley from the garage and set off for Slag Hill. Though he would never admit it openly, he enjoyed night calls. Once the shock of waking was over he could drive along deserted roads and let his imagination roam at an hour when most of his fellow citizens had their cerebral cells battened down. Apart from that, there were few patients he would prefer to visit at any hour than the delicious Yvette. Small wonder that he experienced a genuine tingle of anticipation when he pressed the doorbell of the Tudor mini-mansion on Slag Hill and provoked a carillon of tubular bells.

Titch, wearing an old woolly dressing gown over his regimental pyjamas, opened the door.

—Never hear the end of it if I woke the bloody servants. Fully paid-up Communists, the lot of 'em. The wife's upstairs. Woke in a great tizz. Terrible thumpin' of the heart, she said. Make your own way up. Turn right at top of stairs. Third door on left. I'll be waiting in the library.

He toddled back to the tumbler of whiskey he'd left beside his chair.

Finbar climbed the stairs and knocked discreetly on the bedroom door. There was no response. He pushed gently at the door and it swung open. Yvette lay on the bed. She looked up and greeted him with an emphatically healthy smile.

—Don't be shy doctor. I won't bite.

She'd pulled the black silk sheets tight under her chin and her ash blonde hair sprawled across the black silk pillow. Finbar shrugged off the awkwardness that suddenly afflicted him, stepped cheerfully across the room and pulled a chair alongside the bed. Fighting manfully against the visual distraction, he set about taking a history of the illness. The tale Yvette told was a textbook description of an attack of paroxysmal tachycardia. Yet when

Finbar took her pulse rate, it was a steady 68. Clearly the attack was over.

—Best have a look at what's going on, he said.

—Of course, cried Yvette and flung back the sheet to reveal that her notion of night attire was a few well placed dabs of Eau Sensationnelle.

Clucking like a fussy old hen Finbar quickly re-draped the sheet over her lower half so only her chest was exposed. This was the time, he decided, to stick strictly to the clinical routine he'd learned all those years before from Hutchison and Hunter's textbook on *Clinical Examination*. Inspect, palpate, then auscultate.

First he inspected the affected area, an investigation that provided ample compensation for getting out of bed in the middle of the night. Next came palpation. He placed his hand beneath Yvette's left breast and located the beating apex of her heart. Did he detect a slight vibration, the fremitus of a cardiac thrill? He placed his hand flat across her breastbone to confirm it.

—What are you doing now? asked Yvette.

—I thought I might feel a thrill, said Finbar.

Yvette's eyes opened wide. Without a word she flung back the sheet once more, grabbed Finbar's wrist and moved his hand directly south to a portion of the corpus which only Ovid, and a few dedicated Freudians, would claim had a direct connection with the heart.

—Now, she said, we can both feel a thrill.

At which point, and I tell no lie, Finbar's spectacles fell off.

Yet even as he knelt beside the bed with his right hand firmly locked between his patient's thighs and his left hand fumbling across her pectorals in myopic search for his spectacles, Alan ffitch-Tucker entered the room carrying, and again I tell no lie, a shotgun.

—Dammit man, he cried. What are you doin' with my wife?

—You may find this difficult to believe, said Finbar, but I am carrying out the routine examination devised by teachers who made British medicine the envy of the world.

—Vive La Grande-Bretagne, cried Yvette.

Her husband failed to respond. He just raised his gun, took deliberate aim, and squeezed the trigger. Finbar, hit in the side of the head, went flying across the room, meditating *en route* how surprisingly painless it was to be killed. Indeed, the only disturbing symptom was a strange tinnitus in his right ear that grew louder and louder like an alarm clock.

Damn it all, it was an alarm clock. He reached out his hand to the bedside table and switched it off. But the ringing went on. Not the alarm, you idiot. The telephone. He lifted the receiver and tried to listen through the static that crackled across his brain. Eventually he gathered that Cornelius Molecatcher was having one of his nasty turns. He was back in the land of reality

Finbar felt none too good as he climbed out of bed. His first experience of a double dream, one parked inside the other like a Russian doll. Could it have to do with the glasses of Armagnac he'd had after the Vosne-Romanée … or maybe those hefty slices of pickled pork?

Yet it wasn't indigestion that jellified his legs, made his brow clammy, caused his heart to race. A fortunate man was he, reprieved at the foot of the gallows. As he looked at his bleary self in the mirror, he spoke the words out loud.

—There, but for the grace of you know who went you know who.

He pulled his trousers over his pyjamas and prepared to set off into the night. Maybe this would be the time he'd tell Cornelius that the nasty turns of today are the stars of tomorrow.

EDITOR'S NOTE

Donovan scrawled a note at the end of this manuscript: *As told by Finbar over breakfast much to the delight of this morning's guests: Sara, Arthur, and Stanley.*

Finbar still shaken but unstirred.

Knocked Out

Slagton-on-Sea, Slagshire's bingo-bubbling holiday resort, is today immersed in gloom. Few people brave its streets and those who do wear black arm bands and walk with heads bowed. Big Tom, the bell of the parish church of St Myrtle, tolls a gloomy threnody and the half dozen Union Jacks that flutter proudly at the pier entrance flutter today at half mast. Last night, before a continent of witnesses, Slagton disgraced the nation by coming last in the European Grand Final of *Jeux sans Frontières.**

Not only did Slagtonians cede victory to cunning Frogs, track-suited Huns, and operatic Italians, they even bowed the knee to a bunch of Swiss cuckoo-clockers. Could theirs really be the soil that nurtured the gallant Lord Slagwood, who had a kidney shot away in the service of Wellington, Jolly Jack Slagwell, who danced the hornpipe while cannons roared at Trafalgar, and the indomitable Albert Shufflebottom, national ballroom champion of 1927?

Or, as the *Slagshire Post* hints this morning, has the permissive society so undermined the land of Raleigh, Drake, and Stanley Matthews it no longer breeds men with the determination to scramble up water shutes with balloons balanced on their foreheads?

*Jeux sans Frontières was a pan-European television project initiated, would you believe it, by Charles de Gaulle. The BBC renamed the British version It's a Knock-Out, possibly because it wanted to avoid undue familiarity with foreigners or resented the notion that La Manche was a mere frontière.

Yet last night honour was Slagton's for the taking. Its citizens were playing a home match and had prepared for KO-Day with typical Slagshire thoroughness. The team had had four months' intensive training in the basic skills: carrying leaky buckets of water across ploughed fields, strengthening flabby leg muscles in mammoth treadmills, and racing one another along the promenade on foot-rolled barrels. So great was Slagton's hunger for the prize that, when Slagthorpe's Brigadier Digby Knutsford MP, OBE, TD, LMSSA, RAMC volunteered to provide administrative skills, *annealed*, as he put it, *in the furnace of war*, the Town Clerk appointed him Director of Operations.

By the time of his appointment, force of habit had inspired the Council to devise ways of cheating. The Town Clerk had scoured the county for folk with special skills and the Council had awarded them honorary Slagton citizenship. Digby sought to emulate the Town Clerk's enterprise. He persuaded the governor of Slagcaster Prison to parole Slippery Sid Silvertoes, Slagshire's notorious cat burglar, for use in the rope-climbing event. Then, *calling*, as he said, *on his knowledge as a man of science*, he cajoled the Research and Development Department at the String Vest Manufactory into research on greasy poles – an endeavour which eventually provided Mavis Slapperton with her secret weapon: grease-resistant knickers.

Over the next few months the planning ran unnaturally smoothly and yesterday morning the Brigadier gave an up-beat final briefing to his troops. Intelligence reports, he said, suggested that all teams would pick up points in the middle events but his battle plan was to go for a strong start and a powerful finish. His team's preparation should ensure the strong start and he'd had to make a tactical change to provide the powerful finish.

The final event demanded a 100-yard dash by a woman. One of Digby's undercover agents had discovered that the Hun had stolen a leaf from the Slagshire manual and were running a Scandinavian ringer. They'd granted honorary citizenship to the Danish national sprint champion, Ilse Dossersaltz. In a brilliant tactical riposte Digby recruited Stanley *Lightning* Postlethwaite, Slagshire All-comers Professional Sprint Champion and two time Powderhall winner. In return for a consideration, Lightning agreed to compete in drag with a curly blonde wig over his thinning hair and a pneumatic brassiere beneath his track vest.

Yesterday evening when battle was joined, everything started according to plan. Slagton ran away with the opening events: the first thanks to Slippery Sid's speed up the rope and the second thanks to Mavis Slapperton's knickers.

—These British lads and lasses have made a brilliant start, cried breathless commentator Stuart Hall.

But cautious Eddie Waring sounded a warning:

—The only way to get this gold cup is to win yer Mini-Marathon and yer joker.

Brigadier Digby's prediction of the middle events was also on the button. With only two games to go, the Hun, represented by the beefy burghers of Bad Schlagwein, had a slight lead with the other teams grouped close behind. But every team save Slagton's had played its points-doubling joker and Digby had more than just the joker up his sleeve.

Because this was the European Grand Final, the Mini-Marathon – an intermittent game played by one team at a time between the main events – was neither mini nor marathon. Instead the BBC had devised the sort of test that makes *It's a Knockout* a by-word wherever men talk of skill, courage, and endurance.

Moored to one side of the corporation boating lake were the teams' rowing boats, each packed with 30 helium-filled balloons kept in place by a fisherman's net. A man and a woman from each team had to climb into a boat and on the starting signal – a blast on a hunting horn from the dapple-mounted Master of the North Slagshire Whippets — the woman had to cast off the net and try to restrain the balloons while her mate, using only his hands, paddled the boat to the other side of the lake. A point was scored for each balloon left in the boat when it grounded on the mud beneath the statue of Jolly Jack Slagwell.

Digby, as aware as Eddie Waring of the value of the Mini-Marathon, had imported his team secretly from Ireland. Munster's lady wrestling champion, 22-stone Finoula O'Beese, and a wiry Dublin bartender Seamus Never whose wrists, the brigadier assured us, had been strengthened by a lifetime's drawing of corks from Guinness bottles.

As the hosts, Slagton were the last to go. The other teams, which had already banked their points, smiled not-so-secret smiles when the massive Finoula entered the boat. Her mountainous flesh protected all 30 balloons but the water line rose to within an inch of the rim. They didn't fancy Seamus's chances of making it to the other side.

But then they didn't know about another of Digby's secret weapons. Concealed beneath the murky surface of the lake was the fully oxygenated president of the Slagheaton Underwater Club, Ernie Oldroyd, whose frogman flippers would give the Slagton boat additional propulsion.

Yet even as Digby congratulated himself on his strategy and the Master of the North Slagshire Whippets raised his horn to his lips, the team doctor, Finbar Aloysius O'Flaherty, burst into the Operations Room to announce that he had just dragged an exsanguinated Ernie from the lake. Finoula and Seamus would have to make it on their own.

Ernie, it transpired, had a nasty nose bleed during the opening ceremony when the competitors entered the arena to a rousing welcome from the Slagheaton Colliery Silver Band in which Ernie was an enthusiastic percussionist. As the band hurtled into its finale Ernie, in a moment of ecstatic frenzy on the tubular bells, blew a nasal gasket. Though his nose refused to stop bleeding, he bravely donned the flippers but had donned in vain. Finbar was called when one of Digby's special agents spotted a large crimson patch spreading amid the water lilies

On hearing the news Digby dashed to the Mini-Marathon

finishing line just in time to see the Slagheaton Colliery Rescue Men carrying Seamus away on a stretcher. When the massive Finoula was raised from the bilges, with the aid of a quickly rigged hoist, only six intact balloons were found beneath her person. With the single point earned for completing the course Slagton scored only seven, way behind the eighteen already scored by an Italian trapezist and her hot-blooded partner from Baia Slagizia

Those seven points, while not pushing Slagton into the crushing lead that Digby had anticipated, did at least keep them in touch with the leaders. A win in the last game, the *Fil Rouge*, for which Digby had held back the points-doubling joker, could still bring the trophy to Slagshire.

The honour of the island race now rested on the shoulders of Lightning Postlethwaite. Finbar had, with difficulty, persuaded him to shave the hairs from his legs and when he emerged from the Competitors' Enclosure in his blonde curls and his slightly over-inflated bra he produced a few whistles from the crowd. Those few whistles grew to a consensual crescendo on the arrival of Ilse Dossersaltz. The Germans had picked themselves an outstanding piece of Danish pastry – a tall, Nordic blonde with a slim boyish figure and long slender legs which Finbar, who had given the matter clinical attention, claimed had no tops to them.

This year's *Fil Rouge* was simple in design but testing of performance. Each country was again represented by a man and a woman. Each woman stood at the near end of Slagton's Open Air Lido outside a bathing tent decorated in her national colours. The men stood at the far end. At the starter's signal – this time a rousing chord from the massed trumpeters of the Slagheaton Fusiliers – the men had to don large striped Victorian bathing costumes over their bathing trunks, swim the length of the Lido, climb out, strip off the bathing suits, and hand them to the women.

The women had then to retire into the tents, pull the striped costumes over their one-piece bathing suits (*No bikinis*, said the rules. *Any undue exposure of flesh will be penalised*) then sprint 100 yards over a cinder track to the finish.

The first leg for Slagton-on-Sea was to be swum by the Lido's life guard, Reg Otter, still abrim with confidence after his triumph as the Swimming Skater in the Indoor Baths' production of *The Forsyte Saga on Ice*. Reg would, at worst, hold his own with the other swimmers and give Lightning the chance to exert his masculine superiority over the 100 yards of cinders.

I'll confess that even I, cynical voyeur that I am, felt a twinge of excitement as I stood between Finbar and Digby waiting for the Slagheaton Fusiliers to send the swimmers on their way. The only person who seemed unaffected by the tension was Lightning. Indeed he was in danger of giving the game away by flirting with Ilse as they stood side by side outside their bathing tents. Strangely, Ilse seemed happy to flirt back. I looked around the crowd to see if anyone had rumbled Lightning but everyone's attention was focussed on the starting line.

The Fusiliers sounded their discordant note and the race was on. Reg lost a few precious seconds before he realized he was trying to get his foot through the arm of the bathing suit but he didn't lose his cool and dived into the water just two lengths behind the hairy Hun from Bad Schlagwein. In highly professional style he pared back the German lead and he and the German climbed from the water together, well ahead of the rest of the field.

Things then took a surrealistic turn. As Reg struggled from the bathing suit, Lightning offered him no help. He had eyes only for Ilse. She did help her partner then, as she carried the striped bathing suit into her tent, she cast an inviting smile over her shoulder towards Lightning. Lightning responded by flinging away the Slagton suit and striding after her into the German tent.

Digby's face turned brickhouse red as the walls of the German tent started to twitch and bulge in rhythmic motion. Then just as the other swimmers reached the end of the Lido, an anguished scream soared high above the roar of the spectators. Only those with bat-like discernment heard the cry transmute into a strangulated gargle because the air was filled with the cheers of the Bad Schlagwein supporters as Ilse emerged from her tent like a greyhound from its trap. As she sped down the track, her blonde hair streaming behind her, she was such a magnificent sight that Erasmus Dewdrop, who was on the stopwatch, lost grip of his timepiece.

Thanks to that mishap, the record books were denied an official time but there was no disputing Ilse's margin of victory. In one, dare I say it, lightning dash she had brought the gold cup to Bad Schlagwein and ignominy to Slagton-on-Sea. Lightning never reappeared. When the Slagheaton First-Aiders swooped on his tent, they found him out cold with a large bruise on his temple and a small rubber cosh discarded by his side. When they bore him away on a stretcher, the Germans were already dancing noisily around the prize-winners enclosure.

Finbar and I slipped away from the arena and headed for *Uncle Joe's Fish n' Twopennorth* on the promenade. As we waited for Uncle Joe to bring us some deep battered cod, Finbar revelled in the thought of the Brigadier Digby Knutsford, MP, TD, LMSSA being out-thought and outmanoeuvred by a mere Uber Burgermeister from Bad Schlagwein.

—Let us not be downhearted, he said. We should be on our knees thanking God that they kept him away from the battlefields during the war.